The
Beekeeper's
Promise

OTHER TITLES BY FIONA VALPY

The
Beekeeper's
Promise

Fiona Valpy

LAKE UNION

PUBLISHING

Text copyright © 2018 by Fiona Valpy
All rights reserved.

Published by Lake Union Publishing, Seattle

www.apub.com

Amazon, the Amazon logo, and Lake Union Publishing are trademarks of Amazon.com, Inc., or its affiliates.

ISBN-13: 9781542047036
ISBN-10: 154204703X

Cover design by @blacksheep-uk.com

Printed in the United States of America

For my friend Michèle,
with love

*Go to your fields and your gardens, and you shall learn that it
is the pleasure of the bee to gather honey of the flower,
But it is also the pleasure of the flower to yield its honey to the bee.
For to the bee a flower is a fountain of life,
And to the flower a bee is a messenger of love.*

from The Prophet – *Kahlil Gibran*

*A honeybee performs a 'waggle dance' to communicate the
distance and direction of a new foraging site to her coworkers
in the hive. She dances in a figure eight, moving in a clockwise
semicircle, then in a straight line . . . and, finally in a
counterclockwise semicircle.
In the winter, bees stop foraging and cluster together with
the queen in the center of the hive. They generate heat
by uncoupling their flight muscles from their wings and
'shivering' or rapidly contracting and relaxing these muscles.*

from The Beekeeper's Bible – *Richard Jones and Sharon
Sweeney-Lynch*

PART 1

Eliane: 2017

She knew that this would be her last summer. The warm caress of the late-spring sunlight couldn't roll back the fog-like weariness that crept through her bones these days. But then there had been so many summers. Almost a hundred. She glanced up the hill, towards the little graveyard beyond the vines where those she loved the best were laid. They were waiting, now, to welcome her.

A worker bee, one of the first to venture out of the hive that bright morning, drew dizzy spirals in the air as it orientated itself, sensing the nectar in the flowers that she had nurtured in her garden. It circled around her, drawn by the scent of beeswax and honey that saturated her age-soft skin. 'Good morning to you too.' She smiled. 'Don't worry: I'm not going to abandon you just yet. I know there's still work to be done.'

Beside the whitewashed hives, she set down the basket of frames that she'd been carrying and settled the veil of her broad-brimmed hat over her head and shoulders. She opened the first hive, gently lifting off the sloping roof, and bent closer to inspect the drones, a seething, humming mass of bodies attending their queen. Their honey supplies had lasted well over the winter and already the colony was expanding.

She slotted the new frames into an empty box and set it in place above the mass of bees. 'There you go – room for expansion,' she told them. 'And for this summer's honey.'

Working methodically, she attended to each hive in turn. When she'd finished, she paused, stretching her back to ease the ache from the effort of lifting the boxes of frames. She peered up into the delicate tracery of acacia leaves that cast their dancing, dappled shade over the hives. Any day now they would burst into flower and the cascades of clustered white blossom would turn the trees silver, and then the bees would drink their fill of the sweetest nectar of all. Her jars of acacia honey would be like bottles of summer itself, sweet and golden.

She smiled to herself. Yes, there had been so many summers. But just one more would be a gift.

Abi: 2017

I'm lost. Lost in France, just like in the words of a stupid song that I can't get out of my head as I trudge along the road. I stop for a moment to wipe my face with my shirt, which is already soaked with sweat. The road runs along a ridge that falls away steeply to one side and, I must admit, there could be worse places to lose my way. The view sweeps away in front of me, patchwork fields of green and gold interrupted here and there by dark velvet woodlands. The broad satin ribbon of a twisting river edges the valley floor beneath me.

Peace and quiet in the French sunshine. It's exactly what I'd imagined when Pru and I signed up for the yoga retreat. 'Look, it's just what you need, Abi.' She'd brandished the glossy leaflet at me as we were putting away our mats and pulling our boots back on after the regular Thursday-evening class. '"A week of springtime yoga, meditation and mindfulness in the heart of the French countryside,"' she'd read.

I didn't point out to her that I'd hardly been able to bring myself to leave the apartment for the last couple of years, and that walking to the yoga class and back was the furthest I'd been in months. Besides the hospital visits, that is, where the physios and psychologists had tried to help me stitch the shattered pieces of myself back together.

But the retreat had been a tempting thought. I'd always loved France. Well, more the idea of it really; I hadn't exactly spent a lot of time travelling there – or in any other foreign countries either, come to think of it. French was my best subject at school, though. Something I had been good at, immersing myself in the wonderful world of Maman, Papa and Marie-Claude and their lovely safe, orderly lives, as set out in the textbooks. And I knew I needed to make more of an effort now to get my life back on track, to start getting out a bit more again. Being able to travel with Pru would make it that much easier, I had thought. She's good company and always very organised. We'd bonded over cups of cinnamon chai after she joined the yoga class to help get over her divorce. She's got a good sense of humour and doesn't witter on the whole time, which would set my nerves jangling, so I reckoned she'd make a good travelling companion and agreed to go. She'd signed us up that evening for the retreat and booked our flights too, so backing out wasn't an option – even though I desperately wanted to, the minute she called to confirm the arrangements.

That'll teach me to be spontaneous, I think, as I trudge along the hot tarmac of the road. Nothing good ever comes of it. And now I've no idea where I'm going, up the hill from the centre, through the vines – one vineyard looks exactly like the next, if you ask me. A tiny bit of me has to admit it's rather beautiful, though, that golden light on the flourishes of lush green leaves springing from the gnarled, dead-looking wood.

But I don't want to be distracted from my anger by the beauty of my surroundings. I need to let my fury at Pru – abandoning me like that – simmer and seethe for a while longer. My counsellor would be pleased; she's always telling me that anger is part of the healing process. And at least I'm feeling something. Which may or may not be better than feeling nothing at all.

But so much for the serenity and enlightenment that the retreat brochure had promised. I stomp along a little further. Actually, I know I can't really blame Pru. Most people would have done the same, given half the chance. The thought of a bath and a proper bed, never mind with some fit and flexible Dutchman alongside you, is certainly tempting. I'm just jealous; but still definitely entitled to be furious with her.

She'd met him in the queue for the loos, after lunch on the second day. A fast worker, our Prudence – not one to live up to her name, it turns out. She said they'd both felt an instant connection. 'Kindred spirits' were the words she used when she finally cornered me, plonking herself down next to me at lunch.

'Based on a synchronised need to go to the loo after a plate of spicy lentil stew? It's not exactly soulful,' I retorted, unable to stop myself.

Ignoring my outburst, she said, 'He's paid the extra to stay at a guesthouse nearby. Apparently it's gorgeous. He's got a whirlpool bath, en suite.'

I sighed. 'Well that certainly beats a mildewed concrete shower with someone's grungy old plaster stuck in the corner.'

We'd arrived at the centre three days earlier. It had been evening when we got there and most people were already installed, their tents set up, claims staked, seeming to know their way round. A helper in a tie-dyed T-shirt, his shaved head gleaming in the late sunshine, showed us a corner where we could pitch our own tent. It was very obviously the last available spot: 'handy for the loos' would be the best way to describe it. We managed to get the tent up after a bit, although it took us a while to work out where the poles go. Banging the pegs in with a rubber mallet wasn't easy either, since the ground was as hard as concrete. Eventually, we got three out of four corners staked down quite well, and the fourth a bit more precariously, and two guy ropes in, front and back, so it should stay up. There's been no wind anyway. The weather's been gorgeous – at least the brochure got that bit right. It's been cold at night, but in the mornings the sun quickly warms the air and by midday it's been downright hot.

I jump, nearly out of my skin, at a sudden rustling in the verge beside me, catching sight of a thin yellow-and-black-striped snake slithering away. A snake in the grass. Watch out for them; they're the most dangerous of all. I take a deep breath and sigh it out, the way the counsellor taught me, to help calm myself when the alarm bells in my brain get triggered.

Get a grip, I tell myself. Try to stay in control: that's the key. Don't let the memories overwhelm you. Give it time – that's what everyone says.

I've reached the top of a rise and the road flattens out in front of me for a bit before climbing again. I pause to catch my breath, pressing my fist into my side where a stitch is griping, and then push on, at an easier pace now. I glance at my watch. It's gone six. Supper will be over in the dining hall at the centre, the portions of rice and vegetable stew doled out and consumed, rounded off with a piece of fruit. We're all detox-ing, although so far all this healthy eating seems to have achieved is an awful lot of irritable people with headaches, flatulence and really bad breath – talk about toxicity! But no one's going to put on any weight on this holiday, that's for sure. Unless Pru and her Dutchman are secretly pigging out back in his luxurious guesthouse. I imagine they're probably swigging champagne and eating chocolates in bed.

I plod on, thinking that right now I'd kill for a bacon sarnie. Now there's a sentence you'll rarely hear on a yoga retreat, even if it is what most people are probably thinking half the time when they're sitting on their meditation cushions trying to empty their minds. Or perhaps that's just me.

It had all been a bit overwhelming, the evening of our arrival. After we'd got the tent up it was time for supper so we followed the tide of fellow retreaters to queue at the serving tables. We were all secretly eye-ing each other up while trying to appear yogic and laidback. Pru had changed into a kind of long floaty kaftan-thing, very different from her usual attire. After the wrestling match with the tent, I'd felt grubby and hot. I hadn't bothered changing out of my shirt and jeans, the uniform I wear to cover up the worst of the scars on my arms and leg. I could already feel the mosquitoes biting my ankles above the straps of my sandals too.

Pru got the giggles in the tent that night when I said, 'Do you think we're allowed to kill the mozzies or is that bad karma?' I got my spray out all the same; anything for a good night's sleep. Although the chances of getting much sleep at all were pretty much slim to none, what with the damp chill of the night-time air soaking into the tent and my bites itching and the loo doors banging next to us all night long. I wasn't feeling very serene by the time morning came around and a cock began crowing at a nearby farm, just when I was finally managing to get a bit of sleep at long last.

I walk past a cottage at the side of the road and a dog appears out of nowhere, hurtling towards me with a volley of vicious barking. I nearly jump out of my skin once more, nerves set a-jangling as the panic systems in my brain are triggered all over again. It's a good job there's a fence between him and me. A dangerous place, this, what with the snakes and the rabid dogs.

Now my sandal has rubbed a blister on my heel so I stop walking and reach down to loosen the strap, my fingers still shaking in the aftermath of the almost-too-close encounter with the dog. The skin's raw. It's going to be fun walking back to the centre. I've no idea where I am or how far I've come. There's a tall wrought-iron cross on the crest of the hill a little way ahead, so I limp up to it and sit down on the grass (first checking carefully for snakes, of course). A milestone beside the cross reads 'Sainte-Foy-la-Grande 6 Kilomètres'. There's a blue-topped post beside it with a yellow cockleshell design on – I recognise it as the sign for that pilgrim route Pru was banging on about the other day, when she was reading from her guidebook over breakfast.

I think back to this morning's talk in the meditation hall, which was about karma; what goes around comes around. It was all I could do not to give Pru a death stare at that one, though of course that would have been bad karma so I kept to the moral high ground. She and her

Dutchman were sitting there on their cushions a couple of rows in front of me. She'd called me over to sit next to them, but I'd shaken my head and stayed put. *No thanks. I don't need your charity and I certainly don't want to be a third wheel on your bicycle.* I sat on the little purple cushion with my legs crossed, even though my stiff knee was complaining loudly and I immediately got pins and needles in my foot. It's been nearly two years since the accident, so you'd have thought that with all the physio and the yoga stretches things would have healed by now. I'd closed my eyes so I wouldn't see Pru turning around every five minutes to smile at me. She was probably trying to be conciliatory, but in the frame of mind I was in it just came across as smug.

How on earth do people sit still for so long? It was impossible to get comfortable and I started fidgeting all over the place. My mind started fidgeting too, thoughts crowding in. So much for emptying it. And thinking is the last thing I want to do.

I'm starting to believe I'm not cut out for meditation. We were supposed to be doing it on the walk this afternoon as well. *Being* mindful. Rather than *having* a mind that's full, which is what mine is. The fields around the centre were full of people doing the walking meditation, drifting like zombies, focused on every step – 'staying in the moment', as we'd been instructed to do. I was doing okay for the first few minutes, but then the sight of Pru and Mr Netherlands floating along in tandem set me off again and I stalked off up a narrow path into the trees. I'd suddenly felt that I couldn't bear to be in that slow-moving crowd for another second.

As I'd stomped away from the walking meditation, it was a relief to be in the woods – cooler, and safer-feeling too; less exposed. It's been a while since I've had a full-blown panic attack (the medication has helped), but I'd definitely started to feel my throat and chest tightening, and my head pounding. So now it was a relief to be alone at last. I'm not used to being around other people the whole time.

I wonder how many miles I've walked. The milestone doesn't give me any clues as I've completely lost my bearings. I'm now drenched in sweat and there's a major blister on my heel. I inspect my foot again and find that the skin's ballooning up into an opaque bubble over the raw patch. To take my mind off the pain I scratch viciously at a mosquito bite on my ankle, just below where my yoga leggings end, until it starts to bleed. Then I lean back against the rough face of the milestone and stretch my legs out in front of me, looking around at the view.

Neat vineyards fan out in all directions, with creamy stone buildings nestling among them here and there. Red-tiled roofs glow in the evening light. There's a bit of a breeze now, up here on the crest of the hill. Gratefully, I lift my chin to let it blow on to my sweating neck and burning cheeks. At least it's all downhill from here on in. If I follow the road back down maybe I'll recognise some landmarks, or find a sign for the centre.

I turn to look back the way I came and am horrified to see massive black storm clouds billowing up. I can almost see them growing as I watch, towering higher and then covering the sun, the light suddenly changing from mellow gold to a sickly, bruised purple. There's an ominous silence too and I realise the background chorus of birds and crickets that has accompanied me on my walk up until now has suddenly fallen quiet. I put a hand on top of the milestone and grab the stem of the cross with the other to haul myself up, gingerly putting weight on to my sore foot. I'd better be heading back, and fast, before the storm hits.

Just then I hear the rumble of an engine and a white van pulls up alongside me. I turn, expecting to see a balding Frenchman in a string vest, but the driver is a woman about my age, with long dark hair pulled back into a neat ponytail. 'Jump in,' she shouts over the noise of the van's engine and the wind, which has suddenly begun to whip up little whirlwinds of dust along the side of the road. I look up apprehensively at the clouds, now blackening the whole sky. Do they get tornadoes in this part of the world?

'I was just going to . . .' I tail off, gesturing back along the road in what I believe to be the general direction of the centre.

The first big drops of rain plop into the dust on the road ahead of me and then on to my face. They're ice-cold, making me gasp. I duck my head, closing my eyes against the sudden, angry raindrops, and climb into the passenger seat.

'Sara Cortini – pleased to meet you,' she introduces herself in English (how do they *always* know you're not French?). 'I live just over there.' She points towards the top of the next ridge just as the storm engulfs it. 'Come and shelter for a while and then we'll get you home. Where are you staying?'

'At the yoga centre. My name's Abi Howes.'

Sara nods and puts the van into gear, driving fast up a steep and dusty track to try to beat the oncoming storm. We jump out of the van and hurry through raindrops as hard as hailstones, the cloudburst soaking us in the few seconds it takes to reach the doorway of an elegant stone building.

'What is this place?' I ask, trying, as I run, to take in the cluster of buildings that surround us, perched high on the hilltop.

She bangs the door shut behind us and reaches for a kitchen towel, passing it to me to dry my face and shirt.

And then she says, 'Welcome to Château Bellevue.'

Eliane: 1938

The river's breath hung in a veil of mist above the weir as the sun began to rise. The first rays of late-summer light were as soft and golden as the fruit, ripe for picking, that hung from the branches of the pear and quince trees in the orchard as the first blackcap's fluting song swept the night's silence westwards, heralding the dawn.

The door of the mill house opened and a slender figure slipped out, her bare feet leaving soundless footprints on the dew-soaked grass. Scarcely breaking her stride, she skipped across the moss-capped stones that bridged the mill race where the water foamed and churned in frustration at being constrained into the narrow channel beneath the powerful mill wheel. Transferring the three broad wooden laths she carried to her right hand, Eliane hitched up her skirts with the left and stepped, surefooted, on to the weir.

Her father, Gustave, who had followed her outside to gather an armful of firewood, paused, watched his daughter as she crossed to the far side of the river, her progress dreamlike through the ankle-deep water, her feet obscured by the low-lying miasma of river mist. Sensing his presence, Eliane glanced back over her shoulder. Even from a distance, she could tell from his unusually sombre expression that he was worrying again about the threat of another war, not twenty years after that last terrible war from which his own father had never returned.

She raised the wooden laths in salute and his features creased into his habitual ready smile.

The beehives beneath the acacia trees on the far riverbank were quiet and still when she reached them. Their inhabitants were still safely sheltering inside, waiting for the sun's rays to warm the air enough to tempt them out. Silently, she pulled lengths of thin rope from her apron pocket, tying the wooden laths in place to block the hives' entrance gaps before the bees could begin their busy to-ing and fro-ing. They would be moved up the hill today so that the bees could over-winter in a sheltered corner of the walled garden up at the château.

Eliane's job, as kitchen assistant at Château Bellevue, meant she would be on hand each day to check on the bees and to top up their sugar supplies, if necessary, to see them through the winter if it proved to be another hard one. Monsieur le Comte had agreed readily to her shy request to house the hives. He'd noticed that she had a way with nature, coaxing her bees to produce generous slabs of dripping honeycomb, as well as working miracles in the kitchen garden with her herbs and neatly tended beds of produce. Even the château's cook, the formidable Madame Boin, seemed delighted with Eliane's work and had been heard humming contentedly of late as she bustled between the scrubbed kitchen table and the range.

Back in the mill's cavernous kitchen, Eliane filled a small pitcher with water and arranged a posy of wildflowers in it, setting it in the middle of the worn oilcloth that covered the table. Her father, who was dipping a hunk of bread into his bowl of coffee, paused to ask, 'It's done? The hives are well sealed?'

Eliane nodded, pouring coffee from the enamelled pot into her own bowl. The morning sunlight began to creep its way across the table as she pulled up her chair.

'They're all ready. Is Yves awake?'

'Not yet. You know what he's like on a Saturday morning.' Her father pretended to disapprove of her brother's indolence.

14

'We need to move the hives soon. It's not good for the bees to be held inside as the day heats up.' She traced the line of light – stronger now – that had reached the jug of flowers and was continuing to steal silently towards her father at the head of the table.

Her father nodded, wiping his moustache on a crumpled handkerchief that he stuffed back into the pocket of his blue overalls.

'I know.' His chair scraped on the stone flags as he pushed it back and hauled himself to his feet. He was a sturdy giant of a man, with the well-filled belly and muscular build that a life's work of running the flour mill had endowed upon him. 'I'll wake him now.'

'Where's Maman?' Eliane asked, cutting a slice from the fresh-baked loaf of bread sitting on an oak board beside her father's newly vacated place.

'She's gone to see Madame Perret. Apparently her contractions started in the night.'

'I heard the phone ring in the early hours. Is that who it was? But she still has a month to go . . .' Eliane paused, breadknife in hand.

Her father nodded. 'Your mother thinks it's probably a false alarm. You know what Elisabeth Perret is like; she jumps at the sight of her own shadow.'

'Well it *is* her first baby,' Eliane reproached him gently, 'so of course she's nervous.'

He nodded. 'Hopefully your mother will calm her down with one of her *tisanes* and the little one will decide to stay put for a few more weeks.'

He pushed a dish of white butter and a jar of cherry jam towards her and then she listened to his heavy footsteps, which made the wooden staircase creak as he went to wake Yves.

Seeing her mother, Lisette, wheeling the bicycle into the lean-to by the barn, Eliane picked up her bread and jam and went to help carry in her bag of instruments and the basket of herbal preparations that her mother always took with her on her rounds. As the local midwife, she knew most of the inhabitants of the homes in and around the little village of Coulliac.

'How is Madame Perret?'

'She's fine, just a bad dose of trapped wind. That's what happens when you eat a whole jar of cornichons in one go! Nothing that a few cups of fennel tea won't cure. That baby looks to me as if he's going to stay right where he is for a good few weeks more. She's carrying him high and he's far too comfortable to want to move. A typical boy!' Her mother was uncannily accurate in her predictions of the gender of the babies she was to deliver. 'Speaking of boys, where's your brother? I thought he was going to help you and Papa move the beehives this morning before you go to the market?'

Eliane nodded, setting the wicker basket beside the sink and reaching for the coffee pot to pour a bowl for her mother. 'Papa's gone to wake him.'

'And here he is!' Yves announced his arrival with a grin for Eliane and a hug for his mother. 'As soon as he's had his *p'tit-déj*, he'll set to work.'

At sixteen years of age, Yves had just left school that summer and was very much enjoying the relative freedom of working with his father at the mill in lieu of the rigours of the classroom and exams. He was taller than his mother and both of his sisters, even though they were older than him, and his handsome mop of dark curls and easy-going manner made him popular with his peers. And, indeed, of late it seemed that an increasing number of girls were eagerly offering to help their parents bring the bushels of wheat to the mill for grinding and coming back to collect the bags of soft flour when it was ready, trying to pretend they weren't watching out of the corners of their eyes as Yves heaved heavy sacks on to the back of his father's truck for delivery to the baker.

The Martins' truck crept up the steep, dusty drive of Château Bellevue, Gustave navigating around the worst ruts and potholes carefully in order to agitate the bees as little as possible. The hives, secured firmly in place and covered with branches of elder leaves to shade them from the sun on their short journey, reached their new home in the walled kitchen garden behind the château, where Eliane directed her father and brother to place them close to the western wall, facing east so that they would be warmed by the first rays of the rising sun each morning through the cold months of winter. A large pear tree, its branches weighed down with fruit almost ripe for the picking, shielded them from above.

'You'd better get back in the truck and close the windows,' she told Yves. 'They might be a bit confused at finding themselves in their new home and you know how they like to sting you!'

'I don't get it,' he grumbled. 'You don't even wear a veil half the time and they never sting *you*.'

'They're bees of discerning taste,' teased Gustave as he clambered into the driver's seat and made sure his window was firmly secured.

With deft fingers, Eliane untied the cords and gently lifted off the laths that had sealed the hives shut. After a moment or two, the first bees began to emerge from the narrow opening at the base, sensing the air and then launching themselves in dizzy, zigzagging flight. She smiled as she watched them. 'That's right – you explore a bit, *mes amis*. And then make sure you come back and do your dance to tell the others where everything is. There's plenty for you all to feast on here.'

Already they were starting to cluster around the deep-blue stars of the borage flowers; and one or two of the more adventurous ones were soaring towards the dazzling yellow suns of the Jerusalem-artichoke blooms, intent on seeking out the treasure trove of nectar among the rich brown pollen that dusted the centre of each flower.

At the entrance to the walled garden, Monsieur le Comte stood watching, leaning on his silver-topped cane. 'Good morning, Eliane. Safely installed? They look quite at home here already.'

She smiled at her elderly employer. 'It's perfect. It'll be less damp for them up here away from the river and the walls will give them shelter. *Merci, monsieur.*'

'I'm pleased,' the count nodded. 'And Eliane: word has got around already, as it does so quickly in these parts. I've been approached by Monsieur Cortini, the *vigneron* at Château de la Chapelle. His sister-in-law has another six hives, but she's getting too much arthritis in her hands to be able to work them properly these days. He's heard you are going to tend your hives up here and he asked if we could accommodate those others as well.'

Eliane's calm, grey eyes – the colour of the clear dawn light – widened in surprise and pleasure. 'Nine hives! Just think of all the honey!'

'Is there enough space for them all here in the kitchen garden, do you think? We don't want swarms of warring bees on our hands.'

'*Mais oui, bien sûr.* We'll place the new hives a bit away from mine, over there nearer the far corner, and angle them slightly so that the flight paths don't cross. There shouldn't be any conflict then.'

'Very well. The Cortinis will contact you at the market stall this morning to make the arrangements for transporting them up here.'

'A thousand thanks, m'sieur. And now, speaking of the market, I'd better get going.'

The Comte de Bellevue raised a hand in salutation as the Martins' truck headed back down the hill. He paused for a few moments longer in the gateway of the walled garden, watching Eliane's bees, more sure of themselves now, as they went busily from flower to flower in the neat beds she'd helped the gardener to establish there, earlier in the year.

The marketplace in Sainte-Foy-la-Grande was already abuzz with Saturday-morning chatter by the time Eliane arrived. Her progress was slow as she made her way through the crowd, greeting friends, neighbours and stallholders as she squeezed past the colourful displays of produce. Late-summer berries glowed ruby-red alongside amethyst plums in wicker baskets. Beneath their striped awnings, the vegetable stalls were hung with plaited chains of golden onions and tresses of garlic like strings of pearls.

She waved to Monsieur Boin, the farmer husband of the cook at Château Bellevue, as he tended a rotisserie of his succulent, home-raised chickens, which dripped their fat on to a tray of diced potatoes below that were beginning to turn caramel-brown.

Eliane picked her way through the milling throng to the stall where her friend Francine was cheerfully serving the customers clustered around it. Their jams and preserves were always popular and the jars of Eliane's honey disappeared just as quickly.

'What a price,' grumbled a housewife as she picked up one of the amber-filled jars.

'It's the end of the season, madame, and the finest acacia honey.' Francine smiled, unperturbed. 'These will be the last few jars until spring, so I would advise you to buy today if you want some.' She smoothed the crumpled note handed to her and slid it carefully into the leather money belt she wore before counting the change back into the customer's outstretched hand. '*Merci, madame, et bonne journée.*'

Eliane slipped in behind the stall and kissed Francine on both cheeks. The girls had been best friends ever since they'd met on their first day at school. To many, they had seemed an unlikely pair. Francine was impetuous and outgoing whereas Eliane's calm quietness gave her an air of being more reserved. But their personalities fitted together as snugly as the two halves of a walnut in a shell; even at the age of six they'd discovered that they shared a quick sense of humour as well as a strong nurturing instinct, which had over the years grown into a fierce loyalty. Francine's parents had moved back to their hometown of Pau a couple of years before, to be nearer to her ageing grandmother, but

Francine had decided to stay on to take care of the family's smallholding and make her living from the land.

'Sorry I'm late,' Eliane said.

'Don't worry, I knew you were moving the hives this morning. Safely done?'

'They're in their new winter home,' Eliane nodded. 'The bees seemed to be settling in when I left them. Let me take over here for a while. You must be longing for a coffee by now.'

Francine handed over the money belt and folded her apron, stowing it behind the stall. She waved to a sprawling group of friends who had pushed a couple of tables together outside the Café des Arcades, and gesticulated to them to order her a coffee. 'Oh, I nearly forgot! You see that *mec* over there? The big guy between Bertrand and Stéphanie? – in fact, Stéphanie is almost sitting in his lap, flirting as usual. Well, he came to the stall earlier, asking for you. Says his name's Mathieu something-or-other and he's the *stagiaire* at Château de la Chapelle, here to help the Cortinis with their wine harvest. They told him to come and find you, apparently. Something about moving some more beehives. I'll send him over.'

As she served the next customer Eliane glanced over at the group, who were laughing uproariously at something Stéphanie had just said. Francine pulled up a chair and leaned across to speak to Mathieu, who looked towards Eliane's stall across the busy market square. For a moment, the crowds parted and their eyes met. Eliane's calm, grey gaze seemed to disconcert the young man, who set down his coffee cup and scrambled to his feet so hastily that he almost upset the tin table, sending drinks slopping in all directions, to the amusement of the others – and the obvious annoyance of Stéphanie, who grabbed a handful of paper napkins and dabbed furiously at the sleeve of her blouse.

Mathieu waited, standing to one side and pretending to be absorbed in reading the notices pinned to the board in front of the *mairie*, until there was a brief lull in the queue of customers, and then he approached.

'Eliane Martin?' He held out a sun-browned hand as broad and strong as a bear's paw, but she noticed that, despite his bulk, he moved with an easy, animal grace. 'My name is Mathieu Dubosq. I'm working for the Cortinis. They sent me to give you a message.'

As she shook his hand, Eliane appraised him with her clear-eyed gaze and then smiled, causing his cheeks to flush as red as the jars of Francine's wild-strawberry jam that sat on the stall between them. '*Mais oui*. The Comte de Bellevue has already explained it to me. They have some beehives that need moving to join mine in the kitchen garden at the château, *n'est-ce pas?*'

Mathieu nodded, running his fingers through his thick, black hair, suddenly conscious that it might be in need of a little taming in the presence of this quietly self-possessed girl whose smile seemed to have struck him dumb.

'And they are in *Tante* Béatrice's orchard at Saint André?'

There was an awkward silence as Mathieu tried – and failed – to concentrate on what she could possibly be talking about.

'The bees,' she prompted gently. 'Are the hives in the orchard of Patrick Cortini's aunt? I believe Monsieur le Comte said they belong to the sister-in-law of Monsieur Cortini?'

'Yes. Yes, that's right.'

'*Eh bien*. In that case I will see if my father and brother can bring the truck over before first light on Monday. That will be the best time to catch them still in their hives. I'll bring what's needed.'

'I'll be there, Mademoiselle Martin, to help carry them.'

The light in her eyes seemed to illuminate her entire face as she smiled at him again. 'It's Eliane. Thank you, Mathieu, I shall look forward to seeing you on Monday then.'

He stood back, watching as she served another customer, apparently in no hurry to return to join the group at the café.

Stéphanie pushed her way through the throng, which now filled the marketplace as the church clock struck eleven. She picked up a jar of mirabelle jam from the display, wrinkled her nose and set it back, out of place, on the stall. 'Oh, *bonjour*, Eliane,' she said, as if she'd only just noticed who the stallholder was. 'Come on, Mathieu, we ordered you another coffee to replace the one you spilled and it's getting cold.' She tucked her arm through his, proprietorially. 'And look,' she scolded, tapping his hand with mock-severity, 'you have ruined the sleeve of my blouse. It's a good thing it's only an old one.'

Gently and politely, he extracted his arm from her grasp. He picked up the spurned mirabelle jam and balanced it back in its place on top of the neat pyramid of jars. Then he reached out his bear-like hand once again and – gaining in confidence – returned Eliane's candid gaze with his own shy, dark-eyed smile. 'Goodbye then, Eliane. Until Monday.'

Abi: 2017

The sky outside the kitchen windows is ripped open, time after time, by flashes of lightning and loud thunder cracks, and the rain drums furiously on the roof of the château as the storm engulfs it.

The thunder makes me jump. 'Do you ever get struck by lightning up here?' I ask, nervously.

'Don't worry.' Sara carries on serenely emptying a basket of shopping on to the countertop. 'The château's been here for more than five hundred years. We have a very efficient series of lightning conductors installed nowadays, which protect the buildings. We just have to make sure all the appliances are unplugged, otherwise they can get fried by the power surges.' She stashes cartons of milk into the door of a vast stainless-steel refrigerator and pulls out a bottle of wine. 'It'll soon blow over. In high summer they can go on half the night, but these spring storms never last very long.'

'You speak excellent English,' I venture.

Sara laughs. 'Well, that's a compliment! I *am* English. I moved out here a few years ago. And then married a Frenchman.'

The kitchen door opens suddenly. A man dressed in builder's over-alls slams it behind him and shakes the raindrops from his hair, reaching to pull Sara into his arms. She laughs, not seeming to mind at all that his clothes are both dusty and damp, and kisses him back.

'We have a guest,' she turns to gesture towards where I'm sitting at the scrubbed wooden table.

'Excuse me, madame.' He comes over, wiping his hand on the leg of his overalls before shaking mine. 'I didn't see you there.'

'This is my husband, Thomas. Thomas, this is Abi. We met on the road just as the storm was breaking.'

'You look as if you're an escapee from the yoga centre?' he smiles.

'I suppose the Lycra leggings are a bit of a giveaway. I'm sorry to have invaded your space. Sara very kindly offered me shelter. I'll be heading back as soon as the storm's passed.'

'You'd better have some supper with us.' Sara pours three glasses of the chilled wine and puts one of them on the table in front of me. 'You'll have missed it at the centre by now. I'll run you back afterwards.'

The ache in my leg and the throbbing burn of the blister on my heel urge me to accept her kind offer.

Thomas takes a sip of his wine and then excuses himself to go and change out of his work clothes.

'Can I lay the table?' I ask Sara, as she busies herself sautéing a pan-ful of potatoes with some garlic. The smell fills the air and makes my mouth water as I set out the cutlery, napkins and water glasses. I take a small sip of wine, which is fruity and delicious.

'Are you a vegetarian?' Sara asks. 'I've roasted a chicken, but I can easily make you something else if you'd prefer?'

I shake my head. 'No, chicken would be wonderful. It's incredibly kind of you to have taken me in like this.'

Maybe it's the effect of the wine, or the fact that I'm absolutely starving and the food smells so good, or maybe it's the relaxed warmth that this friendly couple radiate as they share their home and their evening meal with me, but I'm suddenly overwhelmed with emotion at their generosity. My throat closes up and tears well in my eyes.

Don't be stupid, I admonish myself. *You've only just met these people. You don't want them thinking you're completely crazy. It's already bad enough that they found you wandering around the countryside with a storm coming.*

Sara notices my disquiet and, under the pretext of setting a jug of water on the table, comes over to pat my hand reassuringly. 'It's our pleasure.' She smiles. 'You must be tired – that's quite a distance you've walked this afternoon. Are you enjoying the yoga retreat?'

Grateful for the diversion, I describe the yoga classes, which I love – and which are so good for strengthening my injured leg and arms, although I keep that bit to myself – and I tell her about Pru meeting her handsome Dutchman, too, keeping it light.

Sara shakes her head. 'Oh dear, it sounds a bit like your friend has abandoned you.'

I shrug. 'It's fine. At least there's a bit more room in the tent.'

Her eyes open wide. 'You're camping? At this time of year?'

'We booked too late for any of the accommodation in the centre so the only option was the tent. There are quite a few others camping too. It's okay. Most of the time we're in the yoga studio or the dining hall, in any case.'

She glances doubtfully at the windows, which are awash with runnels of rain. I admit she has a point, and for a fleeting moment I wonder how the tent is standing up to the storm. 'It'll be fine,' I say stoutly, more to try to reassure myself than anyone else.

'So tell me,' she says, reaching for a chopping board and beginning to prepare a bowl of salad, 'where do you call home?'

'London,' I reply. I pick up a tea towel and begin to dry some pans sitting on the draining board next to the sink. 'Shall I put these away?'

She nods. 'They go in that cupboard over there. And what do you do in London?'

'Nothing much at the moment,' I admit, wiping my hands on the cloth. 'I was studying for an Open University degree, but I've shelved it for the time being. I haven't been very well for the last couple of years. Nothing major. But there was an accident . . . My husband died . . .' I tail off and there's a moment's silence.

'Well, that sounds pretty major to me. I'm so sorry,' Sara puts a sympathetic hand on my arm. 'No wonder you've not been well.'

I shake my head and attempt to swerve the conversation away from the heavier stuff by saying brightly, 'But I used to work as a live-in nanny.'

'Did you enjoy nannying?'

'Very much. I was with a couple of really great families. I loved looking after their kids.' I don't add that a few months after Mum died – having spent what little money there was left on one final drinking extravaganza while I was sitting the last of my A levels – I'd realised that I had nowhere to live. And so I'd applied to the agency ('Domestic Positions at Home and Abroad') and ticked the boxes saying that I was seeking a residential position and was available immediately. Armed with a set of good references from my teachers at school, I landed a job two days later with a desperate couple who had three children under the age of five and whose au pair had just disappeared off to live in Wales with a guy she'd met at a festival.

'And is there anyone waiting for you back at home?' Sara asks. 'Children? A partner? Who's been looking after you while you've been unwell?'

I shake my head. 'None of the above. Footloose and fancy-free, that's me. I'm much better really these days, though.' I resort to my usual strategy of keeping it light, deflecting questions before they can be asked. And trying to ignore the fact that I still suffer from anxiety attacks, insomnia and – despite many hours talking to a kind and encouraging psychologist – a chronic inability to move on with my life.

Over supper, Sara and Thomas tell me about the business they've established at Château Bellevue. 'During the season, we have weddings here. We'll be on our third one of the year this coming weekend. Mondays are days off for us and our staff, then on Tuesdays and Wednesdays we get all the preparations done, making up the bedrooms and setting everything up before the guests arrive for the celebrations.'

'How many people can you accommodate?'

'In the château itself, anything up to twenty-four. The other guests stay in *chambres d'hôtes* in the local area. But we're expanding a bit. Last winter we bought the mill house down by the river. We're doing it up to provide accommodation for another ten people. It's within walking distance so it'll be a good option for larger parties, or for grooms' families, who don't always take too kindly to being put up elsewhere.'

'It's coming on slowly,' Thomas adds. 'I do bits of work on the mill house whenever I can fit it in; and we have a team of builders, too, but they're working on other projects at the same time. We'll definitely have it ready in time for next year, though.'

Sara sighed. 'Well don't expect to be spending much time down there this season. I'm going to need you to help out here as much as possible.' She turns to me. 'We've had to let one of our assistants go. Actually, that's a euphemism for discovering her in a heap in the wine cellar, having downed a couple of bottles of champagne just before the last lot of wedding guests arrived! Such a shame. It's very hard to find people locally who are prepared to do a seasonal job like this one, which effectively means they have no social life at weekends throughout the summer.'

I nod, sympathetically. 'I can imagine how much hard work it must be. But probably quite good fun at the same time – a bit like having one long, joyous party all summer?'

Sara and Thomas smile at one another. 'You're right,' he says. 'If you enjoy the work it is very fulfilling.'

They tell me more about the business and about the experiences they've had in the last couple of years: how much they've learned, the mistakes they've made, the fun they've had. I watch their faces as they talk, noticing the way they laugh so easily, the way they listen to one another, the looks that they exchange. It's evident that they love their work almost as much as they love each other.

By the end of the evening I feel as if I've known them for years, rather than just a few hours, and I'm reluctant to leave and head back to the centre. But after the salad of fresh-picked tender leaves and a platter of cheeses, which range from hard and tangy to runny and pungent, we push our chairs back from the table. 'Thank you again; that was the most delicious meal.' My body is glowing after falling off the detox wagon so suddenly, and I feel sleepy and replete. Surely these foods can't be so bad for you when they make you feel this good?

Just as Sara predicted, the storm has blown over; and as she drives me back to the centre a few stars are becoming visible where the clouds have parted. It looks like there's quite a party going on outside the doorway of the centre's main building when she pulls up behind the police car that's sitting in front of it. Several of the retreat organisers, Pru and her Dutchman, a few of our fellow yogis and a pair of *gendarmes* are milling around.

As I climb out of the van, there's a piercing shriek from Pru. 'Abi! There you are! Where the hell have you been? We've all been worried sick. No one could remember seeing you since the walking meditation this afternoon. They even called the police . . .'

The *gendarmes* turn to look at me. 'Is this the missing person?' one asks. And then he spots Sara. '*Ah, bonsoir, Sara, comment vas-tu?*'

She replies in rapid-fire French, explaining what's happened.

'There's no need to worry, madame,' they reassure Pru when Sara has finished. 'Your friend has been in the best possible hands.' Laughing, they climb into their police car and the tail lights disappear off down the drive.

Once I've reassured Pru that I'm absolutely fine and have enjoyed a very pleasant evening being wined and dined in a château, she and her Dutchman climb into his car and depart for the unspoken luxury of his guest house.

I'm a bit embarrassed by all the fuss, so I turn to shake Sara's hand. 'Thank you for rescuing me. And for that delicious supper. It's lovely to have met you and Thomas.'

But she seems to be in no great hurry to leave and is gazing around at the group of buildings whose lights illuminate the courtyard where we're standing. 'It's good to have a chance to see what they've done here. I haven't been to the centre since they did it up.'

'I'll show you around, if you like,' I offer. It seems the least I can do after all her kindness. So I give her a brief guided tour of the dining room, the airy yoga studio with its floor-to-ceiling sliding doors that open on to a view of fields and woodland, and the chill-out space where a few people are lounging with cups of herbal tea. I lead her round to the side of the building, saying, 'Some people have rooms upstairs, and some stay off-site at local guest houses, but the rest of us . . .' I tail off.

'Camp?' Sara finishes for me as we both survey the scene of carnage before us.

Most of the tents are, admittedly, still upright, although they are dripping forlornly into wide puddles that gleam where the lights catch them. But one has been reduced to a soggy heap of crumpled material that sits like a lonely, deserted island in the middle of a sizeable pond.

'That's yours, I take it?' Sara nudges me gently.

I nod, not wanting to speak in case doing so releases the barrage of tears that is welling up inside me. I feel defeated, suddenly. Apart from my handbag and phone, which are stashed in the safe in the office (we had to hand them over when we arrived – it's all part of the detox), everything I have with me is under that pathetic-looking bundle of sodden fabric.

'Right,' she says briskly, immediately decisive. 'We need to excavate your belongings and then you're coming back to stay with us.'

I begin to object, but, to be honest, here and now I can't really come up with an alternative solution. Sara ignores my feeble protestations and wades through the puddle to lift up what's left of the tent. Together, we manage to unzip the inner layer and while she holds the muddy, dripping flysheet out of the way I rummage around and find my things. My holdall of clothes is soaked through. My sponge bag is afloat in the puddle. And the two sleeping bags, Pru's and mine, are so saturated that it's an effort to drag them free. As I'm struggling to wring as much rainwater from them as possible, Sara extracts the two sleeping mats and pulls them clear. She spots a length of clothes line stretched between two birch trees. 'Here,' she says, 'let's hang what we can over there. They'll drip dry a bit overnight and we can finish sorting them out in the morning.'

Making it clear that she's not prepared to discuss any other possible sleeping arrangements that I might be able to come up with, she puts my holdall to one side. 'We'll bring that back with us and stick everything in the washing machine. Then at least your clothes will be clean and dry for tomorrow.'

'I'm sorry to be such a hassle, especially when you're so busy. I bet you didn't realise what you were letting yourself in for when you stopped beside me on the road.'

'It's no hassle, and it turns out to be a very good thing our paths crossed when they did. Fortunately, I happen to have a château full of empty bedrooms tonight. You can stay in one of them. And I bet it'll be a lot more comfortable than your tent, even if it had been dry and standing upright.'

I hesitate, and she nudges me again and says, 'Did I forget to mention the en-suite bathroom with a bathtub so deep you can almost float in it?'

I smile and hold up the towel that I've retrieved from the tent, which was once cream-coloured but is now a streaky mud-brown. 'You do make a compelling case. Tell me – are there fluffy white towels too, by any chance?'

Sara grins back. 'You betcha!'

Eliane: 1938

The following week, before setting off up the hill to her day's work at Château Bellevue, Eliane covered her head and shoulders with a shawl to keep out the slight chill of the mist that had gathered in the river valley overnight. As she passed, the door of the mill itself stood ajar and she stepped into the dry warmth of the grinding room to say good morning to her father. She lingered for a few moments, watching as her father primed the millstones with a few handfuls of grain before turning the control wheel to open the mill race. The calm, hushed flow of the river was transformed into a powerful rush as the water began to tumble into the narrow channel, coaxing the mill wheel to begin to turn. As it gathered speed, the rush became a roar and the machinery sprang to life, adding its clattering chatter to the cacophony. Creaking and clicking, the gears began to turn the runner stone and her father opened the grain chute, directing the flow into the hole in the stone's centre. After a few moments, the first powdery grist began to fall into the wooden trough below the bed stone, reminding Eliane of the first flakes of winter snow.

Her father checked the grist and adjusted the speed of the runner stone before he was happy that it was grinding the grain finely enough.

On rafters high above them, the boards of the upper floor creaked as Yves heaved another sack of wheat over to the hopper that fed the millstones. He pulled open the trapdoor in the ceiling above their heads, to check with Gustave that all was running smoothly, and grinned as he caught sight of Eliane. The din was far too loud for his voice to be heard, but she saw him mouth 'Good morning'. She waved back at him, then kissed her father and bade him a *'Bonne journée'* before gathering her shawl around her head once again and setting off towards her own place of work.

As she trudged up the hill, the sounds of the mill faded behind her. In the distance, far away on the other side of the river, the faint, rhythmic rumble of a passing train stirred the air like a pulsing heartbeat before the silence swallowed it. At the top of the ridge she emerged into the autumn sunrise, which would soon evaporate the river's night-time blanket and reveal the mill house to the day.

She paused to catch her breath, glancing back to the valley below. The upper branches of the willow tree were just visible now, and she smiled to herself as she remembered how she and Mathieu had sat beneath the leafy canopy yesterday evening, as they had done on all the evenings since he'd helped her move the additional beehives, and how, at last, he had plucked up the courage to reach out his hand and hold hers.

Madame Boin was already clattering pots and pans when Eliane stepped across the threshold into the warmth of the cavernous kitchen, which was filled with the smell of baking bread.

'*Bonjour, madame.* What do we need this morning?' She picked up the shallow wickerwork basket that sat beside the door, being careful not to track the prints of her dusty boots on to the clean kitchen floor. Her final duty each day was to sweep and mop the slate tiles so that Madame Boin would arrive to find her domain neat and tidy the next morning.

'*Bonjour*, Eliane. I'm making a *blanquette* for lunch today, so bring some carrots and potatoes. We need the peppermint leaves for Monsieur le Comte's *tisanes*. And didn't you say there was something else I could add that would help speed his recovery? I'm still worried about that ulcer on his leg.'

'Thyme is best for circulation and for fighting infection, Maman says. I'll bring you a good bunch. And basil is good for convalescence too, as well as the mint tea. There's still some growing in a pot in the corner of the garden, although I should probably bring the whole thing back inside now if it's to survive the winter.'

Madame Boin nodded. 'And bring me a good handful of sage leaves too, would you? Your sage tea is certainly helping to calm these blasted hot flushes. I slept much better last night.'

Even though summer was well on the wane now, Eliane's *potager* still flourished within the protection of the walled garden. The gardener had let her take over a couple of unused beds for her pharmacy of herbs and medicinal plants. It was useful, especially at this time of the year, to have access to these sheltered, upland plots as well as her more shaded riverside garden at the mill, so that she could grow a wider range of varieties across the two different habitats. When Eliane had asked his permission to cultivate the redundant beds, Monsieur le Comte had been delighted that the château could help to provide Lisette with the plants she used to treat her patients across the community.

The stone walls of the garden were already soaking up the morning sunshine when she pushed open the gate. The first bees were at work mining the sweetly pungent nectar from cushions of thyme and rosemary. They seemed to have a sense of businesslike urgency about themselves today and Eliane knew that they had read something in the softening autumn light that had told them to hasten to lay in their supplies before winter arrived. She wouldn't gather any more honey from the hives now, until the bees could harvest the renewed bounty of pollen next spring, making sure that they had the resources to see them through the austerity of the coming months.

She dug up the vegetables, smiling at the robin who had been watching her from his perch in the pear tree and who immediately fluttered down to search the newly-turned earth for breakfast titbits. From her apron pocket, she took a penknife and cut the herbs, placing everything in the basket. She had a list of ingredients to bring home for her mother, too, but she would gather these at the end of the day when the sun had warmed the leaves, stimulating a good supply of the essential oils that were a vital part of the healing concoctions.

Re-entering the kitchen, she untied her boots and set them on the mat beside the doorway, before slipping her feet into the wooden-soled *sabots* that she wore inside the château and beginning her day's work.

Abi: 2017

For a moment, I can't think where I am. Early-morning sunshine slants across the pillow through slatted shutters and my legs, which ought to be constricted by a narrow sleeping bag, slide freely over smooth sheets. And then I remember: so Château Bellevue and its owners weren't just a lovely dream I conjured up during the best night's sleep I've had in years.

I check my watch. It's early. Thomas said he'd run me back to the yoga centre after breakfast as he'd be going that way anyway. I stretch luxuriantly one more time, making the most of the space and comfort of a proper bed, and then reluctantly throw back the covers and plant my feet on the floor. I'm conscious that the room I'm staying in is part of Sara and Thomas' business and that I've created enough extra work for them already, so I strip the bed and clean the bathroom, leaving the room looking as if I'd never been there.

As I scoop up the bundle of bedding, a memory ambushes me out of nowhere. The simple, everyday gesture of holding an armful of washing suddenly brings back associations for me that touch a nerve running right to my very core. In my mind's eye, I see myself as a teenager again, back in the flat trying to get Mum's bed sorted. She'd have been drinking all day, as usual, and I'd persuade her out of her sodden bed when I got home from school and help her into a bath. Then, leaving her changed and propped in an armchair beside the gas fire, with a silent prayer that she wouldn't set fire to herself and the flat, I'd bundle the sheets into a bin bag and trudge around the corner to the launderette. I'd sit there in the soap-scented warmth, doing my homework while the machines juddered and sloshed around me. If we had enough money that day I'd stick a fifty-pence piece in the dryer and come home with a stack of neatly folded still-warm linen. But more often, and especially towards the end of the month, I'd have to turn the bin bag inside out and stuff the wet sheets back in, my arms aching after hauling the heavy bundle back home to drape them over a plastic clothes horse in front of the fire.

'Caring', they call it these days. To me, it just felt like surviving. I was terrified of the alternative, of being taken away from her. I suppose children almost always want to stay with their parents, no matter what. So even when Mum got really bad I didn't let on; I just looked after her the best I could.

Her own family had made it clear that they wanted nothing more to do with her when she got pregnant with me. I have no idea who my father was – and, to be honest, I'm not sure that Mum really knew either. She told me various stories, over the years, depending how much she'd had to drink and whether she was in one of her full-on happy moods or on a complete downer . . . Maybe he really was a soldier who'd been killed in a friendly-fire incident on training manoeuvres shortly after I was conceived; or maybe he was the Australian backpacker who had disappeared without leaving his number (or even, apparently, his name); or maybe he was just some scummy chancer who'd taken advantage of a girl who'd been too drunk to know what she was doing. Anyway, we were a team, Mum and me, and we managed just fine on our own, so long as she was sober enough to collect her benefits and didn't blow the whole lot in the off-licence on her way home.

I shake my head, rousing myself and shrugging off the memory, and take the bundle of bedding downstairs. Sara is already bustling about in the kitchen.

'Good morning,' I say. 'And thanks for the best night's sleep I've had in ages. Where do these go?' I show her the armful of bedding. 'If you give me a fresh set I'll get the bed made up again. I've cleaned through, but I just need to give the room a quick going over with the vacuum and then it'll be all ready for your wedding guests.'

She nods, approvingly. 'Here, give those to me. I'll stick them in a laundry bag. Thanks for doing that, it's a huge help. I'll give you a hand re-making the bed, but sit down and have your breakfast first.'

Thomas comes in, whistling cheerfully, and we sit around the kitchen table which is set with a red-and-white gingham cloth. I help myself to fresh fruit and a big bowl of cereal, as Sara pours us each a mug of richly fragrant coffee.

Thomas and Sara exchange a glance. 'Look, Abi,' she says, 'I know this is probably going to sound like a crazy proposition, and it's right out of the blue, but how would you like to try working at Château Bellevue for the season? Thomas and I discussed it last night. You seem very practical and I'm sure you'd pick it all up very quickly. Heaven knows, you'd be doing us a massive favour as we're desperate for another pair of hands. We can offer you accommodation in the mill house, as long as you don't mind it being a bit of a building site. But I promise you the room you'd be sleeping in would be as far away from the mess and noise as possible. It would certainly be a lot more comfortable than a tent!'

I laugh. 'Are you serious? You've only just met me.'

'Yes, but I can see that we already get on well. I'm afraid the pay isn't great, but you get your meals when you're working so that helps. I think you'd fit in well as a member of the team. I know this is all very sudden, so maybe you could think about it for the rest of the week while you finish your yoga retreat? And then, if you decide you're happy to give it a try, you can see how it goes.'

I think of the empty apartment waiting for me back in London, of its huge floor-to-ceiling windows, which look out across the docklands on to the vast sprawling city beyond, and of how lonely and isolated I feel among all those millions of people. There's no sense of purpose to my life there. Whereas here, I realise, I'll be busy. I won't spend hours trapped inside my own head as there'll be so many other things to think about. Weddings! Parties to organise. Guests to look after.

But then I hesitate again. Will I be up to the work? What if I let them down? What if I ruin someone's special day because I make some terrible mistake? What if I have a panic attack at being in a crowded room and collapse, gasping for breath, in the middle of someone's elegant reception?

As if she can read my mind, Sara smiles reassuringly. 'Abi, I know you've told us you haven't been well lately, and if it's something that means you can't work then we would completely understand. But it seems to me you are a very capable woman – maybe more capable than you think. You could give it a go on a trial basis and if you decide, at any point, that you don't want to stay on then you can go home straight away. But, honestly, any help you can give us will be better than none. It'll free up Thomas to get on with the work on the mill house during the day; otherwise the project's going to over-run badly and the bank manager won't be very happy. And although the weddings are quite hard work, you might find that it's quite enjoyable too.'

I look from Sara to Thomas and back to Sara again, both waiting for my answer.

And then I decide. And, despite the events of yesterday afternoon, I clearly haven't learned my lesson about the dangers of spontaneity at all, because I say, with a grin, 'Is there room for a yoga mat in the bedroom at the mill house, do you think? If so, I could probably start right away.'

Eliane: 1938

'Pass me the rolling pin if you've finished with it, would you, Eliane?'

Mother and daughter were busy in the kitchen at the mill, preparing food for the holiday weekend. Eliane was slicing the pears that Madame Boin had allowed her to bring home from the château's kitchen garden, and arranging them in a neat fan shape on top of the frangipane tart she was making.

Lisette looked over at her handiwork approvingly. 'Very good; that looks perfect.'

'I've tried to make an extra effort for Mireille coming home. She's probably used to fancy Parisian pâtisseries now and will find our home-made offerings far too ordinary. Do you think she'll have changed, Maman? I imagine she'll be very sophisticated now.'

Lisette laughed and shook her head. 'Not our Mireille. You know *tarte aux poires* is her very favourite dessert. This will be more delicious than anything you could buy in a shop, even in Paris. I'm looking forward to seeing her clothes, though. Working in such a prestigious *atelier* she'll know about all the latest fashions.'

Happily, All Saints Day fell on a Tuesday that year, so Eliane's sister Mireille had been allowed to take the Monday off as well and was coming back to the mill for the first time since she'd left in May to embark on her career as an apprentice seamstress at a Parisian couture house.

Yves entered the kitchen, whistling, accompanied by a flurry of fallen leaves that blew in on the late-October wind as he opened the door. He set a lidded wicker basket on the table with an air of triumph. Lisette came over to inspect.

'*Oh là-là*, what beauties!'

'Eighteen of the finest langoustines the river can offer.' He lifted one of the plump crawfish out of the basket and pretended to threaten Eliane's ear with its fierce-looking claws. She batted him away, unruffled by his teasing, and he picked up a piece of her leftover pastry instead and popped it into his mouth.

The sound of the truck pulling into the barn brought them all to the kitchen door and then Mireille was there, laughing and exclaiming as her family engulfed her, her dark curls blown into a tangle by the blustering October wind.

She set down her handbag and stood for a moment, breathing deep the air of home, taking it all in: the soft rush of the river turning the millwheel; the willow tree trailing its leaves into the pool below the weir; the chickens pecking busily in the dust; the nanny goat and her kid grazing in the pasture beyond the orchard; and, from within, the familiar smells of woodsmoke and something good simmering on the range; the faint under-notes of the herbs and medicinal plants that were hanging to dry beside the chimney breast for her mother to use; and, most of all, the embrace of her father, mother, sister and brother: her family.

'Look at this chic bag,' Lisette exclaimed. 'And your jacket!'

'Ooh, fancy,' Yves mocked, picking up the bag and mincing about the kitchen with it over his arm. 'Mademoiselle Mireille Martin is far too fine for the Moulin de Coulliac these days!'

'Not so fine that I can't still beat up my cheeky little brother.' Mireille pounced on him and pretended to twist his arm behind his back until he surrendered her bag. 'In fact I can't wait to change into my comfortable clothes and *sabots* again.'

41

Gustave brought in her luggage. 'I'll take this straight up to your room, shall I?'

'Come, Eliane.' Mireille linked arms with her sister. 'Help me unpack. I've got some presents for you.'

The bedroom the sisters shared was tucked under the eaves of the mill, its windows looking out across the weir to the fields beyond. Gustave had set the bags down next to one of the single beds and Mireille flung herself on to its sprigged cotton quilt. The room smelled faintly of beeswax and the lavender bags that scented the chest of drawers and the tall walnut-wood *armoire* in the corner. 'It's so good to be home,' she sighed.

Eliane had arranged a posy of autumn berries in a little porcelain vase at her sister's bedside and they now glowed carmine in the pool of sunshine that filtered through the window panes.

'Come,' said Mireille, patting the coverlet. 'Sit down and tell me the news. What's it like working at the château? Have you tamed that dragon Madame Boin yet? And how is Monsieur le Comte's health these days?'

Eliane settled herself on the bed beside her sister, tucking her legs up beneath her. 'It's good. I like the work. They let me do quite a bit in the kitchen garden, so I'm not always indoors, and I have my bees up there now. Nine hives! And there'll be more next summer if they swarm. Madame Boin is alright – her bark is worse than her bite. We get on okay now. And Monsieur le Comte is in better health. The ulcer on his leg is healing well, thanks to Maman's herbs and regular honey poultices. He's a kind boss, a real gentleman as always.

'But tell me all about Paris,' she continued. 'Have you dressed any film stars yet? How do you survive in all that noise and bustle? Among such crowds of people? I can't imagine it.'

Eliane listened, wide-eyed, as Mireille described the basement lodgings that she shared with two of the other seamstresses, her journey to work on a careering, clanging tram, and the demanding *Parisiennes* who came to the *sâlon* for fittings of their expensive new outfits. Mireille rummaged in one of her bags. 'Here, I've brought these patterns for you and Maman. I thought you might like to make some of them – they're very *à la mode*.'

Yves stuck his head round the door of the girls' room. 'Look at you two, gossiping away there. Has Eliane told you about her boyfriend yet?'

He grinned as his sister blushed.

'He's not my boyfriend; he's just a friend. And anyway, he spends more time going fishing with you than he does with me. He's just as much your friend as mine.'

'Ha!' Yves exclaimed. 'If you say so, but he and I don't spend hours sitting under the willow tree together, holding hands and gazing into each other's eyes.'

'I see,' said Mireille, the laughter in her dark eyes belying her serious tone of voice. 'And what is "his" name, may I enquire?'

'Mathieu Dubosq,' Yves cut in eagerly. 'He's a great fisherman, always knows where the big ones are lurking. Knows all about hunting too. And he's almost as much of an expert on mushrooms as Eliane is. He's also coming to have lunch with us in a few minutes.'

'Well, I'm looking forward to meeting him.' Mireille diverted her brother by passing him a small package wrapped in brown paper and tied with rough twine.

Yves whistled through his teeth as he unwrapped a horn-handled penknife. 'Just look how sharp that blade is. Fantastic. Thanks, Mireille.'

'And now . . .' Mireille got to her feet and gathered up an armful of similarly wrapped parcels. 'Let's go and give these to Maman and Papa and help set the table for lunch.'

As they scraped their plates to collect the last crumbs of succulent frangipane and sweet pastry, Eliane surveyed her family gathered around the kitchen table. She'd been concerned that this first meal at the *moulin* might be an ordeal for Mathieu, but he displayed none of his shyness as he answered Gustave's questions about this year's wine harvest and Lisette's questions about his home in Tulle. Eliane had already told her parents that Mathieu's mother had died of a severe haemorrhage – every midwife's dread fear – after giving birth to his younger brother, Luc.

'I'm taking the train home tomorrow to be back for *la Toussaint*. We always put flowers on my mother's grave. I haven't seen my father and brother since the wine harvest began, so it'll be good to catch up. They work on a farm just outside the town – beef cattle and feed crops mostly.'

Gustave set his fork down finally, reluctantly accepting that his plate was empty now. 'And will you go back to cattle farming when you've finished your *stage* at Château de la Chapelle, do you think?'

Unable to help himself, Mathieu glanced across the table at Eliane and a pink glow suffused his deeply sun-browned features. 'I'm not sure. My father wanted me to try the experience of wine farming and I've found it very interesting. I like this part of the world too, so I may stay on with the Cortinis for a while longer. They've already asked me to, so I'll tell my father tomorrow. After all, Coulliac isn't too far from Tulle . . .' He trailed off, suddenly conscious that he may have given too much away.

Eliane smiled at him. The most like Lisette of the three Martin children, she had inherited her mother's intuition and her uncanny ability to see beneath the surface, reading people's innermost thoughts and feelings. She understood Mathieu's unspoken hope that their future would be a shared one. The first tentative flickers of mutual attraction were blossoming into something far deeper than just a friendship and were binding them together more strongly every day.

She stood up from the table to collect the empty plates and, when Mathieu handed her his, her fingertips touched his hand for a fleeting moment, a touch as gentle as the brush of a butterfly's wing and as strong as a promise that had no need of words. He would go home to place his remembrance offering of flowers on his mother's grave, just as the Martins would visit the little churchyard of Coulliac to pay their respects to their forebears, and when *la Toussaint* was over and November well and truly begun, he would return so that they could be together again.

Eliane and Mireille rested their elbows on the stable door and watched the pig as it buried its snout in the trough, snuffling contentedly as it rooted out some turnip tops from among the potato peelings.

Eliane scratched behind the animal's ears with a stick. 'You see, she's forgiven us already.'

It had taken them the best part of an hour to find the pig in the forest, where she'd been turned out to enjoy an autumn feast of acorns, and then to persuade her to return to her sty with the help of a tempting bucket of swill. Perhaps she suspected the fate that was in store for her once the winter weather arrived in earnest. But until that day arrived, she would be well fed and well cared-for.

The sty was more of a small cave, really, hollowed into the wall of limestone through which the river had etched its course for thousands of years. The rock rose abruptly behind the mill house and soared upwards to form the buttress upon which the Château de Bellevue perched, high above them. Ancient underground streams – most long-since disappeared – had carved a network of tunnels through the porous rock across the whole of this region, and one of these tunnels formed an invisible link between the *moulin* and the château. According to Monsieur le Comte, it had been a vital lifeline when the château was besieged in the Middle Ages. The invading army couldn't work out how the Comte's forebears trapped within were able to survive for so many weeks without access to food and water, and eventually they'd got bored and left.

The tunnel had been blocked up at both ends for years, although Gustave had removed the rocks and rubble that had plugged the entrance at the back of the pigsty in order to use a few feet of the tunnel to store wine. This natural larder would also be used when butchering time came, as the cool, dry darkness provided the perfect conditions for curing hams and *saucissons*, as well as preserving the jars of pâté that Lisette would prepare to see them through the winter. An old door, overlaid with several sheets of corrugated tin, concealed the tunnel's opening and made the outer part of the cave into a snug home for the pig, who had now settled down for a nap on her comfortable bed of straw.

Mireille took a handful of acorns from her pocket and tossed them into the trough with a sound like the rattle of hailstones, which caused the pig to open one eye. 'I do miss lots of things about home,' she remarked, 'but I'll be quite happy not to be here when your time is up.' The pig grunted in reply.

'It's hard to imagine you in Paris, wearing your chic dresses and working in that elegant *atelier*. I don't think I'd enjoy living in the city at all.'

Mireille smiled at her sister. 'City life certainly isn't for everyone. One of the apprentice seamstresses has already packed up and gone home to Normandy. She hated Paris. It can take a while to make friends there too. It's strange that you can be a lot lonelier among all those people than you ever would be living in the countryside. But I've made friends with some of the other girls now, and I do enjoy the work – even if some of the clients are impossible to satisfy! Maybe you can come and visit me one day and I can show you round.'

'Maman doesn't like you being so much nearer to Germany. Everyone's been nervous ever since the Nazis marched their way into Czechoslovakia.'

'Don't worry; Paris is safe enough. There wouldn't be so many refu-gees flooding into the city if it weren't. The best thing everyone can do is to get on with their day-to-day lives. Perhaps you and Maman could come and visit me together. I can show you all the sights. The Eiffel Tower is amazing, and the churches are simply huge!'

Eliane thought of the little chapel where they would go tomor-row to put their *Toussaint* flowers on the ancestral graves. Its simple, whitewashed walls and solid oak beams always made her feel safe. And in the churchyard the earthy scent of chrysanthemums would perfume the air, reassuring the souls of the departed that they weren't forgotten and they could rest peacefully. Even as another year ended, there was the reminder that the seasons would turn and, after winter's death, there would be rebirth in the spring.

She spared a thought for Mathieu, who would be in the train by now. Her heart beat a little faster when she recalled the hours they'd spent sitting on the riverbank. With other people, he was usually so silent; but when the two of them were alone together he relaxed, con-fiding to her his hopes and his dreams. She smiled as she thought of the way his dark eyes shone when he described his work in the vines and everything that he was learning in the winemaking *chai*. But then she reminded herself that the trip he was making today wouldn't be an easy one for him . . . How sad it must be for him to lay his offering of *Toussaint* flowers on his own mother's grave, as he had done each year since her death.

As if she had read Eliane's thoughts, Mireille said, 'Mathieu's nice. I enjoyed meeting him.'

Her sister nodded. 'He's a good friend to us all.'

'I get the impression he'd like to be something more than just a friend where you are concerned, *ma p'tite*.' Mireille grinned.

Eliane's cheeks flushed as she studiously concentrated on scratching the back of the pig's neck. Then she smiled in her turn. 'I like him too. Very much. It feels . . .' She tailed off.

'Yes?' prompted Mireille.

'It feels right. It feels like we have a future. I can see us together.'

'Well, if it feels that way, then it *is* right.' Mireille gave her sister's arm a fond squeeze. 'I'm glad.'

Just then Lisette opened the kitchen window, pausing for a moment to enjoy the sight of her two girls exchanging confidences, before she called to them. 'Please can you bring some more wood for the fire when you come in? Supper's nearly ready.'

Abi: 2017

My bedroom in the attic of the mill house is an oasis of calm and order among the chaos of the building project.

'We started at the top and are working our way down,' Thomas had explained. He and his team of builders have created a light, airy room with limewashed beams, and added a bathroom tucked in under the eaves. There's an old-fashioned bath with claw feet, where I can soak to my heart's content, and a wooden towel rack that holds two of Sara's fluffy towels. She insisted on bringing a few finishing touches down from the château – a worn, but still beautiful Aubusson rug; a watercolour painting of beehives beneath a blossom-laden tree; and a canopy of mosquito netting, both pretty and practical, which she drapes above the wrought-iron bedhead. I'll be able to draw it around me as the nights begin to grow warmer, leaving the windows open to allow the cool breath of the river to caress me as I sleep.

Pru was highly disapproving at first when I announced my decision to check out of the yoga retreat and spend the summer living and working at Château Bellevue. But Sara invited her to come and see where I'd be staying and I could see that Pru was impressed. I promised I'd send her regular texts, letting her know how I was getting on and reassuring her that Sara and Thomas weren't actually slave masters keeping me here against my will.

After the first night, even though I was in an unfamiliar room, in a strange house in a foreign country, I felt immediately at home. The whitewashed walls of the attic bedroom emanate calm and tranquillity (even when the builders are busy shattering the peace and quiet elsewhere in the building with their noisy power tools). And the honey-coloured floorboards give off a faint scent of beeswax that perfumes my dreams.

There is a sense of placid permanence about the mill house, standing firm as the river rushes by, the water whipping itself into a froth as it cascades over the weir. The vast mill wheel no longer turns, although Thomas has said it wouldn't take much to get it going again. 'They still used to grind flour here just a few decades ago,' he's told me. 'Ask Sara to tell you the story of the family who lived here. It may look peaceful now, but in the war years this area was occupied by the Nazis. Even today, this community bears the scars of that time. The wounds may have healed a bit, but they are still there, just beneath the surface.'

At his words, I glanced around, taking in the graceful limbs of the willow tree trailing green fingers in the water, the cluster of ancient buildings whose cream stone walls basked in the early-summer sunshine and at the pool beneath the foaming weir where brilliant-blue dragonflies hover. It's hard to picture this place as anything other than harmonious. But as I'd stood there I'd run my hands down the sleeves of my shirt and felt the faint ridges of my own scars, which I keep hidden there. I know as well as anyone that sometimes you have to look beneath the surface to discover the secret history of places. And of people.

And then something Sara said when I moved my things into the mill house echoes in my mind. As I'd set down my small holdall of belongings, I'd mused, 'It's funny, isn't it? The different paths that bring us here from such different backgrounds and places.'

Sara had smiled. 'You know, Abi, we all bring our own baggage along with us. Perhaps that's what we humans have in common – what binds us together. When you get to know this place a little better, you'll begin to see.' Her eyes were like dark pools, fathoms deep. 'There's something about this corner of the world. It's drawn people to it down the ages. Not just the tourists and the people who come on yoga retreats, but pilgrims and others too. Local people say there are three very ancient lines of energy – ley lines – that converge here. And then there are three rivers that converge in this region, the Lot, the Garonne and the Dordogne. Three of the pilgrim routes to Santiago de Compostela from the north meet here too. Who knows? Call it what you like, but maybe there's something that draws people to this place just at the point in their lives when it's most needed.' She shoots me a shrewd glance. 'Anyway, I'm glad that our paths crossed when they did.'

Standing beside the river now, I run my hands over the scars beneath my sleeves once again and I think, *Me too.*

Eliane: 1939

The day after Good Friday was the only time the ancient bread oven at the mill was fired up. Everyone had the modern convenience of a range, or even one of the new electric ovens, in their own home. But it was a tradition in the Martin household, handed down through the generations, to bake the plaited loaves of bread for Easter Day in the mill's original wood-fired oven.

Mathieu had become a frequent visitor, spending all of his spare time with Eliane. In the past month, they could often be seen working alongside one another in the vegetable patch by the river, clearing the last of the winter crops and preparing the ground for spring planting. On that Easter weekend, he came over to help Yves and Gustave stoke the fire and bring the *four-à-pain* up to the right temperature for baking. In the kitchen, Eliane hummed as she helped Lisette and Mireille – who was back from Paris again for a few days – to knead the bread dough and then deftly plait it into three loaves that would prove in the warmth beside the range for a while longer before they were carried out to the oven.

Spring was always one of her favourite times of year, the season of new life and new beginnings. In the walled garden up at the château, the bees were venturing forth on a daily basis now, blissfully drinking the nectar from the abundance of pear blossom that frothed above the hives.

One day last week, Monsieur le Comte had brought a chair and his painting things and begun a picture of the scene. 'It always seems such a hopeful time,' he'd remarked to Eliane as she gathered tender young salad leaves for his lunch, although they were both aware that that year it was overshadowed by the news from beyond France's eastern borders.

Mireille had told them that Paris was filling up with refugees who were flooding in from Austria and Czechoslovakia, which were now under Nazi occupation. What must it be like, Eliane wondered, to wake up one day and find that your country was being run by an invading force?

'Aren't you worried that they may decide to target Paris next?' she asked her sister again.

Mireille shook her head firmly and gave the bread dough another good thump. 'They wouldn't dare! Think of the backlash it would create. France and her allies wouldn't just sit back and let the German army march across the border. Every day in the Parisian newspapers we read of the political and diplomatic efforts that are being made to bring this madness to a halt. They will win through: no one wants another war across Europe.

'I feel so sorry for the refugees, though,' she continued. 'We've got one working at the *atelier* now. She's from Poland – Esther is her name. She's going to have a baby. Imagine how desperate she must have been to leave her home in her condition, carrying only a few belongings. Her husband is in the Polish air force. Sometimes you see whole families, often with young children. Paris is full to overflowing with them these days. There's talk of the French borders being closed to prevent any more coming in.'

Lisette finished rinsing the cooking implements piled up in the sink and wiped her hands on a cloth. 'I wish you'd come home, Mireille, just until things quieten down a bit. We worry about you.'

'Don't worry, Maman, I reckon Paris is about as safe as anywhere else in France. I love working at the *atelier*; I'm getting such good experience, working on all that beautiful *couture*. I wouldn't have such opportunities back here. So I think I'll stay put for the time being. I can always come home if the worst does happen.'

Mathieu appeared in the doorway, his bulk blocking the sunlight for a moment. 'Gustave says the oven is ready whenever you are,' he reported. He came over to stand behind Eliane and peer over her shoulder to see what she was doing. She turned and popped a scrap of sweet pastry into his mouth, then kissed him on the cheek. He put his arms around her and pulled her to him, before remembering where he was and, becoming flustered, glancing over towards Lisette.

From the other side of the kitchen, she smiled at him fondly and said, 'We're looking forward to meeting your father and brother tomorrow, Mathieu. It's lovely that they can be with you for Easter, and so kind of the Cortinis to invite us all to eat together.'

He smiled his shy smile back. 'I know. I'm looking forward to it too.' Gaining in confidence, he wrapped an arm around Eliane once more and said, 'They've been wondering why I've been so busy in the wine cellar, at a time when not much is going on in the winemaking calendar, that I've not been able to come home to see them more often. I told them that pruning the vines has been keeping me occupied, but I think they're growing suspicious!'

Mireille laughed. 'I think they're probably more than suspicious by now . . . Tulle isn't so far away from Coulliac that the gossip can't reach them there!'

'Surely the dough has proved enough now.' To change the subject, Eliane lifted a corner of the muslin cloth that covered the loaves to protect them from any wayward draughts.

'They look perfect to me.' Lisette smiled.

'Here then, Mireille, you can carry one and Mathieu you bring this one. Let's get them in the oven.'

It was the morning of Easter Sunday, and after church the bells, which had been silenced for the past two days since Good Friday, pealed out from village to village in joyful pronouncement that Christ had risen. Dressed in their Sunday best, the Martins drove over to Château de la Chapelle in the neighbouring *commune* of Saint André, bearing gifts of golden, plaited bread and a basket of eggs that Eliane had coloured with natural dyes gleaned from her larder of winter crops: yellow from onion skins, deep pink from beetroot and azure-blue from the leaves of a red cabbage.

It was warm enough to drink their aperitifs outside. The Cortinis were welcoming and hospitable, and especially keen to share their wines with their friends and neighbours. Beneath the generous branches of a walnut tree whose new green leaves were just beginning to unfurl, a table was spread with dishes of pâté, olives and baby radishes alongside a generous array of wine bottles.

Mathieu introduced the Martin family to his father and brother, both of whom were as silent as Mathieu himself at first. Later, though, as the wines flowed and they found themselves in the midst of the most convivial company, they relaxed and became a good deal more talkative. Luc chatted and joked with Yves and the Cortinis' son, Patrick, and Monsieur Dubosq joined in an animated discussion with Gustave and Monsieur Cortini about the state of farming in France and the merits of mechanisation over the use of horses in ploughing. Mathieu and Eliane held hands beneath the table and watched as new bonds were forged between their families.

Finally, they all pushed their chairs back from the dining table, replete with the feast of succulent roast lamb, which had been washed down with several bottles of the Cortinis' finest vintage red.

'So tell me . . .' Monsieur Dubosq turned to Monsieur Cortini. 'Are you going to make a winemaker out of my elder son?'

'He has great aptitude, and he's a dependable pair of hands in the cellar as well as in the vines. I'd be happy to keep him on here, if he'd like to stay.'

'That's good to know. And what about you, Mathieu? Do you think you'd prefer to be a wine farmer than to come back to our cattle and our fields of grain?'

'I . . . I'm not sure, Papa. I know you will need me in the summer to help with the harvest. But I really like it here. I like working in the vines. I like learning how to make wine . . .' He tailed off, unable to say more. Eliane gave his hand a gentle, reassuring squeeze under cover of the tablecloth.

Monsieur Dubosq shot Mathieu a piercing look from beneath his bushy eyebrows and then smiled. 'Don't worry, *mon fils*, I can see that this place has done you good. You're learning a lot and you're growing up. I'm thankful to all these good people who have become your friends.' His dark eyes included Eliane in his remarks at this juncture. 'If Monsieur Cortini is prepared to keep you on then I daresay I can find someone in Tulle to help me and Luc at harvest time. Let's see how it goes.'

Monsieur Cortini clapped his hands. 'Excellent! This calls for a glass of something special to celebrate. I think I have a bottle of Armagnac in the cellar . . .'

That night, as the girls lay in their attic bedroom at the mill listening to the owls softly declaring their territories in the darkness, Mireille whispered, 'Eliane? Are you awake?'

'Yes,' came the reply from across the room.

'It's been a good Easter, hasn't it?'

There was a pause. 'One of the best.'

'I'm glad you and Mathieu are so happy. You're really good together.'

'His family seemed nice, didn't they?'

'Of course they did. Luc's coming over with Mathieu tomorrow to go fishing with Yves. They're already firm friends. And I could see that Monsieur Dubosq approves of you, even if he is a man of few words. I can understand where Mathieu gets it from now!'

As they fell asleep, in the room filled with the hush of the river and lit by moonbeams that stole in through the window by her bed, a smile of contentment played over Eliane's face.

Abi: 2017

'This is Karen, my right-hand woman.' Sara is in the kitchen, sorting dusters and cleaning cloths into three plastic buckets, but she pauses to introduce me to the capable-looking woman who has just appeared in the doorway.

'Pleased to meet you, Abi.' Karen has an Australian accent that is almost as broad as her smile, and a handshake so firm that it leaves my fingers numb for a moment or two. 'Sara's told me about you. I hear you turned up out of the blue to save us, just in the nick of time.'

'Actually, I think it was more like the other way around.'

'How are your digs down by the river? Not too dusty?'

I shake my head. 'The room's perfect. It's so peaceful down there – at night-time at least. When I left this morning Thomas had just turned up with a cement mixer, so it's probably not going to be so serene during daylight hours.'

'You're definitely better off up here in Wedding Land.' She nods, and then turns to Sara. 'What've you got in store for us this week then?'

Sara glances at a bulky folder sitting on the table. 'The MacAdams and the Howards: a full contingent staying here, all arriving Thursday afternoon; one hundred and twenty for the wedding on Saturday; the usual timings for the service and pre-dinner drinks. Caterers and florist booked for Saturday morning. We've got the wines in the cellar. So this morning it's going to be making up the bedrooms. Abi, you can work with me and I'll show you the ropes.'

'This sounds like quite a straightforward one then?' I say hopefully as I pick up my bucket.

Karen grins, picking up her bucket. 'Abi, as you're about to find out, when it comes to weddings there's no such thing as straightforward!'

Château Bellevue is built on the site of an ancient hill fort, Sara explains as we tuck in sheets and shake out pillows, throwing open shutters and windows to air the rooms as we go. The main building houses a dozen bedrooms on its two upper floors; and on the ground floor there's the kitchen as well as several reception rooms, which range in size and feel from cosy and secluded to large and elegant. The main sitting room has tall French windows that open on to a stone-slabbed terrace shaded by a wisteria-draped pergola. Beyond the terrace, a walkway leads to a vast marquee (luckily staked down a lot more securely against the storm than my tent had been), where the wedding receptions are held. And next door to the marquee is a lofty stone barn with a glitter-ball hanging from a central beam, a complicated-looking sound system and a bar stretching along one wall: 'Party Central', as Sara calls it. 'Thomas doubles as the resident DJ and Karen's husband, Didier, is the barman,' she explains. 'We might ask you to help behind the bar occasionally if there's a particularly big crowd.'

She also shows me the walled garden where she grows flowers, vegetables and herbs; the swimming pool; a small cottage where she and Thomas live in the summer months while the main building is full of wedding guests; and a lean-to apartment at the back of the barn where the gardener-cum-groundsman stays. 'His name's Jean-Marc. Our first year, we had several students working for us, but they've mostly moved on now. Jean-Marc's been with us for the last two years. He can turn his hand to anything. Thomas and I couldn't do without him. And here,' Sara continues, 'is the chapel.'

A carved stone cross sits on the gable roof above an ancient wooden door. We push it open and step out of the midday glare into a peaceful hush, where the simple stone walls seem to embrace us. 'It's de-consecrated these days, but we can offer the option of holding services of blessing here if the bride and groom don't want an outdoor ceremony.'

I walk up the aisle between the pews and stop to read a memorial plaque set into the wall on one side of the dais at the front.

Charles Montfort, Comte de Bellevue

18 novembre 1877–6 juin 1944

Amor Vincit Omnia

'He was the owner of the château in the war years,' says Sara. 'A brave man, and much respected in the area.'

'What do those words in Latin mean?' I point to the inscription beneath the dates.

'Love conquers all,' Sara translates. 'Very appropriate for a chapel that is used solely for the blessing of marriages nowadays.'

'There's so much history in this place,' I remark, as we emerge into the courtyard around which the buildings are clustered. 'If only the stones could talk.'

Sara nods. 'You're more likely to get the stones to talk than to hear the history from the people about these parts. The war years are still pretty recent for many of them, just one generation back. People tend not to want to dwell on those memories – they're still too painful. Perhaps some things are best left to heal until it's safe to bring them into the light of day.'

I remember Thomas' comments from the previous evening, about the Nazi occupation and the wounds being still there, just below the surface. And then I recall what he'd said about asking Sara to tell me the tale of the family in the mill house. 'Do you know the story of this place from those years?'

'Well, I don't know the whole story of the house, but I do know one person's story from the war. She grew up in the mill house and worked up here at the château for the Comte de Bellevue. She'd kept it to herself for decades, but I think perhaps she felt it was time, now, for her story to be told.'

Sara pauses, considering, smoothing the embroidered linen cloth that covers a small altar just beneath the plaque. And then she says, 'Her name was Eliane Martin.'

Eliane: 1939

In the walled garden, Eliane had been able to add three new hives to her thriving apiary as a result of early-summer swarms. As the summer wore on, she made extra space in each of the hives by adding empty frames above the brood boxes so that the busy community of worker bees would fill these with honey. They could then be collected without disturbing the queens and drones, whose sole preoccupation was to ensure the continuity of the colony.

Leaning a little less heavily on his stick these days – the ulcer on his leg had healed well – Monsieur le Comte watched from a safe distance just beyond the garden gate as Eliane, armed with a smoker and wearing a broad-brimmed hat draped with a veil, moved calmly from one hive to the next. She worked methodically, first puffing a little smoke in to calm the bees, then removing the wax-capped frames, which were heavy with honey, gently brushing off any bees from them and placing them carefully into tin buckets at her side. She replaced them with empty ones and closed the hives securely again, leaving the bees to set to work on the task of filling the new frames with the next cache of sweet nectar.

The kitchen was its own hive of activity. Francine had come to help prepare the honey harvest for their market stall. She held the frames as Eliane ran a broad-bladed knife over each to remove the wax capping, revealing the honeycomb whose hexagonal cells immediately began to ooze sticky liquid gold. Setting aside a little of the comb honey – le

Comte de Bellevue was particularly partial to it on toasted brioche for his breakfast – Eliane slotted the rest of the frames into the drum of the extractor. Madame Boin then set to, cranking the handle with gusto to spin the precious liquid out of every individual cell, while Francine operated the tap at the base, collecting the honey in sterilised jars.

In the meantime, Eliane gathered up the shards of wax and put them into a squat iron cauldron sat just close enough to the range to allow the warmth to melt them. The girls would then strain this through a clean muslin cloth and pour it into more wide-mouthed jars. The smell of honey-scented beeswax began to fill the kitchen, perfuming their skin and hair until its sweetness seemed to have permeated the core of their very being.

Madame Boin hummed to herself as she cranked the handle of the extractor and the girls chatted and laughed as they worked, filling the château with life.

'I hear Stéphanie's been seen going for an awful lot of walks in the vines over at Château de la Chapelle lately,' Francine remarked as she wrung out a damp cloth to wipe the stickiness off the mouths of the jars.

Madame Boin gave a derisory snort. 'That girl, she's always out hunting – and I don't mean for rabbits, either!'

'Well she needs to look for some other prey than Mathieu Dubosq. She's wasting her time setting her sights on him. Everyone knows he only has eyes for Eliane.'

Madame Boin glanced across sharply to where Eliane continued transferring wax into the cauldron. 'Perhaps he should speak to your father, Eliane, and make it official. Then maybe that Stéphanie would finally get the message and leave him alone.'

Eliane smiled and shook her head, placidly giving the pot a stir, and Francine nudged her with her hip. 'What's that starry-eyed look about then?' she asked her friend.

Eliane pretended to concentrate hard on stirring the melting wax, but the flush on her cheeks gave her away. Francine nudged her again. 'Well?' she persisted.

Wiping her hands on the hem of her apron, Eliane turned to face her inquisitors. She shrugged, abandoning all pretence of trying to cover up her emotions, and her eyes shone like the opalescent sky of a summer's dawn. 'I love him, Francine. And I think he loves me too.'

Her friend laughed, and put an arm around Eliane, giving her a hug. 'Well, that's as plain to see as the nose on your face. Anyone with half a brain can see he adores you.'

Eliane's cheeks flushed an even deeper pink, which had nothing to do with her proximity to the heat of the cast-iron range. She picked up a few more shards of wax and dropped them into the cauldron. Suddenly serious, she turned to Francine again. 'You know, I'm not worried that Mathieu's going to be stolen away by Stéphanie, or anyone else for that matter. I know we will be together. We've already talked about it. We just have to wait until he's finished his apprenticeship and secured a winemaking position somewhere. He knows there won't be a permanent job for him at Château de la Chapelle, unless Monsieur Cortini and Patrick were to expand the vineyard considerably. And that seems very unlikely in these uncertain times.'

Madame Boin shook her head and frowned, cranking the handle even more vigorously. 'Those power-crazy Nazis must be stopped if you ask me. Monsieur le Comte is worried sick that we're going to be dragged into another war, which is the last thing anyone wants. He spends far too much time sitting hunched over that blessed wireless, listening to the doom and gloom that gets broadcast day in, day out. We mustn't let those bullies scare us.'

'I agree. We can't just ignore what's going on,' Francine chipped in. 'I heard they're deporting thousands of people. And the refugee situation is becoming a crisis in Paris. Bullies need to be stood up to, not just ignored in the hope they'll go away. Otherwise we might find that we are their next target. What do you think, Eliane?'

'I think we should promise that we will stay true to ourselves. No matter what happens. No matter how bad things get. We should hold on to that truth. And I think we should all do whatever we can to prevent any more bloodshed. Even if, at the moment, it seems that the only thing we can do is pray. Pray that everyone sees sense.'

'But what if the only way to bring an end to the bloodshed is to fight, spilling more blood along the way?' Francine persisted.

'Then we will fight when the time comes,' Eliane replied, her eyes becoming sad, suddenly. But the expression was fleeting, like a cloud passing across the sun, and then her gaze became clear again. 'Now,' she said briskly, 'pass me those lids and let's get these jars ready for market, otherwise Saturday will arrive and we'll still be standing here worrying about things we cannot change.'

Abi: 2017

The wedding party will be arriving this afternoon, so Sara and I are in the walled garden cutting flowers to put in the bedrooms and the main sitting room, and picking herbs, which she'll be using to flavour tonight's meal. She explains to me that, while they use outside caterers and professional florists for the celebrations in the marquee, she and her team do the day-to-day catering and housekeeping. She was a landscape gardener before she came to live in France, she tells me, and her evident talent is on display all around us.

In the shelter of the walled garden, she's created long beds crammed full of cottage-garden flowers – blowsy peonies and scented roses, starry-blue love-in-a-mist and a foam of mock-orange blossom – with which we fill our baskets before returning to the kitchen to arrange them in Sara's collection of pretty vases and jugs, gleaned from *brocantes*, which will add a welcoming touch to each guest's bedside table.

The gardener, Jean-Marc, waves to us from his tractor-mower as he cuts a swathe through a meadow of marguerite daisies which they've cultivated to one side of the marquee. This grassy walkway will allow the bride and groom to make their way into the heart of the meadow of white flowers, the perfect setting for some stunning wedding photos.

Along the paths that lead to the chapel, the barn and the swimming pool, Sara and Jean-Marc have planted beds of lavender interspersed with a froth of long-stemmed white flowers ('gaura', she says it's called), which dance like butterflies above the blue haze. Cream-coloured climbing roses drape themselves over stonework and around windows, and the heavenly scent of wisteria hangs in the warm stillness of the midday air.

'What a romantic setting,' I remark, imagining how these back-drops must set off the photos of beautiful brides and dashing grooms. It's in stark contrast to my own wedding photo. Zac and I paused on the steps of the registry office as his mother snapped a picture on her phone. She had made it very clear that she thought her son could have done far better than marrying a penniless, family-less nanny.

I remember clearly the day we met. He was staying the night with the family I was working for in London and he'd marched into the kitchen, full of confidence in his perfectly ironed shirt (I found out only later that he'd sent them to be professionally laundered, but that he expected his new wife to do an equally immaculate job as part of her uxorial duties). I was attempting to spoon spag bol into little Freddie and had resorted to the 'train going into the tunnel' game to try to get him to finish what was in his Thomas the Tank Engine bowl. Some of the sauce had spattered on to my grey T-shirt (I'd given up wearing white ones within twenty-four hours of embarking upon my nannying career, two families back), and my hair was scraped back into a messy bun that was way more utilitarian than chic.

He'd ruffled Freddie's hair (carefully avoiding a strand of spaghetti that had somehow ended up there), and then held out a hand to me. 'Zac Howes; pleased to meet you.'

I juggled the bowl and fork, wiped my sticky fingers on my jeans and then returned his handshake. 'I'm Abi. The nanny.'

His blue eyes, which had looked a bit cold to me at first glance, sud-denly crinkled with amusement and I realised he was actually breathtak-ingly good-looking.

'I see, Abi-the-Nanny, what an interesting surname you have.' He grinned and in my confusion I dropped the bowl of spaghetti on to the floor. Freddie clapped his chubby hands and crowed his approval, picking up a wayward strand of cold pasta and flinging it down by way of his own contribution to the general mayhem.

'Here,' said Zac, 'let me get that. You deal with this young reprobate before he trashes the joint.'

Freddie's mother, who wasn't proving to be one of my favourite employers, clicked in on her kitten heels. 'What on earth's going on here, Abi? What's all this mess?' she snapped, before noticing Zac, who was on his hands and knees scooping spag bol off the polished sandstone tiles. Her tone altered immediately. 'Oh Freddie, I hope you haven't been a naughty boy! Abi will take you upstairs for your nice bath.' She made sure she stayed well beyond the reach of her little boy, clearly not wanting to risk getting any of the bolognaise sauce on her pale-pink yummy-mummy jeans. 'Now, Zac, you shouldn't be doing that. Let me get you a drink. Leave it and Abi will sort it out later.'

He shot me a sympathetic glance. Freddie flung his sticky paws around my neck and planted a big, sloppy, spag-bol-flavoured kiss on my nose. 'Come on then, Freddo Frog,' I smiled. 'Let's see if there are any crocodiles in the bath tonight.'

I glanced back over my shoulder as I carried my small charge upstairs. Zac was still watching me appraisingly.

And at the time, if I thought about it for more than a moment, I put it down to the way the light was hitting his face, but from that distance the warmth seemed to have seeped out of those blue eyes of his again.

Eliane: 1939

It was with a sense of numb disbelief that Eliane trudged up the track to her work at the château on the first Monday morning in September. The afternoon before – a golden Sunday afternoon – she and Mathieu had been sitting on the riverbank watching the damselflies dance above the water. It was that moment in the day when the setting sun's rays caught the surface at just the right angle to bounce off again, like stones skimming the river's surface. For a brief spell, the water shimmered with golden light that was reflected back up into the overhanging trees, an alchemy that transformed their leaves into a treasure trove of shimmering gilt.

As suddenly as it had arrived, the moment passed. The angle of the light changed and the colours faded as dusk began to draw its veil over the river. Mathieu stood and then reached out a hand to Eliane, helping her get to her feet.

The peace was shattered, all at once, by the sound of bicycle tyres skidding in the dust, sending a hail of pebbles scattering against the side of the barn. Yves leaped from the bike, leaning it against the wall in such haste that it immediately clattered on to the ground in a heap. Not stopping to right it, he sprinted towards the house.

'Eliane! Mathieu!' he shouted when he caught sight of the couple standing beside the willow tree. 'It's war! We're at war with Germany.'

Eliane felt a chill sweep her body at his words and she shivered, despite the warmth of the evening. She had hoped so hard and for so long that her sense of foreboding would turn out to be misplaced. But in truth, she'd known that this moment would arrive and a great sadness engulfed her. Instinctively, she reached for Mathieu's hand and held on fast. His powerful grip reassured her and strength seemed to flow into her from him. She knew she needed to stay calm, to resist the panic that was rising in her chest, so that she could support her family and her community through whatever was coming.

At Château Bellevue that next morning, Madame Boin was in such a state of distress that she burned the brioche for Monsieur le Comte's breakfast not just once but twice. Eliane sought refuge in the walled garden, checking her beehives and gathering ingredients for the day's meals. She added a good handful of lemon-verbena leaves to her basket, knowing that their calming properties might help to soothe Madame Boin's jangled nerves.

Monsieur le Comte spent much of the day ensconced in his library, listening to the wireless. Eliane heard snatches of the news as she brought him his meals. French troops were being deployed along the eastern front, creating what they hoped would be an impenetrable line that would defend France's borders. Great Britain had joined the mass of Allied Forces too and would be lending their considerable firepower to the fight.

The count tried his best to reassure her, saying, 'Don't worry, Eliane. Our army will soon have them on the run, especially with help from our neighbours. And luckily your young man is a farmer, so he won't be called up – we're going to need to keep production up to feed the country while the war lasts.'

But there was a forced confidence in the way he said this, which didn't quite manage to camouflage the dread that flickered in his eyes as he turned back to listen to the next bulletin.

At first, it seemed to Eliane that the country waited with bated breath for the war to begin in earnest. As she took the last of the summer's honey from her beehives, she looked out from her hilltop perch to scan the sky above the walled garden for signs of enemy aircraft. But all was peaceful and she could see the inhabitants of the village of Coulliac in the valley below going about their daily business. As autumn turned to winter, life continued much as it always had done.

Mireille came home for Christmas and Eliane was grateful for her sister's presence, which went some way towards filling the gap left by Mathieu, who had returned to spend a week with his father and brother in Tulle.

At the mill house, the family were preparing their usual Christmas feast. Mireille turned the handle of the mincer as Eliane fed in morsels of home-raised pork, seasoning the minced meat well, before the sisters wrapped patties of it in a lattice of caul as fine as lace to make the tasty *crépinettes* that would be fried and served at the start of the meal. Lisette was preparing the capon for the oven, and before long the house began to fill with delicious smells of roasting meat.

'I wish you would reconsider, Mireille,' said Lisette, as she scooped potato peelings into a bucket for feeding to the hens later. She was worried about her elder daughter continuing to work in Paris now that the country was officially at war with Germany. But Mireille dismissed her concerns.

'Honestly, Maman, life goes on the same as ever. Our wealthy clients are still ordering couture; the cafés and shops are all open and it's business as usual. They're calling this the *drôle de guerre* – it's a joke as nothing at all is happening. Perhaps the Nazis realise they've gone far enough and will begin to think again.'

That winter was a bitterly harsh one – the coldest in living memory for even the most elderly inhabitants of Coulliac. On a day in early January, when the surface of the river had frozen as hard as iron and the weir had become a sheet of pure white ice, Gustave went to the barn to start up the truck and warm the engine. It was time to drive Mireille to the station now that her holiday had come to an end.

Lisette could scarcely bear to let her elder daughter go. 'Take care of yourself, Mireille, won't you?'

'Don't worry, Maman. I'll be fine. You know I love my work – and besides, what would I do if I came back here? Sewing curtains and letting out waistbands would bore me rigid.'

She turned to hug Eliane. 'Look after them all for me,' she murmured and Eliane nodded.

After Mireille had left, Eliane walked up the hill to check the beehives and smiled when she saw how the bees were keeping their queen warm by clustering together around her and shivering their bodies to generate heat. As she put extra supplies of sugar into the hives to give the bees the extra energy they'd need to see the colonies through until spring arrived once more, she said to herself, *Perhaps the weather has frozen the war and not just the land.* Glancing northwards, she spared a thought for the soldiers who held the Maginot Line, defending France against the possibility of a German attack, and as she did so the chilblains on her own toes burned and itched in sympathy with them.

Abi: 2017

'So that's your first wedding out of the way,' Sara says. It was a successful one, by all accounts, even though one of the bridesmaids had overdone the pre-event Prosecco while helping the bride get ready and had tumbled, spectacularly, down the main staircase when making her grand entrance. Luckily, she'd been at the front of the bevy of bridesmaids preceding the bride and so hadn't taken anyone else out on her way down. Equally luckily, she'd been in such a relaxed state when she fell, that – apart from a few nasty bruises and a rip in the skirt of her dress – she hadn't done any serious damage to herself. Karen and Sara had helped her into the library, where they'd laid her on a sofa in the recovery position with a bucket beside her head, and I'd sat with her for a while until she'd suddenly come to. Hearing the strains of the party coming from the barn, she'd tottered off to join the dancing, once I'd made her drink a large glass of water and pinned together the tear in her dress as best I could. I'd had a quick word with Karen and she went to tell her husband, Didier, who was behind the bar, not to serve the girl anything alcoholic for the rest of the evening. She'd appeared for breakfast the next morning wearing a large pair of sunglasses but apparently none the worse for her tumble.

Sara and I are cleaning windows, which are thrown open to allow the fresh air to erase the lingering smells of perfume and aftershave left by the bedrooms' recently departed inhabitants. The warm breeze replaces the harsher, chemical odours with the heavenly scent of the wisteria, whose trailing clusters of flowers drip from the pergola covering the terrace beneath where we're working.

'How are you finding the work?' Sara asks.

I polish the last smudges off the pane of glass I've been cleaning. 'I love it. I don't think I'm quite ready to face a whole crowd yet, but I'm fine doing the behind-the-scenes stuff, if that suits you and Karen.'

She nods, wringing out a cloth into a bucket of soapy water. 'Don't worry – we're not going to chuck you in at the deep end straight away. Take your time. You seem to be picking everything up really quickly and it's a great help to us all having you here. Now, if you give the mirror and tiles in the bathroom a polish, I'll start next door.'

I try to finish the job as quickly as I can so that I can catch up with Sara and ask her to tell me more of the story of Eliane, the girl who, like me, once lived in the mill house and worked at the château. As I clean, I catch sight of my reflection in the mirror. My cheeks are still sunken and the bruised-looking skin beneath my eyes appears even darker in the bright overhead light. But there's also a faint flush of colour across my cheekbones and my collarbones don't stick out quite as sharply as they did before. The regular meals of fresh, hearty food, which I've been helping to prepare and serve up three times a day, are doing me good. As I rub the glass vigorously to make it shine – the energy that Sara and Karen bring to their work is catching – I notice that my suntanned arms are shaped with a new, muscular definition. I like the new-found feeling of strength this gives me.

At the end of each day, once supper has been cleared away, I walk down the hill to the mill house and sit for a while beneath the sheltering canopy of the willow tree, watching the darkened river flow quietly by. Those moments of utter peace are balm for my soul and soothe away the tension in my body and the anxiety in my head, which I've carried with me everywhere I go for so many years. When I climb the wooden stairs to my attic room at night, my muscles ache with the satisfying tiredness of physical labour rather than the shooting pains of chronic stress. And then, lying beneath the veil of the mosquito netting, softly lit by moonbeams, I drift into a calmer, deeper sleep than I've known for a very long time, kept company by the murmuring of the river and the softly hooted conversation of the owls in the trees along the riverbank.

Only once in the past week have I woken in the darkness gasping for breath, shaken by one of the nightmares that used to surface every night. I'd panicked even more when I couldn't think where I was for a few moments. But then the fluting song of a bird called me back, reminding me that I was safe beneath my veil of netting and that I'd survived another night with dawn about to break.

And it's funny, but the more Sara tells me of Eliane's story, the more I seem to feel the ghost of her comforting presence, too, calming me and watching over me in the attic room.

Eliane: 1940

The anti-climactic *Drôle de guerre* or 'Phoney War' continued as – at last – the bitter winter gave way to spring. In April, the plum and cherry trees burst into exuberant clouds of white blossom and the bees resumed their busy to-ing and fro-ing, as the colonies in each of the hives began their annual expansion. Eliane loved to watch the way the returning worker bees would weave their dance steps to tell their comrades where they had found the best sources of nectar. Observing closely, she noticed the way the dancing changed as the fruit trees began to drop their flowers like falling snow and the acacias donned their own snowy draperies for May Day. This was a critical time for the first collection of the year: in a few weeks, she would take the combs filled with pure acacia-flower honey and extract their sweet harvest, which was as pale and clear as champagne.

In the fields, a foam of meadowsweet and ox-eye daisies hid shy purple orchids. But the bees knew they were there and they danced their coded minuets to tell their co-workers where to drink from the secret caches of precious pollen and nectar.

Mathieu was kept busy in the vineyard, ploughing between the vines to keep the weeds down and tying in the burgeoning shoots as they reached out along the trellis of wires that in the fullness of time would support the heavy bunches of grapes. But in any spare moment he had he would walk over to the mill house to see Eliane. On the first day of May, the traditional workers' holiday, he arrived bearing a newspaper parcel of wild *mâche*, which he'd gathered among the vines, and a bunch of lily-of-the-valley. Half of the flowers he presented, wordlessly, to Lisette, and he gave the rest to Eliane.

Lisette lifted the sprigs to her face to inhale their sweet scent. 'Ah, *les muguets*,' she sighed. 'Thank you, Mathieu, I'm sure they will bring us luck.'

It was a beautiful day outside and Eliane had packed a picnic into her wicker basket. She and Mathieu picked their way across the weir and then wandered a little way along the riverbank on the far side. Mathieu spread a rug in the shade of a wild cherry tree that grew at the side of the meadow and lay down alongside Eliane as she set out the things for their lunch. He stretched his strong limbs, enjoying the unaccustomed midweek rest and the sensation of the sunlight dappling through the leaves. He squinted up into the branches and smiled. 'It's going to be a good year for the fruit.' He pointed upwards and she glanced at the clustered bunches of green cherries that were just beginning to blush with colour here and there where the sun's ripening rays brushed them.

She nodded and passed him a hunk of bread spread with homemade pâté. 'An exceptionally good year. The bees have been busy. I think they're making up for lost time after such a long, hard winter.'

After they'd eaten, Mathieu sat with his back against the trunk of the tree and Eliane lay on the rug, resting her head on his thigh, which was as broad and comfortable as a bolster. He plucked a stem of grass and began to plait it, his thick fingers surprisingly nimble and precise.

'According to Monsieur le Comte . . .' she began, but he gently pressed a finger against her lips to stop her.

'No talk about the war today, please, Eliane. It's a holiday, remember? So let's take a holiday from that as well.'

She smiled up at him, gazing into his wide brown eyes until his mouth curved upwards into the generous smile that he reserved mostly for her. She closed her fingers around his hand and kissed it. And then he took her hand into both of his, the smile fading as his expression grew more serious.

'Eliane . . .' he began, but then had to stop and clear his throat. She stayed silent, still gazing up at his face, waiting. He went on, 'You know we've talked about our future together, and that we can't really make plans until I've finished my training as a *vigneron* and can find a permanent placement somewhere . . . And things have been a bit uncertain with this idiotic war – which, after all, we're not going to talk about today . . .' He lost the train of his thoughts for a moment and she remained still, quietly looking up at him with her clear grey eyes that both reassured him and at the same time caused such a confusion of emotions to rise up within him. 'What I mean to say is – because I've never exactly asked you – well, not in so many words . . .' She smiled and kissed his hands again, giving him the confidence to go on.

'Eliane, I want to marry you!' He blurted the words out suddenly, and his brow creased into lines of anxiety as he awaited her reply.

'Well, Mathieu,' she replied calmly, 'that's a very good thing indeed. Because I want to marry you too.'

His features relaxed then, into a smile as big as his heart. He took the plaited grass and tied it carefully around the fourth finger of the hand he held. 'One day it will be a proper ring, I promise.'

'That promise is worth more than any ring ever could be, my Mathieu.'

They stayed on the far bank of the river as the golden May Day afternoon wore on, in a world where only the two of them existed.

And then, just ten days after that picnic on the riverbank, the voices coming through the wireless in the library up at the château became shriller and more strident, transmitting a new sense of panic, as the news came through that the German army was launching concerted attacks on the Netherlands, Luxembourg and then Belgium. The Panzer divisions, supported from the air by the Luftwaffe, moved inexorably westwards towards the French border.

'The Maginot Line will hold, don't worry,' the count assured Eliane and Madame Boin as he recounted the day's bulletins to them. He had started taking his afternoon *tisane* in the kitchen so that he could tell them the latest news. 'The British and French have troops in Belgium. We're strategically placed to turn back Monsieur Hitler's army.'

But then one afternoon in the first week of June, Monsieur le Comte came into the kitchen looking grave. 'It's bad news today, I'm afraid.' His tea stood untouched, growing cold, as he told them that the French and British troops had been driven back to the Channel, that they were fighting a desperate rearguard action trapped along the coast at Dunkirk. 'The remaining French divisions are still holding the Maginot Line, though. There's still hope.'

And then every last scrap of that hope was dashed when the elite German battalions smashed through the last line of defence. By the middle of June, the invading forces reached Paris. All was chaos and confusion as the war engulfed France like a tidal wave, powerful, unstoppable, unrelenting. The president resigned and key members of the government fled, leaving what was left of the French army without leadership. The army fought on, bewildered but brave, but were quickly overwhelmed by the ruthless efficiency of the German war machine.

Mathieu came to the mill house one evening and, as they sat around the supper table, he asked Gustave and Lisette for advice. 'I'm worried about my father and my brother. I haven't heard from them. I know my brother was desperate to sign up for the army and go and fight, but my father needed him to help with the farm. I don't know what to do . . .'

Without hesitation, Lisette replied, 'You should go and see them. Family is the most important thing there is. Make sure they're alright. Find out what your brother is thinking, support your father. The situation is changing on a daily basis at the moment. It would be best for your brother to sit tight and see what happens before he takes it into his head to go charging off to fight. And, after all, your father needs him.'

Gustave nodded slowly. 'That probably would be best. If only for your own peace of mind. You need to reassure yourself that they are alright. It's not so far to go, if the Cortinis can spare you for a few days?'

Mathieu nodded. 'They've said I can go. We've just finished lifting the trellises, so the work in the vineyard is up to date for the moment and as long as this good weather lasts the vines will be fine. But . . .' He glanced up from his plate and met Eliane's calm gaze.

She smiled at him. 'You need to go, Mathieu. And then come back once you know for sure that all is well.' Her voice didn't betray the unease she felt at the thought of his absence. But, after all, things seemed a little calmer at the moment, now that the negotiations in Paris were under way. All everyone was talking about was the armistice, hoping it would bring peace and stability to the country once again. ('"Armistice" is just another word for "surrender", if you ask me,' Monsieur le Comte had grumbled earlier that day.)

She walked with Mathieu along the river as darkness fell and the chirping of birds and crickets gave way to the singing of the frogs. The couple stood a long while together beneath the shelter of the willow tree.

'I don't want to leave you,' whispered Mathieu, taking both of her hands in his.

'You're not leaving me,' she replied. 'I'm keeping you right here with me, in my heart. And it's not for long. The sooner you go, the sooner you'll be back again. Give my love to your father and to Luc.'

He nodded, miserably, knowing that she was right. And yet, an unspoken anxiety seemed to pervade the air around them, as nebulous as the river mist that hung above the surface of the water, shifting and deceiving, creating phantoms of fear that haunted everybody's minds nowadays.

They kissed one last time and he eventually let go of her hand and made his way back to the vineyard to pack and set off for Tulle early the next morning.

By the time the armistice agreement was signed, just a few days later, the French army was decimated. Hundreds of thousands of troops had been killed and almost two million rounded up as prisoners of war, according to the sketchy reports that still trickled through on the wireless. Marshall Pétain was empowered to establish a new French government – ('the puppets of the Nazis,' declared the count with contempt) – in Vichy to run the south-eastern third of the country, which was all that the Germans had allowed to remain unoccupied.

And a line was to be drawn on the map to define the area now under Nazi occupation.

'They've barricaded the bridge!' Yves burst through the kitchen door, having been out delivering flour to the local bakeries.

'Who have barricaded which bridge, *mon fils?*' Lisette asked, as she wiped the table where she'd been preparing the evening meal.

'The Germans. In Coulliac. They've drawn the line of demarcation and it runs along this part of the river. The village is now in occupied France – so that means we are too. And just over there –' he gesticulated through the doorway in which he stood – 'just across on the other bank, it's unoccupied territory, run by the government in Vichy. Did you ever hear anything so crazy? I had to turn back because they wouldn't let me drive the truck across the river to finish my deliveries on the other side.'

Eliane sat, frozen, where she'd been shelling peas into a colander. Lisette shot her a worried glance and then said, trying to sound reassuring and with more conviction than she really felt, 'Surely they can't have closed the bridge for long. It's probably just temporary, until they have a proper checkpoint in place. After all, people live and work on both sides, so they'll need to be able to cross.'

Yves shook his head. 'The mayor was there. I asked him what was going to happen and he just shrugged and said that everything had changed. The soldiers were taking down the flag outside the *mairie* and, as we watched, they raised their own one in its place. I tell you, Maman, there is a swastika flying in the middle of Coulliac right now.'

'Well, some arrangement will surely have to be made.' Lisette kept her voice calm, trying to sound reasonable, even though it felt that their world had suddenly been turned upside down. 'What happens when I need to go across to help deliver Madame Blaye's baby next month? And how will we get the flour to Sainte-Foy?'

Eliane spoke then, at last, but her voice was weak and shaken. 'And how will Mathieu come back?'

Lisette hugged her tightly. 'Don't worry, *ma fille*, he'll find a way. And in the meantime you can be reassured that at least he's safe and sound in the unoccupied zone.'

Then Eliane began to weep as she voiced the other question that they'd all been asking themselves over and over during the past, tumultuous days. 'But, Maman, what about Mireille? What will happen to Paris now that it's in German hands?'

From the phone at the mill it was only possible to make local calls, so Gustave went and queued for hours outside the telephone kiosk at *La Poste* in Sainte-Foy-la-Grande to try to place a call to the *atelier* where Mireille worked. But when the phone at the other end did finally ring, his call had gone unanswered. They were frantic for news that Mireille was safe, and waited desperately for her to contact them. The newspapers reported bombings, and a mass exodus from Paris as the Germans had moved in. The Martin family prayed that Mireille had managed to find transport and was on her way back to the safe haven of the mill house at that very moment.

A phone call, a letter, a message passed on via a friend or neighbour – they longed for anything that would let them know Mireille was safe. But the minutes stretched into hours and the hours into an agonising eternity of days as they waited to hear from her.

Abi: 2017

I wonder how must it have felt for Eliane in those first days when the war began in earnest. After so many months of stand-off, perhaps she'd imagined life would simply carry on that way, with the French army holding the country's borders. Perhaps she'd relaxed a little as she worked in the kitchen and the walled garden at the château. Or perhaps she carried the tension with her – day in, day out – as she went about her duties, her muscles tensed and her fists clenched, waiting . . .

I set down the bulky laundry bag that I've heaved up the stairs on my own today. Karen phoned earlier to say that she slipped and fell on a patch of spilled cooking oil while shopping in the local supermarket and is currently sitting in the local hospital waiting to have her wrist put in plaster. I roll my head from side to side, easing the tension in my neck. The soreness of my muscles is due to hard physical work these days, but I remember the times when they have ached for other reasons: the hours of physio to regain strength in my arms; the yoga classes, which helped me on the road to my recovery but which always left me stiff and sore. And before all of that, I remember how I carried myself carefully, my shoulders tense and knotted, waiting for the next angry outburst from Zac. The anger was easier to deal with than the coldness that always followed it, as inevitably as night follows day.

Zac changed almost the moment we got home from our honey-moon. Or am I kidding myself, and did he always have those moments of coolness, when he withdrew his love like a rug that he could yank from under my feet any time he chose? Thinking back now, I can remember that the signs were there. But I missed them.

He'd phoned the house the day after we first met.

'Hello, is that Abi-the-Nanny?' he'd asked. 'This is Zac Howes.' His voice had sounded self-assured and faintly teasing. At the time, I'd interpreted it as friendliness – maybe even pleasure at hearing my voice. But now I realise it was more the satisfaction of a cat that's spotted its prey and is about to relish the sport of the chase.

I'd thought he must be calling to thank his hostess for last night's hospitality. 'Hello, Zac. I'm afraid they're all out at the moment. Can I take a message?'

'No, that's okay. It's you I wanted to talk to, actually.'

I was confused at first; I couldn't think what he could possibly want to say, unless it was to ask if he could pass on my name to a friend who occasionally needed a babysitter. But then he said, 'I wonder if I could take you out to dinner one evening? I presume they do allow you out every now and then?'

'Well, yes, Monday's my evening off. And I get some time at the weekends too. Not usually the evenings though . . .' I could hear myself beginning to blabber nervously, and silently told myself to shut up and let him do the talking.

'Okay, good. Are you free next Monday then?'

I pretended to think. 'Let me see, what date's that?' Although I knew full well that I had precisely nothing on that evening – nor any other Monday evening either, for the foreseeable future. I usually spent my free time slumped in front of the TV in my room at the top of the house, next to Freddie's, with the volume turned down low so as not to disturb him. If he knew I was there, he'd want me to give him his bath and put him to bed, reaching his chubby hands to pull my face close to his for a damp goodnight kiss. 'Er, no, I think I'm free next Monday.'

'Great, I'll pick you up at eight. See you then.'

'Thanks Zac. Looking forward to it.' I'd tried to sound nonchalant, but then the second he hung up I'd run up the stairs to my room and thrown open the door of my narrow wardrobe, desperately trying to think what I could wear.

By the time Monday evening came around, I'd settled for my newest pair of skinny jeans, with a tunic and a cropped jacket, hoping my get-up exuded an air of chic sophistication. I'd washed the mashed potato out of my hair (a remnant of Freddie's enthusiastic approach to his lunch that day), and had been a good deal more attentive than usual with the hairdryer and straighteners.

In spite of my efforts, I still felt gauche and under-dressed as he held open the door of his BMW and helped me in. But he seemed not to mind the fact that I was young and nervous. He questioned me, attentively, over dinner that first evening, fixing me in the full beam of his piercing blue eyes. In the beginning, I felt like a scared rabbit, caught in the headlights, but as the evening wore on – and as he topped up my wineglass again and again – I began to relax and even to bask in the warmth of his attention. It was a sensation to which I was completely unaccustomed. But I liked it. And I wanted more.

When he kissed me goodnight, he was tender and loving. Gently, he pushed me away from him a little, appraising me with his amused, blue gaze.

'Little Abi,' he said. 'How perfect you are.'

Just six words. That's all it took.

I mistook the web he was spinning around me for something else: for the promise of safety and security. I mistook it for love.

Eliane: 1940

Not knowing was the worst thing of all, thought Eliane, as she wrung out her mop and leaned it back in its bucket. They were all trying to keep things as close to the normal routine as possible and she had just finished another day's work at the château. She closed the door on the freshly washed kitchen floor and trudged down the hill as swifts circled and darted above her in the evening sky.

The count had told them that there were reports of air attacks further north and that sketchy news was coming in of civilian casualties. For a moment, Eliane imagined what it might feel like if, instead of birds soaring above her head, there were aeroplanes armed with deadly weapons. She felt panic rising in her throat and her heart began to pound.

'Please, Mireille, where are you? Come back to us safely. Please come home.' She said the words out loud, but they sounded fragile and ineffectual as they were carried away on the faint breeze that stirred the leaves of the acacia trees along the roadside.

As she approached the turn-off to the track that led to the mill, a pair of crows suddenly launched themselves from a fencepost where they'd been perching further up the road. The explosive beating of their wings and raucous, angry cries startled her, making her jump. She looked up the road to see what had disturbed them. A huddled figure was limping towards her, stooped and weary. At first, Eliane thought it was an old woman, but as she moved closer the figure raised her dusty, dirty head and she realised who it was.

'Mireille!' she screamed, and ran forwards just as her sister seemed to stumble, her legs giving way beneath her.

'Take her,' mumbled Mireille, thrusting a bundle of rags into Eliane's arms, and then she crumpled into a dead faint at her sister's feet.

The bundle of rags that Eliane now held was surprisingly warm and heavy. And then it began to wail; the thin, feeble cry of a baby, weakened with thirst and hunger.

Eliane sat on Mireille's bed in the attic room and stroked her hair as her sister told the story of her flight from Paris and the last few hellish days on the road in the company of thousands of others who flooded out of the city. Some were refugees from Poland, Czechoslovakia, Austria and Germany who had already fled their homes once and were now on the move again. Others were Parisians who feared for their lives and those of their children as bombs fell on the city and the enemy vanguards began to arrive. And some, like Mireille, simply knew that they needed to be with their families at a time like this.

She had set off with Esther, her colleague from the *atelier*, and Blanche, Esther's baby, who had just turned nine months old. Esther had arrived from Poland, alone and pregnant, the previous spring. 'My husband thinks I'll be safer in Paris,' she'd explained on her first day at work as she balanced her sewing on her gently rounded belly and stitched up a hem with fine, quick stitches. 'I hope this will be a good place to have our baby.'

After the Germans invaded Poland in the autumn, she'd received word that her husband had escaped to join Polish forces in England to continue the fight from there. He'd written that she and the baby should stay safe in Paris until he could come and get them once the war was over.

But when Paris fell, Mireille had urged her to come to the mill house, 'We'll go together. My parents will shelter you and Blanche there.'

'But then Herschel won't know where to come and look for us,' Esther had protested, clutching Blanche to her so tightly that the baby started to cry.

'Better that he eventually finds you both alive and well than that he has to look for you in the debris of a bombed-out basement,' Mireille had argued. 'Come, Esther, bring what you can for Blanche. A friend of mine has a car; he'll squeeze you in. But we have to leave now!'

When she recounted this part of her story, Mireille began to cry. Eliane held her tight, smoothing her hair. 'If I hadn't made her leave, she might still be alive,' choked Mireille.

Still holding her and rocking her gently, Eliane said, 'Or she might have been killed in Paris by a bomb. Or, if she'd survived, she and Blanche might well have been rounded up and deported as soon as the Germans arrived. We've all heard the reports – people disappear off to these "work camps" and are never heard of again. Those camps would be no place for a mother with a small child. You can't blame yourself, *ma soeur*.'

When, at last, she'd managed to calm her sobs, Mireille continued with her story.

The day's car journey they'd envisaged had rapidly turned into a drawn-out nightmare. The roads south from Paris were packed with a slow-moving tide of refugees on foot, on bicycles and in horse-drawn wagons filled with their personal belongings, blocking the way for the cars that tried, impatiently, to get past even though there was no space ahead, just more and more people.

The car Mireille and Esther were in crawled onwards at a walking pace. But they were thankful, at least, that the vehicle offered some protection from the milling throng that pressed around them, as well as from the heat of the June sun.

And then they began to have to manoeuvre the car around other vehicles that had been dumped in the middle of the road when they'd run out of fuel, there being no more to be found anywhere along the route. In the end, inevitably, their car also ran empty and they had to abandon it. Mireille's friend, the car's owner, said he would walk back to a garage they'd passed a few kilometres previously, where it had looked as if there might be a chance of some fuel. 'You two take the baby and start to walk. Orléans isn't too much further. When you get there, see if you can find a room for the night in the main square – there are cafés and hotels there. I'll come and find you once I've got the car on the road again.'

And so Mireille and Esther, carrying Blanche, had joined the slow-moving flood of people making their terrified, weary way south.

'Did you find somewhere to stay in Orléans?' asked Eliane.

Mireille shook her head. 'No chance. Everywhere was full. People were barricading their doors against looters and chasing refugees out of their gardens where they were scavenging for something to eat. It was as if a swarm of locusts had swept through the countryside before us, taking everything, and that's how the locals saw us too. We slept that night under a hedge, holding the baby between us to keep her warm. Esther tried to feed her, but her milk was drying up and anyway Blanche is already being weaned on to solids so she was hungry for more. We begged a little bread from another family the next morning and soaked it in some water for her. But otherwise there was nothing to eat – the locusts had got there first.'

Their mother Lisette brought in a bowl of chicken broth on a tray, balancing Blanche on her other hip. The baby was already looking a little better-nourished, having been fed sips of goat's milk and some of the broth too.

'Eat, Mireille,' Lisette ordered. 'We need to get you back on your feet so that you can help look after this pretty little one, don't we, my sweet?' She placed a kiss on top of the baby's dark curls.

After she'd sipped the broth and managed to swallow a bite or two of bread, Mireille went on with her story.

They'd rejoined the frightened and weary procession and continued on their way southwards and westwards, reasoning that it would be better to keep moving forwards, towards the hoped-for safety of Coulliac, than to wait there, where there was nothing to eat and no shelter, in the hope that their friend would turn up with the car again.

'A situation like that shows people in their true colours,' Mireille commented as she paused to take a sip of water from a glass beside her bed. 'Some people behaved with the most extraordinary compassion and generosity, like the family who'd shared their bread with us that morning. But others displayed selfishness, envy and malice. I suppose they were terrified, as we all were, and just desperate to survive.'

They'd been on a stretch of road somewhere around Tours, Mireille thought, although she'd lost track of the distance they'd covered, with progress so slow and so haphazard. They'd tried taking by-roads, which weren't quite as crowded, but ended up losing their bearings and so had found the main arterial road once again, where it ran alongside a railway line. 'Someone said they thought it was the main line to Bordeaux, so we knew we were heading in the right direction,' said Mireille.

The midday sun had been beating down and they had sat in the shade of a plane tree to rest and give Blanche some shelter. She had been crying with hunger for more than an hour now. Esther had tried again to feed her, but the baby just grew angrier and more frustrated as she attempted, unsuccessfully, to suckle at her mother's breast. Exhausted, Esther had handed Blanche to Mireille and done up the buttons of her blouse. 'Here, see if you can calm her down a little. I'll go and ask around in case anyone can spare something for her to eat.'

Esther had limped back into the road and Mireille had begun to sing to Blanche, rocking her.

And then there had been a shrill, high-pitched scream. Mireille had looked up, bewildered, to see who was making the noise and for what reason. The scream went on and on. As if in slow motion, she saw that all the other refugees on the road were also looking around, equally bewildered, trying to pinpoint the source of the noise.

Then, one by one, they raised their faces to the sky. 'Like a field of sunflowers – that was what I thought in that moment,' said Mireille, unable to suppress a sob. She took a deep breath and then went on. 'It was an aeroplane. A German one. It made that terrible screaming sound as it dived. And then the noise became something worse. A rattling hail of bullets and screams and groans from people standing in the road. A woman just in front of me looked into my eyes and saw that I was gazing, in horror, at the blood that was spreading across the front of her dress. It was only when she looked down and saw it herself that she folded in half and fell at my feet. I turned and held Blanche tight between me and the trunk of the tree, with my back to the road. The pilot came back twice more, and each time there was that horrible screaming sound as he dived again and then the sound of the guns. I couldn't breathe until the noise of the plane had gone completely. And when I did breathe, I could smell the dust. And then the blood.'

Mireille's eyes were dry as she recounted the final part of her story – because the sight she'd seen when she'd turned around was too terrible for mere tears. Her voice, as she went on with her telling, had become a hard monotone.

'I stumbled over the people who'd walked past me just moments before, slipping in their blood, which covered the road. Most of them didn't move, but one or two reached out, begging for help. But I knew there were others who could try to help them and I had to find Esther. I called her name again and again. I was holding Blanche tight but she cried inconsolably, as if she already knew her mother was gone. Then

I saw a piece of the blouse that Esther was wearing. It was the same blouse that she'd just re-buttoned in those moments before the attack, and yet that now seemed such an age ago. The blouse wasn't white now, though. It was soaked with blood. Her blood. From her wounds. Where the bullets had hit her in the chest.'

Mireille stopped there, unable to find any more words. But Lisette and Eliane needed no further explanation. They could read the shock and trauma written across Mireille's face, in the way her normally strong features had collapsed and dissolved into an expression of complete helplessness, and in the pain that was lodged deep in her dark eyes.

Lisette passed the now-sleeping baby gently to Eliane and gathered Mireille into her arms. 'Hush now, hush now,' Lisette soothed, as she rocked her daughter, weeping the tears that Mireille could not.

Abi: 2017

From the window of my attic bedroom in the mill house, I can see the moonlight playing through the branches of the willow tree, its leaves cascading like silvered tears into the deep pool below the weir. I pull the shutters to, although they don't close properly as the iron catch is broken, hanging loose where the screws are missing, letting moths and mosquitoes slip through. Thank goodness for the netting draped over my bed, which protects me in the night, letting me sleep deeply as their wings whirr harmlessly in the background.

From the lamp beside my bed, a circle of golden light pools on the floorboards, which exhale their faint scent of beeswax, letting it mingle with the fragrant posy of lavender and white roses that I brought back with me from the château today. Jean-Marc had appeared with it just as I was leaving. He offered it to me with a shy smile. 'I thought a few flowers might cheer up your room down there,' he said, with a nod of his head towards the valley below. He'd been at the mill house earlier, helping Thomas put up some plasterboard in what was going to be the new kitchen.

As I gaze around my bedroom, I can picture Mireille lying in her single bed at one end of the room, with Eliane and Lisette trying to comfort her after the ordeal of her journey home from Paris when the war broke out in earnest.

Sara had told me that, in her traumatised state, Mireille had lost the ability to cry.

I did, too, eventually. But in the early days of my marriage, I cried a great deal: a river of silver tears.

After the first year, I grew to know the pattern of Zac's behaviour as surely as I knew the London weather. I could watch the clouds from behind the vast sheet of wall-to-ceiling glass in Zac's loft apartment in the docklands – (it never felt like *our* apartment, always *his*) – as they gathered over the Thames beyond the cityscape of tower blocks, sweeping towards us from the west, just as I could sense the change in atmosphere between us, see his anger building, towering over me like a dark storm cloud, threatening. Waiting . . . Then breaking.

Like that first Christmas we spent together. I was determined to make it all perfect, playing at home-making as I'd always longed to do. Together, we drew up a list of the people we would send cards to. They were mostly Zac's friends and family, but I added a few of my own friends as well as the families I'd worked for. Together, we chose the cards, although Zac told me that the ones I preferred were either too mawkish or naff and so we settled on a selection of tasteful images painted by Old Masters. He left me to write them, and I took such a pride in including a little personal message in each and in signing them from the two of us. Each time I wrote our names, it was a public affirmation that we were officially a couple now.

Zac came in just as I was writing the last few to add to the pile of neatly addressed envelopes that I would take to the post office tomorrow, so that they'd reach their destinations in good time for Christmas. He came to look over my shoulder. '*Love from Abi and Zac,*' I wrote and then I turned to kiss him. But his face had grown blank, the non-expression that I'd begun to recognise as the precursor to something much worse.

He reached over me, and I remember I'd automatically flinched as his hand came down. But he didn't touch me then; he just leaned forward and picked up the card I'd been writing, a frown creasing his forehead.

'How many have you done like this?' he asked, the anger already making his voice sound as cold as the winter rain that ran in runnels down the windows, blurring the city lights beyond like tears.

'Like what, Zac? I don't understand . . .'

'Like *this*.' He drew his finger over our names, making the ink smudge slightly where it hadn't quite dried. '"Abi and Zac".'

I'd glanced at him, wondering if it was a trick question, but he was shaking with rage now. Quickly, I dropped my gaze to the patterned rug beneath the glass-topped coffee table, fixing my attention on its grey, geometric design as if the logic of it could keep me safe.

He picked up the pile of envelopes and began ripping them open, wrenching out the cards to read them and then throwing each one on to the floor as he spat the words, '"Abi and Zac" . . . "Abi and Zac" . . .'

He grabbed my arm then and pulled me to my feet. 'You never, ever put your name before mine.' He hissed the words into my face and I had to resist the urge to wipe the droplets of spit from my skin, knowing that would make him even angrier. 'You stupid girl. What a waste of my money. Now we're going to have to buy a whole load more cards and you're going to write them again, this time with our names in the right order.'

A and Z. I hadn't even thought about it, I'd just written our names like that because it sounded right in my head. I should have thought. Stupid girl.

The rain beat on the glass and the lights were blurred against the backdrop of the cloud-darkened sky.

The bruises on my arms were like storm clouds too, purple and black beneath the sleeves of my shirt. But eventually I knew they would fade to the sickly yellow of a London sunset and then they could be disguised with a bit of concealer. The dark, angry clouds would go and Zac's eyes would be as clear as a blue summer sky again and he would hold me and say that he loved me, that the anger was my fault, again, but that he forgave me. And I would try to relax, to let my clenched fists uncurl, but I was always tense, waiting . . .

I grew more and more isolated, shut in behind the glass of those vast windows in that oh-so-desirable London apartment, cut off from the world outside.

Eliane: 1940

The notice, with its stark black swastika emblazoned top and centre, was posted outside the *mairie* in Coulliac and word passed quickly from neighbour to neighbour throughout the community.

> *By order of the new administration, all inhabitants of the commune of Coulliac are to present themselves at the mairie for the purposes of registration of the population and the issuing of identity cards, which are to be carried at all times. Henceforth, anyone found not to be in possession of the necessary documentation will be arrested and may be deported.*

It was shocking to see the signature of the mayor – their elected representative – at the bottom of the notice. Many people grumbled that he had so readily capitulated to the demands of the invaders, but those who had access to a wireless or newspaper pointed out that it was now official policy, adopted throughout the occupied zone. What choice did he have? What choice did any of them have, for that matter?

The Martin family arrived after breakfast the next morning to find that a long queue already wound around the small square at the heart of the village, and they took their places at the end of it. Local people continued to arrive at a far faster rate than those leaving the *mairie*, and the *place* quickly filled. Ordinarily such a gathering, for a market or a fête, would have had a lighthearted atmosphere; a cacophony of laughter and neighbourly chatter would have reverberated from the walls of the shops that lined the square and bounced off the balconies and shuttered windows overhead. But today the crowd was subdued and ill at ease. People addressed one another quietly, if at all, muttering greetings and asking one another in hushed tones what this could all be about. The atmosphere of occupation was oppressive. Most of those standing in the queue kept their eyes fixed on the ground in order not to have to look at the red, white and black flag that had replaced the French tricolour on the *mairie*'s flagpole, and so that they wouldn't catch the eye of either of the German soldiers who stood on each side of the entrance with guns slung over their shoulders.

As they shuffled slowly forwards, Eliane recognised Stéphanie in the line just ahead of them. She smiled when Stéphanie looked around and noticed her, and was rewarded with a cool nod of acknowledgement in return. And then Eliane caught sight of Francine, who had just emerged from the *mairie*. She held her new ID card in her hand. She was reading it as she came down the steps, with a bemused expression on her face. As she passed, her attention still fixed on the document, Eliane reached out and tugged at her sleeve. Francine's features relaxed into a smile at the sight of her friend, and she embraced Eliane warmly.

'What is it like in there?' Eliane asked softly.

'Strange,' Francine quietly replied. 'There are more soldiers, with guns, who are supervising the mayor and his secretary. There are forms to fill in, asking all sorts of questions – who you are, where you're from, who your parents are and your grandparents, your address, your date of birth and your religion. And then this is what they give you.' She held out her card for Eliane to see.

'What does that mean?' Eliane pointed to the large letter 'J' that had been stamped across Francine's ID card.

'I wasn't sure at first. I noticed not everyone had a letter stamped on theirs, so I asked the mayor's secretary on the way out. She says they've been instructed to stamp the cards of anyone who's Jewish.'

'But why?'

Francine shook her head, still keeping her voice low. 'I'm not exactly sure. But I certainly don't think it's a good sign.' She paused and turned to Lisette, who was holding Blanche. 'Is this the baby you told me about? *Comme elle est mignonne!*' She moved closer to embrace the older woman; and as she did so, Eliane noticed that Francine whispered something in Lisette's ear.

Raising her voice a little, so that all those queuing nearby could hear what she said, Francine exclaimed, 'How sad that your husband's cousin and his wife were killed in the bombing, Madame Martin. But it's lucky that you were able to take their baby in. I can't think of a better household in which she should grow up. I'm sure your cousin would have been relieved to know his daughter is with members of the family.'

Lisette nodded, then found her voice. 'Yes, it certainly was lucky that our Mireille was able to find Blanche in Paris and bring her to us in Coulliac. Imagine having another baby in the family at my age, though!'

On hearing this exchange, Gustave looked a little startled, but Lisette gave him a reassuring smile. 'I'm sure we'll adapt to being new parents, won't we, *chéri*? After all, family is family.'

It took Eliane a moment or two to register why Francine had said this, but then she realised the significance of what her friend had just done for their family and for Blanche.

All around them in the queue, people smiled sympathetically and nodded their support. Although Stéphanie, who had also been listening to the conversation, shot a piercing glance at the baby in Lisette's arms and then scowled with her usual bad grace.

Francine hugged Eliane once again, taking her leave. 'Now that the bridge is closed, the mayor is going to allow a market to be held here in Coulliac instead of Sainte-Foy.' She pointed towards another notice pinned to the board outside the *mairie*. 'So I'll see you on Saturday as usual then? Have you got that new batch of honey ready?'

Eliane's grey eyes were filled with a mixture of sorrow and love as she squeezed Francine's hand tightly and bid her farewell until the weekend.

When Lisette explained that all the family's papers had been destroyed in the bombing, it hadn't taken much persuasion for the harassed and over-worked mayor to issue an ID card for Blanche with her surname given as 'Martin'. The baby's birth certificate, which Esther had put in the little bag of belongings that she'd packed so hastily when she and Mireille fled from the city, had been surreptitiously removed from the bundle of papers that Gustave had been holding, and thrust deep into the pocket of his overalls. When they returned to the mill house, Lisette had taken it and carefully smoothed out the creases, folding it into quarters and tucking it into the pages of her heavy book of herbal remedies, which sat on a shelf in the kitchen.

The following Saturday morning, when Eliane came down early to gather together what she'd need for the market stall in the new venue of Coulliac, her father was already at work in the barn. She heard him whistling, and the sound of a saw and then a hammer. The noises stopped at the sound of her footsteps approaching the door, which was slightly ajar.

'What are you making, Papa?'

Gustave relaxed when he saw it was only Eliane, and he grinned. 'I'm making a sign, *ma fille*. Inspired by the efficiency of the new administration, I've realised that, for the safety of the general public, we have been remiss in not warning people about the dangerous weir and strong currents in the river here. It would be a terrible thing if someone were to lose their life trying to cross it.'

Eliane laughed. 'Surely this is one of your jokes?'

His expression was grave, suddenly. '*Non, ma fille*, this is absolutely serious. It's only a matter of time before the *Boches* realise that they haven't quite managed to seal off every crossing point to the unoccupied zone. So I'm going to camouflage what we have here, just in case it should ever be needed.'

'But, Papa, if the Germans come to check, all they need do is walk on to the weir and they'll find how easy it is to cross.'

Gustave smiled again. 'You've never seen the river when all the sluice gates are closed, have you?'

She shook her head. 'You always leave one set open – either to bypass the mill wheel or to make it turn.'

'That's right, and that maintains the balance of the flow. But if I close both sets of gates, all the water coming down the river has to flow over the weir itself. It's quite something to behold: the water level rises and the weir becomes a torrent. Anyone trying to cross then would be swept away in an instant.'

Eliane nodded slowly, considering her father's plan.

'I know it may seem a bit crazy, what I'm doing . . .' Gustave picked up the sign he'd been making. 'But maybe crazy times like these call for crazy plans like this. I have to try, at least. The Germans will probably seal off the whole riverbank in any case, but if we can make it look as if this small section is so hazardous that it needs no defending then it might just be of use to someone, sometime.' He picked up a sledgehammer, a sharpened wooden stake and the sign, which read: 'Warning! Hazardous Weir. Danger of Death!'

'Want to come and hold this for me while I set it up? And then I'll give you a lift to the market.'

Eliane smiled at her father. 'Since it is our duty for the greater protection of the public at large? But of course, Papa!'

By the time Eliane arrived with her basketful of jars of honey and beeswax, Francine had already set up a trestle table in the square, as far as possible from the swastika flying outside the *mairie*. She had covered it with a brightly checked cloth and was setting out pyramids of jam jars and conserves. A few other stallholders were setting up shop, but this makeshift market in Coulliac was a far cry from the hustle and plenty of the one in Sainte-Foy.

A German soldier wandered around the square, a rifle slung casually over one shoulder, and came to inspect each of the stalls. When he reached the girls' table, he paused.

'What is that?' He pointed at the jar Francine was holding. She froze. Then, dropping her eyes, replied, 'Reine Claude preserve, m'sieur. It's made from a type of green plum.'

'It's good to eat with bread?' The soldier's French accent was hard-edged.

Francine nodded. Her hand shook as she passed the jam to him for closer inspection.

'How much?' He balanced his rifle against the table as he fished in his pocket for some coins. 'Thank you, miss. Good day.'

Eliane continued to set out her own produce, but said softly, 'Are you alright, Francine?'

'Sorry, it's stupid of me to be so nervous. But it doesn't feel good, living like this. Soldiers and guns should have no place in day-to-day life. What is happening to us?'

Eliane sighed. 'War is happening to us. And I'm very much afraid this is just the beginning.' She, too, felt tense and off balance. She wanted to tell Francine not to worry, that she had nothing to fear, that everything would be alright. But she found that she couldn't give her friend that reassurance because Eliane, too, could sense the threat that hung over Francine's head as clearly as she felt the glare of the sun beginning to beat down on them from above. 'Come on, here come our first customers. Give me a hand with this umbrella,' she said briskly, giving Francine a quick hug. 'Otherwise the beeswax is going to melt.'

The customer, who was making her way purposefully across the square towards the girls' stall, was the mayor's secretary.

'Good morning, Eliane. Francine.' She'd worked in the *mairie* for as long as the girls could remember and knew everyone in the *commune* by name. 'I need some more of your beeswax, please, and a jar of *confiture aux myrtilles* also.' She counted the exact money on to the table and as she did so she smiled at Eliane. 'How is the baby today?'

'Blanche is fine, thank you.'

'And your sister?'

'She's much better now. Her feet are mending well.' This was true, although Eliane knew Mireille's mental scars would take far longer to heal.

'I'm pleased to hear that. Give my best wishes to your parents.' As if as an inconsequential afterthought, she added, 'Oh, and you might like to mention to them that the *moulin* has been scheduled for a visit on Monday. Sometimes it's nice to be able to prepare for visitors in advance.'

Then, with a businesslike nod, she scooped her purchases into a string bag and continued on her way.

⁂

That Monday, the sound of the jeep pulling up in front of the barn was drowned out by the noise of the river flowing over the weir in full spate. Gustave and Yves were heaving sacks of flour into the back of the truck. An officer and official translator, both in uniform, got out and stood for a moment, assessing the scene before them. Gustave's sign looked as if it had been in place for years, thanks to a light going-over with a sheet of sandpaper and the application of a couple of smudges of river mud. The officer picked up a stone and threw it towards the crest of the weir. The water snatched it greedily and swallowed it into the depths.

He raised his eyebrows and instructed the translator to make a note on the clipboard he was carrying.

Only then did the officer turn to acknowledge the presence of Yves and Gustave.

'Good morning. I'm looking for Herr Martin, the owner of the water mill.' He had to shout to be heard above the roar of the river.

'You've found him,' replied Gustave, heaving the final sack on to the truck and then dusting the flour off his hands before pulling the tarpaulin cover into place.

'Perhaps we could go inside, where it's a little quieter?' the translator said with careful courtesy, his manner a little less abrupt than that of the officer. 'We are sorry to disturb you at your work, monsieur, but there are a few things that we need to sort out with you.'

Gustave led the way and showed them into the kitchen, where the Germans pulled out chairs and seated themselves at the table, gesturing to Gustave to do likewise. Yves, who had followed them inside, remained standing, leaning against the doorframe with his arms folded.

Consulting his clipboard, the translator said, 'Just a few questions, if we may, Monsieur Martin? You live here with your family: your wife, two daughters and one son.' Here he glanced up at Yves. 'And a baby who is the daughter of your deceased cousin?'

'That is correct,' Gustave replied.

'Her parents were killed when you dropped your bombs on them,' Yves chipped in, but was silenced by a glance from his father.

Ignoring Yves' remark, the soldier continued, 'And you have how many vehicles?'

'Just my truck, which you saw outside.'

'Bicycles?'

'One, which we all share. My wife is the local midwife so sometimes she needs transport to get to her patients at short notice.'

The man nodded, translated this for the officer and made a note on the papers in front of him.

'You use your truck for delivering flour to the bakeries in the area?'

'Yes. And I need to be able to cross the bridges at Coulliac and Sainte-Foy to be able to continue my deliveries over there.'

The officer shook his head categorically and spoke in rapid-fire German.

'This is no longer permitted under the new administration,' the translator said. 'The unoccupied zone will have to sustain itself as far as foodstuffs are concerned. From now on, you will deliver one-third of your flour to a depot that we are setting up on the edge of town. It is needed for workers in Germany. The remainder you can deliver to your clients on this side of the river, as normal.'

'And my wife?' asked Gustave, calmly. 'What is she supposed to do when there is a baby to be delivered on the other side? Do those women, in the unoccupied zone, have to fend for themselves?'

Again, there was some discussion to and fro between the two soldiers.

'It may be possible to allow her to have a permit to travel into the unoccupied zone for cases of medical necessity. There is a seven-kilometre area on the other side that will be closely patrolled, and anyone found there without the correct papers will be handed back to the authorities here and dealt with accordingly. Your wife will need to present herself at the *mairie* so that we can organise a permit for her. And we will also issue you with a permit to drive your truck to make your deliveries, since you are contributing to the war effort now. The vehicle will be officially designated for public service. Each week you will be allocated vouchers for enough petrol to carry out these necessary duties.'

The German officer spoke again – a harsh tirade of words that were unintelligible to Gustave, who nevertheless clearly understood their implicit threat. The soldier translated in a milder tone: 'You will please remember, Monsieur Martin, that you and your wife are in a position of some privilege with these extra allowances. You would be well-advised not to abuse them. Please remember that acts of hoarding or sabotage are punishable offences. With advantages such as you have been given comes responsibility. We will be observing the two of you closely, to ensure you both comply with these responsibilities.'

'*Vous comprenez?*' The officer spat the two words of French at Gustave, loading them with menace.

Gustave met the officer's glaring eyes with equanimity, his own expression calmly bland. 'I understand very well indeed, m'sieur.'

The translator made a few more notes on his clipboard. 'You and your wife should present yourselves at the *mairie* at your earliest convenience. The administration will be expecting you.'

They stood, and Yves stepped aside to let them leave. Father and son watched as the soldiers drove off up the track, the tyres of their jeep throwing up a scattering of stones and a cloud of dust.

Following the progress of that dust cloud, they saw it rise anew as the jeep turned off the road and continued to climb the hill behind the mill.

'They're going to the château next,' said Yves.

'Looks that way.' Gustave nodded. Then he turned towards the truck. 'Come on, let's get this delivery done as best we can.' He loosened the tarpaulin and began unloading some of the sacks.

'But what are you doing, Papa?' Yves asked.

'If we have to give the Germans one-third of our production, we'd better make sure that our "production" is reduced accordingly,' Gustave grunted. 'Here, help me stash these in the tunnel behind the pigsty.'

Eliane was checking her beehives when she heard the sound of the jeep pulling up in front of the château and then the double clunk of the car doors being slammed shut. The sight of the military vehicle and the soldiers seemed particularly grotesque in that peaceful setting, against the timelessly elegant stonework of the buildings.

Monsieur le Comte, who must have seen them approaching from the library windows, stood on the top step, scarcely leaning on his stick at all as he drew himself up to stand tall. The soldiers saluted him, clicking their heels together in that abrupt way of theirs. After a few peremptory words, they followed him back inside and disappeared.

Eliane hastily set in place the frames she'd been adding to one of the hives – a newly established swarm that she'd collected from the branches of the pear tree earlier in the summer – and hurried back to the kitchen, removing her gloves and broad-brimmed, veiled hat as she went.

'They're here! Did you see them?' she asked Madame Boin, breathlessly.

The cook nodded, pressing her lips together disapprovingly as she continued to chop an onion with a good deal more force than was strictly necessary. 'I did.'

'What are we going to do?'

Madame Boin turned to face Eliane. 'We are going to do absolutely nothing, my girl. Get this straight: the best way to get through whatever lies ahead is to carry on as normal. I intend to ignore our new so-called rulers and get on with things just as we have always done. I take my orders from Monsieur le Comte and no one else. He's been my boss for twenty-seven years now, and it will take more than the German army for me to abandon him. Here . . .' She handed Eliane the knife she'd been wielding. 'You finish chopping these vegetables. I need to get my bread in the oven or it'll be over-proved.'

Just then, the count appeared in the doorway. 'Ah, Madame Boin, please would you be so good as to prepare a pot of coffee for our visitors? And a lemon-balm *tisane* for me? We are in the library.'

Eliane carried the tray through because, despite her categorical assertion that she was absolutely fine, Madame Boin's hands shook so hard with scarcely contained rage as she set the kettle on the range that the water slopped everywhere, sending boiling droplets skidding across the top of the stove and creating a spitting, hissing cloud of steam.

The men fell silent as Eliane entered, waiting for her to finish pouring the coffee and leave before resuming their conversation.

It was more than an hour later before the soldiers could be heard leaving, the doors of the jeep banging again and another cloud of dust left hanging in the air in their wake.

The count came into the kitchen, awkwardly balancing the tray in one hand. 'Thank you, Madame Boin, Eliane. That calming *tisane* was much appreciated. We have some adjustments to make around here. Those visitors are about to become longer-term guests at Château Bellevue. They are going to billet themselves and, no doubt, a few more of their colleagues, in our rooms.'

Madame Boin gasped and sank into the nearest chair, fanning herself with the dishcloth she'd been holding.

Eliane plucked up the courage to ask, 'But what about you, monsieur?'

'They said I could stay in my own room. But I think it would be a good deal more relaxing to be independent of them. With your assistance, I hope, I shall move into the cottage. That will be the best solution to this unwelcome situation, I believe.'

'And us?' Madame Boin fanned herself even more vigorously. 'Where are we supposed to go? And who's going to look after you, monsieur?'

He sat down at the table opposite her, and gestured to Eliane to pull up a chair as well.

'Ladies,' he began and then cleared his throat. 'I don't have to tell you that these are extraordinary times in which we find ourselves. I'm not going to ask either of you to do anything that you feel uncomfortable with. If you wish to leave Château Bellevue while it is occupied by our enemies, then I will quite understand. And at the end of this war, if we are all still standing, your jobs will be waiting for you here should you wish to return.'

A tear ran down Eliane's cheek and she wiped it away, silently. Madame Boin looked aghast.

The count cleared his throat again. 'However, I am also going to offer you an alternative. You may wish to take some time to consider it carefully. Again, I want to emphasise that I don't expect you to do anything you feel unhappy about. But we have an opportunity up here at the château. A unique opportunity. These Germans have told me that they intend to set up a wireless station here. Our hilltop location makes it ideal for sending and receiving messages. We can monitor their movements and perhaps even their communications. And that just might enable us to help our countrymen fight back against these invaders. There is a French general in London who has been broadcasting over the past few weeks. His name is De Gaulle. I first heard him just before the armistice was signed and he sent a message of hope to all of us here, in the midst of our despair. It was reprinted in the newspaper and I carry it with me as a reminder.' He fished a folded piece of flimsy newsprint out of the breast pocket of his jacket and read from it: '"France has lost a battle! But France has not lost the war! I invite all Frenchmen, wherever they may be, to join me in action, in sacrifice and hope. Our fatherland is in danger of dying. Let us all fight to save it!"'

'Did you really just drink coffee with those Germans with that piece of paper in your pocket?' Madame Boin asked in disbelief.

'Actually, I drank lemon-balm tea, as you will recall. But yes. So, if like me you decide to heed the call of General de Gaulle, then I'm asking you to consider staying at your posts here. I know it will involve some distasteful duties – not least, providing meals for the enemy soldiers under our roof. But it may also give us useful insights into their plans and activities; we may be in a position to help save our fatherland and free it from German oppression.'

Madame Boin looked from Eliane to the count and back again. Her laugh was unexpected and startled Eliane. 'We make quite an unlikely secret force, the three of us! If you'll pardon my saying so, m'sieur,' she added hastily, remembering her manners.

The count smiled. 'And that, my dear Madame Boin, is precisely why we just might be an effective one. Who is going to suspect the three of us up here at the château?'

The cook nodded slowly, considering this.

'I'm not asking you to make a decision right here and now,' said Monsieur le Comte. 'Our world has turned upside down this morning, so take your time to consider what I've said. However . . .' He raised a finger in warning. 'I intend to do what I can, come what may. So I would ask you not to discuss this with others, even with your families. We live in treacherous times and war puts many unforeseen pressures on everyone it touches. If the Germans realise that my motivation for welcoming them into my home in such a civil manner is not, in fact, capitulation to their New Order – rather the opposite, indeed – then I am under no illusions as to what the repercussions will most certainly be.'

Madame Boin threw down her dishcloth. 'I don't need time to consider,' she declared stoutly. 'You are going to need looking after, m'sieur. More than ever in a house full of Germans. I'll stay.'

Eliane hesitated, remembering Madame Boin's words from earlier: 'The best way to get through whatever lies ahead is to carry on as normal.' Would that be possible now that there would be German soldiers living at Château Bellevue? A sudden vision of Mireille limping up the road towards her with the baby in her arms – and the thought of what the Germans had done to Blanche's mother – made her catch her breath. She thought of Mathieu, of whom there had been no word for more than a fortnight now; was he stranded in the unoccupied zone, unable to reach her? Or had he decided to stay with his father and brother now? Had he tried to contact her, as she had him? Had her letters reached him? How – and when – could they be together again? Her longing for him was lodged in her chest, a sickening ache, the contraction of loss that constricted her breath and made her heart feel as if it were closing in on itself. How could this have happened? How could someone, somewhere, decide one day to draw a line on a map that would keep them apart like this? That same line had cut like a scalpel blade through communities and families, severing France in two.

She realised, then, that of course it wasn't possible to carry on as normal. The world was no longer 'normal'. It was time to fight for the things that mattered. They were living with the enemy; it was time to do what she could to resist.

Abi: 2017

The night air is as thick and heavy as a blanket. I lie under the drapery of my mosquito net with the windows and shutters thrown wide open, in the hope that if there's any breath of a breeze it will be tempted in.

From up the hill, the faint, throbbing beat of dance music from the barn fades out and falls silent as the latest wedding party draws to a close. I'm getting used to the routine now, although each event takes on its own personality within the framework that Sara and Thomas have established. I'm getting my confidence back a little too. While Karen's broken wrist was mending, I took on some extra duties to help out and did some of the front-of-house work for a change. I'll admit, I was so anxious beforehand at the thought of being in a crowded space that I was nearly sick, but Jean-Marc was there helping out too, working behind the bar, and it was good to see his reassuring smile whenever I hurried past, and to know that Sara and Thomas were around as well, of course. And then the guests were all so friendly and were having so much fun that it was impossible not to relax and enjoy the party along with them.

Most weddings are happy ones, I suppose. Perhaps I was just unlucky.

As I toss and turn in the stifling darkness of the attic room, I think about the choices that Eliane and her family had to make. Madame Boin had said the best approach would be to try to keep going as normal, to try to ignore the war. But that sounded pretty impossible to me. I know some people collaborated with the Germans. Some probably did it because they believed in what the Germans were fighting for; but most were probably terrified, faced with impossible choices, resorting to collaboration as a means of self-preservation.

And then others chose the path of resistance.

I ponder what Sara has told me about Eliane. She was clearly such a peace-loving, gentle character and, like her mother, Lisette, she believed in saving lives, bringing new life into the world and tending those who were old and sick, like Monsieur le Comte. But she chose resistance without hesitation when the choice was presented to her.

I feel ashamed that I resisted only at the end. It took me years to find the strength, because I quickly became entangled in Zac's web of control. Systematically, he dismantled my sense of identity, which had perhaps never been very strong in the first place. It was easy for me to become isolated in my glass-paned tower overlooking the river; easier to stay inside rather than stepping out to explore my new neighbourhood; easier to give excuses to my few friends than to endure another evening of Zac's rudeness and coldness towards them, sensing the subtle shift in his mood which I knew boded badly for me when we returned home.

After a while, we socialised only with his friends. I tried seeing my friends on my own a few times, but when I returned to the apartment Zac would inevitably have spent the evening drinking alone. And when he was drunk, things were even worse for me. So it became safer, ironically, to let go of the friends who might have helped me escape from my marriage if they'd known what was going on. I'd become trapped in Zac's web now, and escape became impossible.

I tried to convince myself that the times when he was loving and solicitous were what mattered and that the storms of his temper were mere clouds passing across the blue sky of our life together. And anyway, everyone has arguments and hiccups in their relationships, don't they? Do they? I didn't know. There was no one I could ask, no friends I could casually compare notes with to try to work out where the boundaries lay for 'normal' people.

I knew by then that I wasn't 'normal', because Zac told me so, repeatedly. 'If I'd realised how damaged you are, I'd never have married you,' he remarked coldly one day, finding me curled on my side on the bed, weeping silent tears. 'Perhaps my mother was right.'

But then, too, he'd present me with gifts to try to make me feel better (or was it to try to salve his own guilty conscience?). He bought me an expensive new phone. I was delighted when he gave it to me, producing it at the dinner table one evening. But then he'd taken it from my hands and insisted on setting it up for me. 'And look here,' he'd said, flicking screens and pressing buttons, 'you can turn this on –' he clicked the icon marked 'Share My Location' – 'and I'll be able to track exactly where you are on my own phone. That way, I'll be able to picture where you are and what you're doing when we're apart during the day.' I suppose I should have felt flattered, that he wanted to stay so close to me.

He said all the right words, but why did they always seem to mean something else?

He'd buy clothes for me to wear, too – nothing like my usual style: tailored dresses, straight skirts, silk blouses. Expensive clothes, for which I ought to have felt grateful but which constrained me and made me feel like someone I wasn't.

I missed my jeans and the sticky-fingered hugs of the children I'd looked after and one evening I plucked up the courage to suggest that I might look for a job again – nothing full-time, of course, as keeping the apartment clean (Zac had high standards) and cooking his dinner took up so much of each day – just, perhaps, a few hours every morning for a frazzled working mother in need of help.

Zac's eyes grew dark, then, and I steeled myself against his anger, shrinking back against the cushions of the sofa where we were sitting. He was always able to do that with his gaze – to fix me to the spot when he focused it on me that way. He looked at me for a few moments and it was hard to read his expression. I glanced away, trying not to let the beam of his attention make me freeze, focusing instead on the twinkling lights of the city pooled beneath the single, blinking light of a plane as it made its way along the in-bound flight path towards its destination. He put a hand on my arm and I flinched again.

'Oh, Abi,' he sighed. His voice was soft, despairing. 'I've tried to give you everything you wanted. Most women would be delighted not to have to worry about going out to work. This apartment, everything we have, I've worked so hard for it. And this is how you thank me? By wanting to go and look after other people's children? What about my needs? What about having a baby of our own?'

My blood froze at his words. I'd have loved a child of my own, or two or three, but the thought of how that would trap me – and them – in his web, so tightly that there could be no escape, ever, terrified me.

He took me by the hand. 'In fact, let's start trying now, tonight!' His expression was tender again, concerned that I'd tried to pull away, that I was struggling against the silk threads of the web that he'd bound me in. 'Throw away your pills, my love, and come to bed.'

In the bathroom, I opened the mirrored cabinet above the sink and took out the box of contraceptive pills that was kept there. I knew he'd check. So I left a half-used pack in the box and chucked it into the bin beneath the sink. But I took the other packs and tucked them into the sleeve of my shirt, waiting in the bedroom until he'd gone to brush his teeth before I slipped them into the inner pocket of an old handbag that I kept on a shelf in the wardrobe.

Looking back, perhaps that was my first act of resistance. Perhaps I shouldn't feel so ashamed of myself, after all.

PART 2

Eliane: 1940

As the summer wore on, Eliane was relieved to see her sister's strength returning. Being at the mill slowly worked its magic on Mireille and the combination of simple but nourishing home-cooking, the loving care of her family and peaceful days spent playing with Blanche beside the river began to heal her wounded spirit. The sluice gates had now been opened again, so that the deafening roar of water over the weir had reverted to its more usual hush in the background of life at the mill. By late August, the vivacious spark had returned to Mireille's eyes and then, one miraculous Sunday afternoon, Lisette and Eliane smiled at one another as the sound of Mireille's laughter rang out once more, as welcome and as joyous as a peal of church bells.

'Just look at this naughty little monkey!' she exclaimed as she handed Blanche to Lisette. 'She managed to crawl all the way to the edge of the pool and then started trying to eat the mud!'

'She's covered in it!' But Lisette couldn't help laughing too. 'And you're no better, Mireille. What a mucky pair! Look at you – you've got just as much mud on your hands as she has.' She wiped a smudge from Mireille's cheek with a corner of her apron.

'Well, since she was in a bit of a mess already, it seemed like a good opportunity to make a few mud pies,' Mireille grinned.

Lisette washed Blanche's hands and face and then whisked her upstairs to change her out of her muddy clothes. Mireille sat down at the kitchen table and idly began turning the pages of last week's newspaper.

'How is Monsieur le Comte bearing up?' she asked Eliane. 'It can't be easy for him, living in the cottage while the château is full of *les Boches*.'

'He's doing okay. He's a courageous old man.' Eliane didn't elaborate – the count had continued to impress on her the need to stay silent, even with members of her family. 'At a time like this, knowledge can be a very dangerous thing,' he'd told her. 'You will be keeping your family safe by not telling them about anything that goes on up here. For the same reason, I do not intend to explain to you the details of what I am doing: if the Germans were to find out, it would be better for you and Madame Boin if you did not know.'

Indeed, it didn't seem to Eliane as if much was going on at all in the way of subversive activity. Sometimes she wondered whether Monsieur le Comte was becoming a little delusional – it would have been perfectly understandable, given his age and the upset of having his home requisitioned by the enemy. He spent quite a bit of time reading in the château's library – a room that the Germans were happy to allow him to use in light of how accommodating he'd been in welcoming them into his home – and he took his meals in the kitchen. He usually spent much of the afternoon taking a nap in the cottage and often retired early to his bedroom there once the women had given him his supper, leaving them to clear away and get home in time before the curfew.

Madame Boin refused to leave her kitchen, now that the château was 'infested with *les Boches*', as she put it. She prepared meals for the Germans, as the count asked her to, but with as much bad grace and clashing of pans as she could manage. On the count's instructions,

Eliane would set everything out in the dining room before the Germans' mealtimes and wait until they'd left to go back and clear away, so her path rarely crossed with theirs. The only exception was the translator – Oberleutnant Farber – who acted as a go-between, passing on requests (which were, in fact, orders) from the officers billeted in Château Bellevue. He was a pleasant enough man, Eliane thought, although his uniform made her nervous. The insignia on his jacket – the silver eagle with wings outspread and the sharp geometry of the swastika – seemed to her to be brutal icons of dominance and persecution.

One Friday evening, as Eliane was finishing up her week's work by mopping the kitchen floor, she'd looked up, startled, when a figure appeared in the doorway. It was Monsieur le Comte, who put a finger to his lips and then handed her a sealed envelope. She took it, puzzled, and then saw that her father's name was written on it in the count's distinguished handwriting. He gestured to her to put it in her apron pocket and then, with a nod of his head, disappeared back down the darkened path towards the cottage. As she watched him go, it seemed to Eliane that he deliberately kept to the shadows, avoiding the few strips of light escaping from the edges of the badly fitting blackout on the château windows, which illuminated the gardens here and there.

She had handed the envelope to her father when she got home. Gustave had simply nodded and put it in his pocket without opening it, and Eliane had known better than to ask him any questions about it.

She didn't mention that letter to her sister now, either, as Mireille began to read aloud from the newspaper. "'With Paris virtually deserted, employers there are calling for workers to return. Following reassurances that there will be no further bombing raids by the Luftwaffe now that the armistice is in place, for a limited period of time additional trains will be run from Bordeaux to the capital, to ensure employees can return to their posts.'"

Eliane had taken over from her mother when she'd left to clean Blanche up after her mud-pie-making exploits. Lisette had been preparing her medicaments for the week ahead, so now Eliane was carefully transferring essential oils from glass-stoppered bottles into the smaller vials that Lisette carried with her on her rounds. She paused for a moment to look over at Mireille, as the words she'd just read hung in the air, mingling with the medicinal scents of peppermint, for heartburn in pregnancy, and cloves, for soothing the gums of teething babies.

'Will you go back?' she asked.

Mireille gazed out of the window; but whether she saw the river and the willow tree, or whether the visions of the carnage she'd witnessed still played before her eyes, Eliane couldn't tell.

Slowly, Mireille nodded, making up her mind. She turned towards Eliane. 'I'm strong enough again now. I know I'm needed at the *atelier* – so many of the girls left at the same time when Esther and I did. I wonder who else will go back. I wonder who else is left . . .'

'Maman won't like it,' Eliane said, returning her attention to the array of bottles in front of her.

Mireille sighed. 'I know. But there's nothing for me here. You and Maman take such good care of Blanche, you don't need me to help with that. In Paris I am needed, though. I had a postcard the other day from Monsieur le Directeur. He's been told that if he can't carry on as usual, the Germans will take over his business and put their own people in to keep the *atelier* going. Surely it's better if it remains in his hands? He's been a good boss. And he's tried to help people like Esther. Perhaps there will be other women like her who can be given shelter and work. Perhaps I can help with that in some way too . . .'

As she spoke, Mireille's voice grew stronger and her words carried more conviction than they had done since her return to the mill. At that moment, Lisette entered, carrying a freshly washed and dressed Blanche, who was perfumed with the scent of the massage oil – a mixture of tarragon, lavender and mint – that Lisette used as a sooth-ing balm to heal colic and calm the babies in her care. She handed the baby to Mireille to bounce on her knee.

'In that case,' said Lisette, clearly having heard what Mireille had been saying, 'you are going to need to make sure you've got the strength to go back, *ma fille*.'

Mireille's face lit up. 'Will you let me go then, Maman?'

'I will do so at the beginning of September, providing that I'm satis-fied that you are completely well again.' Lisette smoothed a lock of hair from Mireille's forehead, looking deep into her elder daughter's dark eyes. 'I know you. I know that keeping you here will not help your soul to mend and rebuild itself. You will find ways to do that in Paris – of this I am sure. But just remember, you can always return here to the mill if you find that you need to leave Paris again. This is your home. This will always be your home.'

A small tear trickled on to Mireille's cheek and she buried her face in Blanche's curls, which were so like her own.

Lisette continued stroking her daughter's hair, soothing her. 'And now I know you are getting better,' she smiled. 'Because you are able to cry again, at last.'

On Monday morning, Eliane went, as usual, to the walled garden to check the beehives and collect the ingredients that Madame Boin had requested for the day's menus. The upper frames in each of the hives were full of summer honey, capped off with neat beeswax seals. This week she would take the last collection of the year, making sure that she left a good supply to see the bees through the coming win-ter. If it was anything like as harsh as the last one they'd be needing a bit extra, especially now that rationing was making it harder to save any sugar.

As she settled the frames she'd been inspecting back in place, she heard the gate open and turned to see Monsieur le Comte.

'*Bonjour, monsieur.*'

'*Bonjour*, Eliane. How are your charges today?'

'Thriving, thank you, sir. The colonies were much depleted after last winter, but they have survived and are back to full strength again now.'

He stooped a little lower, leaning on his cane, to examine a worker bee that had just landed at the entrance to the hive and was busily weaving her dance to tell her comrades where to find the richest sources of nectar.

'It never fails to fascinate me, the way they do that.' He straightened up and smiled at Eliane. 'They are so clever, the way they work together as a community, each with its own role to play to ensure the colony continues to thrive.'

Beckoning Eliane to follow, he moved a little further away from the hives, so as not to get in the way of the bees' flight paths and agitate them. 'Show me what you are cultivating in this bed,' he asked her.

She'd been spending more time in the walled garden since the gardener had left. He'd joined up a few months before the armistice was signed and, as far as anyone now knew, he was one of the thousands of captured French soldiers who'd been sent to labour camps in Germany.

Eliane began pointing out the late-summer crops of courgettes, beans and tomatoes, but the count's attention seemed to be elsewhere. She fell silent. Still gazing at the neatly hoed beds as if intent on the produce, he said quietly, 'Like that worker bee, would you be prepared to help your community, Eliane?'

Taking her lead from him, she too continued to face the garden, as if studying the plants. Her voice was soft as she replied, '*Bien sûr, monsieur.*'

'I don't want to put you in a position of risk. So all I'm going to ask you to do is to perform a sort of dance to send a message to others. You don't need to know who they are, nor where they are. When I give you the word, you'll just put on this headscarf . . .' He fished a folded square of richly patterned red silk out of his pocket. 'And then take your basket for a little stroll around the outside of the garden walls. It's important that you wear the scarf and that you walk in a clockwise direction: those are the parts of the dance that communicate the message. Would you be prepared to do this?'

Eliane looked down at the bright scarf that he held out to her. Silently, she took it from him and slipped it into her apron pocket. After she had done so, she murmured, 'But, m'sieur, this is too fine a headscarf for a girl like me to wear. Silk of this quality, and so intricately patterned . . . Won't people think it's a little odd?'

'It belonged to my mother,' he said. 'But I'd like you to start wearing it often; and if anyone asks you about it, perhaps tell them it was a gift from your sister in Paris. She has access to such finery – people will believe that. And, if you are stopped by any of our "guests" on your walk, say that you're searching for some of the wildflowers you and your *maman* use to make your healing potions.'

'Very well, monsieur. But how will I know when to go for my walk?'

'I shall be in the library as usual this morning. I understand that our "guests" have an important briefing that they must all attend at the *mairie* today. When the coast is clear, I'll come into the kitchen and ask Madame Boin to prepare a peppermint *tisane* for me. That will be the time to dance your dance, like your bees, and send the message.'

'Understood.' Her voice was almost a whisper, but he heard her reply clearly.

'Thank you, Eliane.' He pointed towards the vegetable plot again, as though their conversation had been about that all along, and then sauntered back to the château.

Deep in thought, as she collected the ingredients that Madame Boin had requested, Eliane deliberately omitted to pick any peppermint.

There was the usual coming and going of German soldiers at Château Bellevue that morning; a motorcycle courier puttered up the drive to deliver documents for the general; a couple of soldiers marched past the kitchen window on their way to relieve the patrol at the checkpoint on the bridge in Coulliac; and a military truck pulled up at the main door.

'Two more of them moving in,' tutted Madame Boin, as she and Eliane made up additional beds in an upstairs room. 'We'll be full to bursting if this goes on much longer.'

The door of the adjacent room opened and they heard the crackle of a radio and German voices. The wireless station had been set up there and Eliane realised suddenly that it was directly above the library, where the count spent so much of his time these days.

Oberleutnant Farber knocked on the open bedroom door. '*Mesdames*, there is no great urgency to finish that. The new arrivals have been ordered to leave their bags in the hallway for the time being as there are other things to attend to now. If you could have the room ready by this afternoon then that will be fine. And there is no need to put out anything for lunch today; we will be making other arrangements.'

'*Oui, monsieur*,' Madame Boin said. And then, once the sound of his footsteps had faded away down the corridor, she resumed her grumbling. 'First they give us no notice of these new arrivals and then they change their plans for the midday meal. How am I supposed to run the kitchen under such conditions? Talk about high-handed . . .'

From the bedroom window, as she finished putting a bolster into its linen cover, Eliane watched several of the soldiers climbing into the truck and then Oberleutnant Farber bringing the jeep to the front entrance for the general. As he was pulling away, the oberleutnant glanced upwards and caught sight of Eliane standing there. He smiled, and gave a very slight nod in acknowledgement, before turning the vehicle and following the truck down the steep driveway towards the town.

As the dust settled behind them, the château fell silent. Eliane hurried downstairs to join Madame Boin in the kitchen and set to work topping and tailing a colander of green beans. After a few minutes, she heard the slow footsteps and tap of a walking cane that signified the approach of the count.

He smiled at the scene of peaceful domesticity as he came through the door. 'Madame Boin, please would you be so kind as to make me my morning *tisane*? I think I'd like peppermint today.'

'*Oui, monsieur.*' She put the kettle on to boil. 'But Eliane, where is the mint? I asked you to bring me some this morning.'

'Did I forget it? Oh, I'm sorry, madame. I'll go and gather some now.' She picked up the wicker basket that sat by the kitchen door and stepped outside. As soon as she was out of Madame Boin's sight, she set the basket down and took the scarf out of the pocket of her apron. It was one of the most beautiful things she'd ever seen: a square of scarlet silk, patterned with exotic birds and flowers. She shook out the heavy folds and then held it by two corners to make a large triangle to cover her hair. She tied it behind the nape of her neck, peasant-style, and then picked up her basket again. She walked right around the outside of the walled garden, going clockwise as the count had directed, feeling self-conscious as she knew that somewhere someone was watching her. Indeed, she felt exposed and conspicuous as she progressed around the outside of the garden walls, aware that she must be visible from Coulliac, where the Germans were, as well as from the surrounding countryside. Her scalp prickled with fear beneath the covering of the headscarf, but she walked determinedly onwards.

After completing the circuit, she removed the scarf and carefully re-folded it, secreting it back in her pocket. Then she pushed the gate open and hastily gathered a bunch of sweet-smelling mint leaves to take back to Madame Boin.

About half an hour later there was the sound of a vehicle driving past and pulling up by the main entrance.

'That had better not be any of those *Boches* coming back and wanting their lunch after all,' scolded Madame Boin.

Craning to look, Eliane was surprised to see her father's truck. 'It's Papa!' she exclaimed.

Gustave got out, whistling cheerfully, and unloaded a sack of flour from the back. He came to the kitchen door and knocked loudly. 'Good morning, Madame Boin. *Et re-bonjour, ma fille.*' He smiled at Eliane. 'After my deliveries today I discovered that I had one extra bag, which I must have accidentally omitted to hand in at the depot. I thought, rather than wasting precious gasoline going all the way back again, I would see if it might be of any use to you. I know you have a great number of "guests" to cater for these days.'

Eliane thought it odd that he used the same jokey term as Monsieur le Comte did when referring to the Germans. She also thought she heard the sound of the truck door opening and then softly closing again, but Gustave was chatting animatedly to Madame Boin, so perhaps she was mistaken.

Her father seemed to be in no great hurry to depart, discussing the latest news reports and passing on snippets of local gossip gleaned on his rounds that morning. 'Lisette had a tiring day yesterday. Madame Leblanc's labour lasted seventeen hours! So she was up all night long. But all is well – a bouncing boy finally delivered at five this morning. Lisette was catching up on her sleep when I left . . .'

He tailed off as the count appeared. 'Bonjour, Monsieur le Comte.' The two men shook hands. 'As you can see,' Gustave pointed at the sack of flour propped against a chair, 'I've just made an extra delivery.'

'That is greatly appreciated, Gustave. Thank you for thinking of us. All is in order.' It sounded to Eliane more like a statement of fact than a question.

The miller nodded. 'Well, I'd better be going. If Lisette's woken up she'll be wondering why I'm taking so long to finish my rounds. Good day, monsieur; Madame Boin.' He paused in passing to plant a kiss on the top of Eliane's head, saying, 'See you later, *ma fille.*' And then, having climbed back into his truck, he gave them all a jaunty wave as he drove past, heading for home.

≈≋≈

When she got back to the mill that evening, Eliane paused beside the river for a few minutes, standing beneath the sheltering canopy of the willow's branches. She had got into the habit of doing so almost every day since Mathieu had left, spending a few minutes thinking of him and remembering the times they'd spent together on the riverbank. She gazed across the river at the fields and then the woods beyond the fields, visible as dark shadows in the moonlight. On the far side of the woods, the faint rumble of a passing train faded away into the distance.

Mathieu was out there, somewhere, beyond those woods, over the railway line and across yet more fields, on the other side of the steep, narrow valleys of the Périgord where the higher land opened out to become the meadows and pastures of the Corrèze, helping his father and brother manage the farm near Tulle. She wished, with all her heart, for a message from him. Just a few words to let her know that he was safe and well and that he was still thinking of her. She thought back to the days they'd spent beside the river, picnicking in the sunlight and idly making plans for a future that they'd been so sure of sharing. She'd known then, with such certainty, that they were destined to be together. But who could have foretold that France would become a country divided by a line drawn on a map? And that that line of demarcation would so quickly become an un-crossable barrier?

Just then, the darkness of the blackout was illuminated for a moment as the door of the mill house opened and light spilled from the interior across the dusty grass to where Eliane was standing, concealed, behind the veil of the willow's leaves. Lisette stepped out, closing the door again quickly behind her; and, as Eliane watched, her mother walked over to the barn carrying something carefully before her. Eliane heard the soft clink of china rattling on a tin tray and caught the fleeting smell of something savoury – soup, perhaps? Or a stew that her mother had made?

How strange. Her mother was taking a meal out to the barn. But then it had been a strange day, with the morning walk in the silk headscarf and her father turning up at the château like that. Eliane stepped out from the shelter of the willow tree just as Lisette hurried back out of the barn, empty-handed now.

'Oh!' she gasped, pressing her hand to her throat. 'It's you, Eliane. You startled me!'

'Sorry, Maman, I didn't mean to.'

'How was your day?' asked Lisette.

'Oh fine. The same as usual,' Eliane replied. Although she was curious as to who could possibly be eating their supper in the Martins' barn, she knew better than to ask questions if her mother didn't want her to.

'Papa is in the kitchen. I think he wants a word with you.'

Eliane followed her mother inside, blinking in the light.

'Here she is!' Gustave pulled out the chair next to his and gestured for Eliane to join him at the table. 'You did a fine job today, *ma fille*. That walk you took was an important one.'

She shrugged. 'It was just a walk.'

He grinned at her and ruffled her hair. 'It was a walk that enabled things to happen. Things that must stay behind the scenes for the moment. But things that will make a difference.'

She smiled back at him, tucking her straight, honey-coloured hair back behind her ears. 'And is one of those things eating supper in the barn right now?'

Lisette gasped. 'I told you it was too much of a risk letting him stay there,' she scolded Gustave.

'Don't worry, *chérie*. Eliane has already played a part in this and she knows not to say anything to anyone outside of this house. It's only fair that she be told. In any case, he'll be gone tomorrow when Yves and I deliver him to his new digs, along with the flour for the bakery. And it's after the curfew now, too late to move him safely tonight.'

Gustave turned to face Eliane. 'As you have gathered, we have a "guest" at the *moulin* for the night. Like your "guests" at the château, he's a foreigner – he's English. He crossed the weir today, having parachuted into the unoccupied zone last night. He'll be around for a while, helping out behind the scenes. More than that, you need not know.'

'I see.' Eliane nodded, thoughtfully. 'And did my walk today have something to do with his arrival?'

'Indeed it did. You let certain people know when the coast was clear. You helped keep him – and others – safe.'

'May I ask you one more question, then?'

'Just one more. But I can't promise you an answer.'

'Did you deliver more than just a sack of flour when you came to Château Bellevue today?'

He looked into her candid grey eyes, considering his reply. 'The answer to your question is "yes", Eliane. But I cannot say any more than that.'

'That's okay. I understand, Papa. I won't ask any more questions.'

When she'd climbed the stairs to her attic room, Eliane took the scarlet headscarf from her apron pocket and spread it out on her bed, running her fingertips across the smooth, richly coloured silk. She knew it was a beacon, and that today it had sent an important signal out from the hilltop to the countryside around. Against the white counterpane, the scarf seemed to blaze with a triumphant message of hope. She willed it to keep the stranger in the barn safe, and to protect her family here and in Paris; she thought of Monsieur le Comte, whose mother had worn the scarf once, and hoped it would surround him with light up there at the château, whatever he was up to in the midst of all those German soldiers; and, most of all, she prayed that it would somehow be a beacon, like the beam from a lighthouse sweeping across a darkened ocean, that took her love to Mathieu on the other side of their divide.

⁂

There was a strange man sitting at the kitchen table when she came downstairs the next morning. His clothes were non-descript and workmanlike, but his features were distinctive: an aquiline nose and square jaw suggested a physical strength that was softened by the faint expression of amusement in his eyes, which were the shade of the dark-blue cornflowers that grew along the edges of the wheat fields. At the sight of Eliane, he set down his bowl of coffee and scrambled to his feet.

She stooped to kiss her father, who was seated at the end of the table nearest the door. '*Bonjour, Papa.*'

'*Bonjour*, Eliane. Allow me to introduce you to Jacques Lemaître.'

The stranger stretched out his hand to shake hers. '*Enchanté, mademoiselle. Je suis ravi de faire votre connaissance.*'

His French was flawless, with perhaps just the faint hint of an accent that was difficult to place. Without knowing otherwise, one might assume he was from further south – the Basque country, perhaps, or maybe the Languedoc.

'Jacques will be working at the bakery in Coulliac and staying in the apartment above it. He's a friend of the family's who's come to lend a hand now that Monsieur Fournier's arthritis is so bad these days.'

She nodded. 'They'll be pleased to have your help, m'sieur.'

Jacques smiled. 'That is a very beautiful scarf you're wearing, Eliane.'

'Thank you. It was a present from my sister in Paris.'

It felt as if they were all practicing their roles, rehearsing them in private so that they would be prepared for a more public performance.

Downing his coffee, Gustave pulled a large, spotted handkerchief out of his pocket and wiped his moustache. 'Right then, Jacques, let's get going. Monsieur Fournier will be wanting his delivery of flour before the rest of Coulliac wakes up.'

'*Au revoir,* Eliane,' the stranger said. 'I look forward to seeing you again soon.'

'Welcome to Coulliac, Monsieur Lemaître,' she replied. 'I hope you will settle in well.'

Abi: 2017

It's a Monday – the day of rest for the staff at Château Bellevue – and I'm sitting on the riverbank, dabbling my feet in the water. Thomas and Jean-Marc have been working on the mill house this morning, but they've gone back up the hill for lunch. It's way too hot to work outside in the middle of the day.

I've grown brave enough, now, to swim in the river. Jean-Marc has shown me that you can walk out on to the weir and dive into the deep pool upstream there, as long as you keep to the middle of the river, away from the sluice channels. The mill wheel is still these days, frozen in space and time, a silent testimony to those war years when it was used to grind the grain for the community's daily bread. But the sluice gate in the bypass channel stands open and the water is drawn into it in a ribbon of blackness that is churned to foaming white as it drops back into the river's course below the weir once again. In the centre of the stream, the water in the deep mill pool is dark and cool, and then it leaps over the top of the weir, cascading joyfully into the golden-brown pool below, where fish swim in the eddies beneath the willow as the river gathers itself before flowing onwards to join other, larger waterways and eventually pour itself out into the ocean.

I pick my way over the river stones next to the bank and sit down with my back against the trunk of the willow tree. The bark is rough, riven with cracks and crevices. Sara's told me that this bark is a source of the main component of aspirin, and that Eliane and Lisette would have made use of a tea brewed from it as a mild analgesic when manufactured drugs were in short supply during the war years. I rest my head against the healing bark and close my eyes, letting the glimmers of sunlight that filter through the willow's elegant leaves make patterns of warmth and light play over my eyelids. I think of Eliane, standing in the shelter of the tree, dreaming of Mathieu on that night that Jacques had arrived at the mill.

What would it feel like, I wonder, to be loved by a man like Mathieu Dubosq or Jacques Lemaître? A good-hearted man.

The faint rumbling rhythm of a train pulses by, far away in the distance, rousing me from my daydreams. It's so peaceful here (now that Thomas' cement mixer has, thankfully, fallen silent) that you can pick out each layer of sound: the fluting call of a bird overhead; the far-off heartbeat of the passing train; the sigh of the weeping willow's leaves; the hushed rush of the river. It's very unlike my view of the Thames from the apartment in London, whose sounds are drowned by the noise of the city all around it; and those city sounds, in turn, are sealed out by the hermetic glass panes of the tall windows so that, inside, there is a silence so absolute that it is anything but peaceful.

I used to play music or have the radio on all the time, when I was in the apartment on my own each day, so that I wouldn't hear that silence.

Zac must have sensed how lonely I was. And something had shifted, that night when he suggested trying to start a family. Although, outwardly, I thought I appeared the same as ever, I was no longer the passive collaborator I had been at the start of our marriage. My small, secret act of defiance in hiding my birth-control pills gave me strength each day when I took one out of the evening bag hidden on the shelf in the wardrobe and swallowed it down with a sip from the glass of water beside the bed.

Perhaps somehow, Zac sensed that shift, too, a tiny loss of control, in a way that he couldn't quite put his finger on. Anyway, whatever his reasoning, he presented the idea of me returning to my studies with an air of triumphant benevolence.

Why was it that every time he gave me something, I felt something was being taken away from me?

'You could study for a university degree,' he suggested, 'while we're trying for our family. What do you think? You've said you always regretted not being able to continue your studies after you left school.'

I was amazed, and then grateful. So he *did* have my best interests at heart, after all.

I beamed from ear to ear. 'Oh Zac! Really? I'd *love* that!' I pictured myself in a packed lecture theatre, and drinking coffee with other students (I'd be older than most of them, of course, but not ridiculously so), carrying a bag of books home on the tube and settling down to write an essay . . .

I realised my mistake immediately, as his expression turned from warm to cool. I'd dropped my guard, let him see a glimpse of my true feelings, and that had given him power.

'Of course, it's going to cost a great deal. But I was looking online at the Open University. It's cheaper to study through them and you won't have all those added travel costs. I'm not made of money, after all.'

There it was again. Given with one hand, taken away with the other. And, although the thought of doing a degree through the OU still filled me with excitement, why did I feel that the walls of the apartment were closing in around me, the views of the city skyline receding even further into the distance, becoming even more unreachable beyond the plate-glass windows?

But, I told myself, if I got a degree I would be empowered. I could go out and get a good job, stand on my own two feet. The tiny voice of my lost Self whispered in my ear: *And then you could earn enough money to get away.*

It was a step. And, right then, a step in any direction was better than sitting, frozen, behind those tall panes of glass.

Eliane: 1940

Instead of retiring to the cottage for his usual nap, the count began to spend most of his afternoons in the chapel. At that time of day, once lunch had been cleared away, the château tended to lapse into silence, with most of the Germans either at their posts in Coulliac or, on their days off, sleeping off the wine from the château's cellar, which they'd enjoyed with their midday meal courtesy of their host.

'Put out a bottle or two each day,' Monsieur le Comte had directed Eliane. 'Like your bees, our "guests" need a regular supply of nectar to keep them happy.'

For Madame Boin, the steps that led down into the cellar from the corner of the kitchen were impossible to navigate. Their steepness made her dizzy, she claimed. So it was Eliane's job to go down into the cool darkness beneath the bedrock on which the château sat and bring up the wine. 'Start from the left-hand side of the racks,' the count had told her. 'The very best bottles are on the right – we will save those for our own celebrations one of these days, God willing.'

Three wooden barrels sat in a row at one end of the cellar, wedged with wooden chocks to keep them from rolling out of place. The first time Eliane had gone down there, the count had instructed her to look closely at the barrels and tell him whether she noticed anything about them.

'The middle one sits a little lower than the other two, which is strange because they seem to be the same size,' she'd remarked on her return.

Monsieur le Comte had nodded. 'When you next go down, Eliane, look again. You've heard the rumours of a secret tunnel that links the château to the mill? Well, they are true. That middle barrel sits on a trapdoor set into the floor, which is why it is that tiny bit lower.'

She had never been into the tunnel, but now thought of it often when she went to fetch the wine: a hidden passageway that linked her place of work with her home.

One afternoon, having descended the cellar steps to fetch some bottles so that the wine could rest above ground and gently come to the correct temperature for serving that evening, she realised that the racks on the left-hand side were almost empty, thanks to the count's generosity. There were some boxes piled up in front of the racks on the right, stamped with the name of a local wine producer and the year 1937. Was this part of the count's precious supply of the finer vintages? Or could she place the bottles in the left-hand racks to replenish what had already been consumed? She would need to check . . .

A little later, she was on her way to work in the walled garden for an hour or two before helping Madame Boin prepare the evening meal, when she thought she would look in at the chapel to ask the count the question about the wine. The chapel was one of the oldest parts of the château, and its stonework slumbered in the afternoon sunshine, mellowed by time and prayer. The ancient cross on the peak of the gable over the entranceway pointed heavenwards, rising above the roofs of the adjacent buildings. She knocked softly on the weathered wood of the door, not wanting to disturb the count if he was at prayer. Oddly, she thought she heard two voices from within, but as she pushed the door open, Monsieur le Comte rose from where he'd been sitting, evidently in peaceful solitude, beside the altar, just in front of the statue of Christ on the cross. *He must have been praying out loud*, she thought.

When she explained the situation in the wine cellar, the count smiled broadly, his eyes crinkling in amusement. 'Ah, yes, I'd forgotten about those cases of wine. Nineteen thirty-seven was a dire vintage, tannic and harsh. The winemaker couldn't sell those wines, so he gave me some for nothing as part of another order. It won't have begun to age yet and when it does it may still turn out to be undrinkable. That will be the very thing to serve to our German visitors; the perfect solution! By all means, Eliane, you may transfer those bottles to the empty racks. Please just make sure you don't serve any to me, though!'

He sat back down on his chair beside the altar. As if it had just occurred to him, he added, 'Oh, and Eliane, I may need to ask you to take another of your walks tomorrow, so make sure you have the scarf with you.'

She patted the red silk around her neck and he nodded approvingly. 'I'll let you know,' he said.

She left him in the quiet of the chapel, sitting where a ray of sunlight filtered through the diamond-paned window above the statue of Christ. The light made the dust motes dance around his head in the cool air and illuminated his hands, which were clasped loosely on his lap. As she pulled the door softly to behind her, she heard his voice again, an indistinct mutter on the other side of the thick walls.

She'd be prepared to walk again tomorrow, as she had done not frequently but on several occasions since that first time. The direction and number of circuits she was told to make varied sometimes; although she never knew what she was communicating, nor to whom. But she hoped that – along with the count's afternoon prayers – the messages she sent out into the wide blue yonder might, somehow, be making a difference.

Abi: 2017

Karen and I are cleaning the chapel this morning. The summer sun has cranked the thermostat up to 'high' today, so it's a relief to step through the door and into the cool half-light. We sweep the flagstones, collecting the detritus of the last wedding in our dustpans; a few of the dried rose petals that Sara provides as an alternative to confetti; a couple of discarded order-of-service sheets; dust from the soles of so many pairs of smart new shoes, bought especially for the occasion. The polished wood of the pews gleams where a ray of light filters through the lead-paned windows.

Together, Karen and I shake out the laundered linen cloth and spread it over the little altar that sits before the statue of Christ. She flexes her wrist, which is still a bit stiff at times, though it's mended pretty well, and then glances at my arm. I notice her looking and pretend to smooth a non-existent wrinkle out of the altar cloth to cover my self-consciousness. In the heat, I've had to discard my usual long-sleeved shirts for once. I know it's not a pretty sight. The bones splintered when they broke, tearing through the skin. The pins they put in to fix it have created more scar tissue, so my arm is lumpy and misshapen. The scars from the lacerations stand out as hard, white wheals against the faint tan that I've picked up while sitting by the riverbank in my swimming costume on my days off.

Karen fixes me with her candid gaze. 'Here I am feeling sorry for myself because my wrist's a bit sore. That must have hurt you a whole lot more, I reckon.'

I shrug, trying not to remember. Trying to blank out the images that come, unbidden, into my head. 'Yeah, I suppose so. But it was a while ago. Nearly healed now.'

She looks at me searchingly for a moment. 'You're doing okay, you know, Abi. I've seen a few people come and go in my time, and you're one of the good 'uns.'

I'm not sure whether she's referring to the work I do around the château or whether she's talking about something else, but her gruff kindness brings tears to my eyes. I duck my head and bend down to gather up my dustpan and brush so that I can regain my composure. From the yard outside, the sound of Jean-Marc's mower passes, growing louder and then fading. He must be on the way to park it in its shed, on his way in for lunch.

As I straighten up, Karen's still looking at me appraisingly, and then she grins, saying, 'And I reckon I'm not the only one around here who thinks that, y'know.'

As we leave the chapel, I pause for a moment before stepping back out into the glare of the midday heat, and I think of the count spending his afternoons here. And in that moment, in the hushed half-light of the chapel, it's as if I can hear the faint whisper of voices, transmitting their messages from the past.

Eliane: 1942

Word spread quickly through the market in Coulliac that the new season's honey was available. There were serious food shortages now, despite the strict rationing that had been in place. Sugar was one of the most precious commodities, and one of the scarcest, and so a queue quickly formed at Francine and Eliane's stall.

People were resigned to queuing for everything these days – queuing at the *mairie* for travel permits and petrol coupons; queuing at the bakery to collect the dwindling daily rations of bread and at the butcher's shop to pick up a meagre square of horsemeat; and queuing at the checkpoints that sprang up on roads where, previously, they had been able to go freely about their everyday business.

People padded out their rations as best they could with whatever was available: fish from the river, sometimes; wild salad leaves – dandelion, chickweed and *mâche* – from the hedgerows; and when the supplies of wheat fell short, as they so often did these days, Gustave and Yves would grind chestnuts into a coarse flour that could be made into heavy loaves of yellow bread that sat in the stomach like a brick. But no one was complaining. After a winter of surviving mostly on turnips and root artichokes, everyone welcomed the relative plenty and variety that came with spring and early summer. The dense chestnut bread filled a hole in an empty stomach. Some honey, though – now that would transform even the mildewed heel of a loaf of bread into a treat.

Instead of charging a king's ransom, which was what most people would have been prepared to pay for a jar, had they had the resources, the girls charged a token amount, distributing the precious supplies as widely as they could among the families of Coulliac. In some cases, they weren't averse to participating in the *marché amical* (a far friendlier name for it than 'black market'), and would quietly exchange a jar of honey for a chunk of dried sausage or a few wizened apples, the last of the previous year's crop. These items were hastily secreted behind the stall.

On the surface, Francine appeared to be her usual cheerful self. But, a few days ago, she had been ordered to present herself at the *mairie* where, after standing in the obligatory queue for over two hours, she was issued with a yellow star and told it was to be worn on her outer clothing at all times. Eliane could sense her growing anxiety. And no wonder – the newspapers carried reports of deportations with increasing frequency. Jews, in particular, were being rounded up and sent to labour camps in the east, and the tone of the reporting was becoming more and more openly anti-Semitic.

When Oberleutnant Farber stepped up to the stall to buy – at full price – one of the few jars of jam they'd been able to make that year (the shortage of sugar having limited their usual production), Francine's hands shook so much that she scattered his change across the cobbles of the square. Jacques Lemaître, who was next in line, helped gather up a few of the stray coins and handed them to the soldier.

'*Merci, monsieur,*' the oberleutnant said.

Jacques simply nodded pleasantly and then, waiting until the soldier had strolled off towards the *mairie*, turned to Eliane and Francine. 'A jar of your very fine honey, please, mesdemoiselles,' he said gallantly. 'And how are your parents? And your brother?' he asked Eliane. 'Have you had any word from your sister in Paris lately?'

Stéphanie, who'd been standing behind him and had been intently watching the exchanges with both men, reached across in front of

Jacques on the pretext of examining the last remaining jar of jam, made from wild plums that the girls had gleaned from the roadside in the spring.

'Allow me, mademoiselle,' he said politely, passing the jar to her.

'Why, thank you, m'sieur. I don't believe we've met? I think I've seen you working in the bakery, though.' She introduced herself and extended a well-manicured hand, simpering as she did so.

'*Enchanté*,' he replied. 'That's right; I'm Monsieur Fournier's assistant.'

'Hello, Eliane,' said Stéphanie, suddenly redirecting her attention. 'What a pretty scarf that is! I've seen you wearing it a lot. Where on earth did you get something like that, I wonder?'

'From my sister, Mireille,' Eliane replied.

'Really? Not from one of your grateful German soldiers up at the château?'

Refusing to rise to the bait, Eliane replied firmly, 'No. A grateful client in Paris gave it to Mireille and she passed it on to me as a birthday gift.'

'I see.' Stéphanie's laugh was brittle with insincerity. 'I wonder whether that client was female or male. And how is that charming baby your mother so thoughtfully took in? She must be getting quite grown-up these days.'

Eliane could sense Francine tensing with anger beside her. She smiled calmly at Stéphanie. 'Yes, Blanche is doing really well now. She's a happy child, with quite a will of her own.'

Stéphanie sniffed, and then handed the jam jar back to Jacques, turning the full focus of her attention to him once again. 'Please could I ask you to be so kind as to replace that for me, monsieur?'

Francine glared again as Stéphanie blatantly fluttered her eyelashes in his direction. 'Just a jar of honey, please, Eliane.' Stéphanie's gaze swept over Francine, her eyes deliberately lingering on the yellow star pinned to the front of her blouse. She stashed the honey in her basket and then extended a hand to Jacques once more. 'Until we meet again, monsieur.' She swept off across the *place*, smoothing back her glossy black hair.

'Goodbye then, Eliane, Francine.' Jacques' smile took in both of them. As he was moving off, the mayor's secretary bustled up to him.

'Good morning, Monsieur Lemaître,' she said. 'I have that newspaper article that you were asking about the other day. I hope you will find it interesting.'

'Why, thank you, madame. That is most thoughtful of you and greatly appreciated. I'm sure I shall.' He took the rolled-up newspaper that she pulled out of her shipping bag and tucked it under his arm. 'Good morning to you all, ladies.'

And then Jacques walked briskly across the square, purposefully making for the door to his tiny apartment above the baker's shop.

The next day, Sunday, Eliane was scattering some scraps for the chickens, assisted by Blanche, who was now a sturdy two-and-a-half-year-old. The little girl laughed as the rooster flapped his wings, trying to assert his authority over the hens – who ignored him and carried on pecking busily at the ground. Both of them were surprised to see Jacques Lemaître walking down the track towards the mill.

'Good morning, Blanche and Eliane. Are your parents and Yves at home?' he asked as he approached.

'Of course. Please come in.' Having ushered him inside, she offered him a seat at the table and went to find Lisette, Gustave and Yves. 'They're just coming,' she told him on her return. 'Can I offer you something to drink? Our so-called coffee is made from acorns these days I'm afraid. But there are *tisanes* – lime-blossom or lemon balm?'

He accepted a lime-flower tea, breathing in the summer scent of the dried blossom as she set it before him to steep. Eliane pulled up a chair and sat Blanche on her knee. Jacques watched the pair as they began to play a game of pat-a-cake and Blanche giggled, demanding that they do it '*Again!*' as soon as it was over.

As her parents entered, she gathered Blanche into her arms and stood, intending to leave them in private, but Jacques gestured to her to sit down again.

'What I'm going to say concerns you all,' he said, his expression grave. 'Ah, *bonjour*, Yves.' He stood to shake Yves by the hand, clapping him on the shoulder in a way that implied a greater degree of friendship than Eliane had been aware existed between the two young men.

'I have received a copy of a list.' Jacques turned to address them all, without preamble. 'All Jews registered in the *commune* of Coulliac are to be rounded up for deportation to camps in the east. It's part of a much wider programme that is planned throughout the occupied sector.'

Eliane gasped, unwittingly hugging Blanche so closely to her that the little girl wriggled and protested.

'There are several people on this list who are your friends and neighbours.' Jacques' eyes met Eliane's.

'Francine.' She whispered her friend's name, her blood running cold suddenly, despite the warmth of the day.

He nodded. 'Her and two others in the immediate area. We are trying to get word to the other people on the list, too, to warn them.' Here, he stopped and glanced at Yves, who nodded.

'Just tell me who they are. I'm meeting a friend for a bike ride this afternoon. We'll work out the route to pass their doors.' As Yves spoke, Eliane looked at him in surprise. Her little brother suddenly seemed to have grown up into someone she hardly knew.

Jacques nodded. 'Thank you, Yves. We have very little time. But remember, take no risks.'

'I know the drill. Don't worry.'

'But for Francine and the other two,' Jacques continued, turning back to Gustave and Lisette, 'I've been able to get word to a *passeur* – an agent who will guide them to a safe house. From there, they'll be moved through the network to safety. However, we need to get them across the river and through a stretch of the unoccupied zone that is patrolled. The Germans have stepped up their vigilance there lately, so it's more risky than ever.'

Gustave glanced at Lisette, who had been listening with her head bowed. 'We can get them across the weir,' he said, 'but then how can they get to the rendezvous point?'

Lisette purposely avoided returning her husband's look and instead raised her head to meet Jacques' steady gaze.

'I'm the one who has the permit to cross into the unoccupied zone. And it just so happens I have a patient on a farm near Les Lèves – in fact I'm overdue a visit to Madame Desclins. When are you planning on going?'

Jacques reached across and squeezed her hands, which were clasped, as if in prayer, on the table before her. 'Thank you, Lisette. You know we wouldn't ask unless there were no other alternative. But we're going to have to move fast. It has to be tonight.'

'It will be an emergency visit then. I know Madame Desclins will be pleased to see me – she's an anxious first-time mother. I have some medication that I need to deliver to her.' Lisette smiled as she released her hands from his and stood up. 'Nothing out of the ordinary. Let's do what we have to do.'

'Stop!' Gustave's voice broke as he stepped forward and seized her arm to prevent her moving away from him. 'Lisette, I can't let you do this. The risks . . .'

She put her hand gently on his and smiled at him, although there was a sadness behind the smile. 'You know, Gustave, my attitude has always been to try to carry on as normal, ignoring the war as much as possible, just concentrating on getting my family and my patients safely through it. But there's a question I ask myself every day.' She looked past him, out of the window towards the weir. 'When do you cross the line? What does it take to reach that point? For your country to be threatened? Your way of life? Your neighbours' homes? Or your own? For your friends to be in danger? Or your children?' She turned back to face him. 'Every one of us has to make that decision for ourselves. Whether we win or lose this war, we will have to live with the consequences of our decisions. I've asked myself: "What will be on your conscience when all this is over? What will your decision be when you get to that crossing point?" Well, I'm at that crossing point now. And I've made my decision. Just as all of you –' she glanced around at Eliane, Yves and Jacques – 'have done already.'

Gustave released his grip on her arm and nodded. But Eliane had never before seen such a look of anguish on her father's face.

⁘

A young couple slipped into the mill house just as dusk was falling. Eliane recognised them from the market – a young man who had made his living mending watches and clocks before the war put an end to such luxuries, and his pretty, vivacious wife. Lisette greeted them warmly. 'Daniel. And Amélie – how is the morning sickness now?'

'Much better, thanks to those *tisanes* you gave me,' the girl replied. Looking more closely, Eliane could just make out a slight rounding of her belly; although, like most of them now, the woman was so thin that her ribcage and hip bones protruded above and below it.

There was a gentle tap at the door and Eliane went to answer it. Without saying a word, she enfolded Francine in her arms and drew her into the kitchen, quickly shutting the door behind her. She held her friend tight, as Francine wept.

'*Courage*,' Eliane whispered. 'You will all need to help each other in order to stay strong . . . And to help my mother to do this.'

Francine nodded, wiping her eyes and making an effort to pull herself together. She turned to Lisette, who was pulling on her boots. 'Madame Martin, we cannot thank you enough.'

Lisette smiled reassuringly at Francine. 'Don't worry. You will be safe. The journey to freedom won't be easy for any of you, but I know you'll make it.' She picked up her basket of essential oils and the leather case containing her midwifery kit.

Yves put his head round the door and said quietly, 'The truck is ready, Maman. We've secured the tarpaulin in place.'

Eliane could hardly bear to watch as Gustave embraced Lisette before she clambered into the cab. The look on his face was one that wrenched at her heart – a tortured mixture of pain and fear. Lisette just smiled at him as she drove out of the yard and reached a hand through the truck's window to pat his shoulder on the way past. She appeared her usual calm, capable self. 'I'll be back soon,' she promised him.

The others waited for a few minutes in the safe haven of the kitchen, allowing enough time for her to negotiate the checkpoint on the bridge at Coulliac. She would have her documents examined thoroughly when her turn came to cross, and it was very likely that the truck would be searched too. All would be in order: just the local midwife making an urgent visit to one of her mothers-to-be on the other side of the river.

When the time came, Francine hugged Eliane as if she would never let her go. 'I won't ever forget what you and your family have done for me. For all of us,' she choked.

'Go now,' urged Eliane. 'Maman should be waiting for you in the lane on the other side of the field any minute now. Good luck. And Francine – I know I'll see you again one day.'

Francine, Daniel and Amélie picked up their boots and stepped, barefoot, on to the weir. Gustave led the way, reaching out a helping hand to Amélie as she scrambled up the bank on the far side. Hurriedly, they pulled on their boots and fastened them.

'Stay in the trees along the edge of the field,' Gustave whispered. A dimmed set of headlights could be seen coming along the lane on the far side. They flickered off for a second and then on again. 'That's her. Go now, *dépêchez-vous!*'

The three figures slipped along the line of acacias that bounded the field and then cautiously made their way along the hedgerow, crouching to keep their heads below the cropped line of hawthorns. The truck pulled up beside the gate and its headlights went out, so that the only light was from the pinpricks of stars in the night sky above them. Lisette got out of the truck and came around to loosen the cover and lower the tailgate. Daniel jumped up and then reached back to help Francine and Amélie scramble into the back. Quickly and quietly, Lisette pulled the tarpaulin cover taut again, sliding the toggles through the loops that held it in place. Without a word, she climbed back into the cab and pulled away, putting the headlights on once more as she navigated her way through the country lanes and back roads that she knew so well.

At the mill, Gustave walked back across the weir to where Eliane and Yves stood waiting in the doorway of the darkened kitchen. He nodded at them. 'And now we wait. And we pray.'

Abi: 2017

I can't begin to imagine the courage it must have taken Francine and the others to leave. I suppose that they had reached a crossing point of their own, just as Lisette described. For them, though, it was also the point of no return: flee or be sent to the death camps. The possibility of life or the certainty of death. There was no choice left to be made.

I know how living in a state of fear creates an inertia. It saps your strength and drains your energy, until you become trapped like a fly in a spider's web. The more you struggle, at first, the tighter the silken threads are woven around you, until finally escape becomes impossible.

Why didn't I leave Zac? It's a question I've asked myself often, since. I can see people thinking it, too, in physiotherapists' treatment rooms and in survivors' support groups. The counsellors and psychologists explain it to me in their clinical terms of codependency, a lack of self-esteem, a secret, shameful belief that I deserved the emotional and physical abuse, which was delivered with an addictive mixture of just enough attention and love (of a kind) to keep me there.

But maybe my reality was simpler than that: I had nowhere else to go. I had no family, no job, no friends. And by the time things got so bad that I should have left, I'd lost the strength to do so. The fear of the unknown world on the other side of the plate-glass window became stronger than the fear of what might happen within the four walls of the apartment. That's why I stayed.

That, and maybe, too, the tiny flicker of hope inside me, which he never quite succeeded in extinguishing – a hope that things would get better. That somehow, if I just did this or wore that, the way he wanted me to, he would change. That's what made me stay.

Eliane: 1942

It was the longest two hours of their lives. A feeling of panic was beginning to flutter in Eliane's chest, like a trapped bird, when at last they heard the crunch of the truck's wheels on the gravel of the track.

Both Yves and Eliane scrambled to their feet.

'Wait!' ordered Gustave. His son and daughter exchanged a frightened glance, realising that she might have been followed; or that perhaps it wasn't even their mother who was driving the truck if she'd been caught.

After what felt like another small eternity, they heard footsteps and then the door opened. Lisette set her bags on the floor and bolted the door carefully behind her.

Then she smiled an exhausted smile. And she nodded at the three of them and said, 'Another successful delivery by the local midwife.'

In the golden half-hour before dusk, when Eliane was shooing the last recalcitrant chicken into the hen house and Gustave and Yves were closing up the mill for the night, the Germans arrived.

From the window of the grain loft, Yves had caught sight of the jeep and the army truck coming along the road at speed. As he'd watched, the vehicle slowed and turned into the track, picking up speed again as they careered towards the mill.

'Papa!' he shouted. 'The sluices!' He almost tumbled down the ladder in his haste to get to the mechanism that closed the gate to the channel beside the mill wheel. It took Yves and Gustave's combined strength to shift the gears against the powerful force of the water, but just as the Germans pulled up in front of the barn, the river reared above the top of the weir in a thrashing torrent.

Eliane's hands shook as she slid the bolt into place to lock the chicken-shed door. Taking a deep breath, she stepped forward to meet the soldiers, giving Gustave and Yves an extra moment or two to finish what they were doing. The general got out of the jeep, accompanied by Oberleutnant Farber. Half a dozen more soldiers jumped out of the truck, their loaded rifles at the ready.

'Good evening, Mademoiselle Martin,' Oberleutnant Farber said. His tone was even, but the look in his eyes was grave. 'Messieurs.' He acknowledged Gustave and Yves. 'Is Madame Martin at home?'

Lisette appeared in the doorway, soothing Blanche, who'd been startled by the sudden, angry roar of the river when the sluice gates closed, as well as the sounds of screeching brakes and slamming doors,

'Please, Madame Martin, you will come with us.' The officer took a step towards her.

'May I ask what this is all about?' Lisette asked, calmly. Eliane could scarcely hear what her mother said above the rushing of the river and the frantic pounding of her own heart.

'We rather hope you will be able to tell us, madame.' His words were almost pleasantly conversational in tone, although the glower of the general standing behind him was in marked contrast.

'Eliane,' Lisette beckoned her daughter. 'Please take Blanche and get her ready for bed.'

Gustave stepped forward as Lisette walked to the jeep. 'I'll come too.'

One of the soldiers raised his rifle, sliding off the safety catch, and took aim at the miller. Lisette gasped.

'Lower your weapon, sergeant.' Oberleutnant Farber's voice was still calm and reasonable. 'Monsieur Martin, that will not be possible at the present time. You and your son will stay here. This work party –' he gestured to the group of soldiers behind him – 'have a job to do. It would be in everyone's best interest for you not to hinder them. We are taking extra precautions to seal off further potential crossing points along the demarcation line.'

The soldiers began unloading rolls of barbed wire from the back of the truck.

'But it's impossible to cross here, as you can plainly see,' objected Yves.

The general glared at him and barked a stream of German, guttural and angry.

'Nevertheless,' said Oberleutnant Farber, 'the river will be sealed off here. After all, one cannot be too careful these days.'

Gustave, Yves and Eliane stood and watched, helplessly, as the jeep disappeared back up the track, carrying Lisette away from them.

As the remaining soldiers began to hammer stakes into the riverbank and stretch the vicious-looking, spiked wire along it, Blanche's sobs mingled with the sound of their blows and the roar of the river.

That first night, when they'd taken Lisette away, there could be no sleep for Eliane, Gustave and Yves, left behind at the mill.

During the day, Eliane tried to calm Blanche and sing her to sleep, but the little girl was frightened and fretful, disturbed at having witnessed her '*maman*' being taken by the soldiers – and by the sounds of hammering, which went on even as darkness fell.

At last, the men climbed back into the military truck and it rumbled off up the track. Eliane drew the blackout curtain aside cautiously and looked out. Her father stood there looking wretched, his strong, capable hands hanging uselessly at his sides, as he surveyed the riverbank. In the moonlight, the barbs of the wire winked with malice, glinting their threatening message into the darkness. It needed no translation: attempt to cross here and you will be cut to ribbons.

⁂

Without Lisette, it felt as though the very heart of the mill house had been torn out. Eliane's own heart felt tight and heavy and it raced with the fear of what might be happening to her mother. Where was she? What would they do to her? Had someone seen her smuggling Francine, Daniel and Amélie across the unoccupied zone to the rendezvous with the *passeur*? You couldn't trust anyone nowadays: neighbours would denounce neighbours for any number of reasons – to gain privileges, to settle old scores, to protect members of their families or to save their own skins. But if the Germans had known for certain that the weir had been used as a crossing point then they'd have arrested Gustave, and probably Yves as well.

Another thought occurred to Eliane, which made her shiver with dread: perhaps Francine and the others had been caught and had given Lisette's name to the Gestapo. Francine certainly wouldn't have betrayed them, but what about Daniel? If he'd thought it might save his wife and their unborn child, surely he wouldn't have been able to stay quiet. What if they'd been tortured . . . ?

It was unbearable. And yet, they had to bear it.

The hands on the kitchen clock crept round with an agonising slowness that made Eliane want to wrench it off the wall. All she could do was what Lisette would have wanted – to look after Gustave, Yves and Blanche, supporting them as best she could and staying strong. That thought, and a sudden vision of her mother's face – calm, kind, smiling – made Eliane gather herself. They had to keep going, for Lisette's sake, and in the fervent hope that she would come back to them soon.

They kept Lisette at the Gestapo headquarters in Castillon for three long nights and three long days. And then the miracle the family had been praying for happened.

Eliane was up at the château on the afternoon of the third day since Lisette had been taken. She'd left Blanche in Gustave's care, in the hope it would be a good distraction for him to have to look after the little girl instead of sitting at the table with his head in his hands, helpless and despairing.

Madame Boin had taken one look at Eliane's strained expression and pale cheeks and had insisted she could manage in the kitchen on her own, sending the girl outside into the fresh air.

Away from the oppressive, anguish-filled atmosphere of the mill – even if only for an hour or two – Eliane willed herself to concentrate on her work. As she picked up her hoe she took a crumb of comfort from the bees, who were carrying on about their business as usual.

Being in the garden grounded her, and she felt she could breathe just a little more easily as she focused on her tasks, weeding and watering, tending her lovingly planted herbs. The scents of thyme, rosemary and mint reminded her of Lisette's healing concoctions. And then, all at once, she knew that her mother would come back to them. She could feel it in her bones and in the blood that coursed through her veins. It was more than hope: it was complete certainty.

She was dead-heading the roses that clung to the wall by the garden gate when she looked up, startled, at the sound of a vehicle. Her hands began to tremble as she caught sight of a grey uniform. Oberleutnant Farber leaned out from the driver's seat and beckoned to her, urgently.

Tightly gripping the pair of clippers she held, Eliane walked towards him. The jeep's engine was still running.

'Come with me, mademoiselle. Don't be afraid. Your mother has been released. She's in Coulliac. I'm going to get her.'

Eliane hesitated, then raised her eyes to meet his. She had seldom looked at him directly – or at any of the soldiers – but now she saw, beyond the sombre uniform, that his face was open and honest-looking and that his eyes, which were almost as blue as Jacques Lemaître's, held a look of gentle compassion. Her hands were still shaking, but she set down the clippers and got into the passenger seat. She was acutely aware that this was the vehicle that had carried Lisette away three days earlier and, for a moment, a chill of fear seized her. Could she trust his words, or was she, too, being arrested? But that expression she'd glimpsed in his face was so honest and so utterly human that, instinctively, she knew she did trust him.

Lisette was sitting on the wall beside the fountain in the middle of the square. How she'd got there from Castillon no one knew. She had simply appeared, limping into the *place*, not looking to her left or her right as she made her way towards the water that splashed in the stone *bassin* surrounding the fountain. The women queuing outside the bakery to collect the meagre rations of bread for their families watched her cautiously, casting sidelong glances towards her. Stéphanie, carrying an empty shopping bag, whispered to her neighbour.

Lisette's hair had come loose from its usual neat plait and her clothing was dishevelled. Despite there being no obvious outward signs of physical injury, everything about Lisette seemed to have been broken. She scooped up a little water in her hands and used it to wash her face.

Then one of the women left her place in the line and went to her. She sat beside Lisette and offered her a frayed handkerchief, before taking her hands and whispering words of comfort and encouragement.

When the jeep pulled into the square, the woman sitting beside Lisette hastily got to her feet. Seeing Eliane, she looked relieved. 'See, Lisette,' she urged. 'Your daughter has come to get you.'

But Lisette just sat, looking blankly at the water that sparkled where the sunlight played with the drops cascading from the fountain.

Eliane gathered her into her arms. 'Maman,' she whispered. 'I'm here. Come back to us. They took you away. But you can come back to us now.'

Slowly, Lisette's eyes focused on Eliane and she raised her hand, tracing her daughter's cheek with her fingers. She still didn't speak, but she nodded, barely perceptibly, and let Eliane help her to hobble to the jeep. They sat, side by side, in the back. Eliane wrapped an arm tightly around her mother, as if that might make the strength and life flow back into her, but Lisette gasped and flinched in pain so Eliane quickly loosened her grip.

Oberleutnant Farber, who had remained in the driver's seat, put the car in gear and drove them out of the square towards home. As they passed the queue outside the baker's shop, Stéphanie turned to watch them go. 'Special treatment for some,' she remarked, loudly enough for everyone to hear. Most of the women standing in the line ignored her, but one or two pursed their lips in disapproval and nodded.

When the oberleutnant dropped them back at the mill, Gustave came to the door at the sound of the jeep's engine. Tenderly, gently, he took Lisette into his enveloping embrace and held her for a long time, standing beside the barbed wire that clad the riverbank. Eliane took Blanche inside and began heating water, which she carried to the bathroom for her mother.

Only when she had washed and changed into the clean clothes that Eliane had put out for her did Lisette begin to return to them in spirit. She held Blanche on her knee; and Gustave kissed her wet hair, then gently began to comb out the tangles in its smooth lengths. Blanche cupped her *maman's* face in her little hands and planted a kiss on her cheek. As Lisette hugged the little girl, and as the love of her family began to permeate to her core, the light started to return to her eyes and the colour to her face.

'Do you want to talk about it?' Gustave asked her later that evening, once Blanche was in bed and Yves had gone out to shut up the mill for the night. Eliane froze in the middle of clearing the table of the supper that her mother had hardly touched.

After a moment's hesitation, Lisette began to weep, quiet tears of despair. Then she spoke, her voice low, the words fracturing here and there. 'They were beating a boy in the room next door. I heard his screams. I kept thinking, *That could be Yves.* I kept wanting the noise to stop. But then when it did stop, the silence was even more awful.'

The tears rolled down Eliane's face as she watched her mother, not wanting to move in case Lisette stopped talking again.

'And you?' Gustave whispered. 'What did they do to you?'

She shook her head and then looked round at him, her expression determinedly defiant. 'They did nothing to me, Gustave. Because I didn't let them. Whatever they did, it couldn't touch me. You see, I decided that I wasn't there, in that grey-walled room. I was back here, at the *moulin*, with you.'

Gustave wept then, too, and she held him and rocked him, hushing him as she would do a baby.

When there were no more tears left to cry, Lisette smiled at them both. 'But, you know what? They got away. Francine, Amélie and Daniel. The others, too. It was obvious from what the Gestapo were asking me. And, in the end, they had to accept my story. After all, the truck was searched both going and coming back across the bridge and it was empty. Eventually, they sent the police to speak to Madame Desclins. She verified that I'd been to visit her on Sunday night and showed them the medicaments I'd left for her. They had to let me go.'

Yves came back in from shutting down the mill for the night and she turned to him, her eyes suddenly as bright as they'd ever been, the woman they so adored restored to them again. 'They got away, Yves! They all got away.'

Abi: 2017

Dissociation, I think they call it, when you go somewhere else in your mind so that you can bear the unbearable. That's what Lisette managed to do during those three days and nights of untold horror when she was being questioned by the Gestapo. Sara told me that Lisette had been able to remove herself from what was being done to her, to imagine that she was somewhere else, to transport herself away from the grey-walled room and back to the love of the *moulin*. Now that's strength. 'Resilience' is another word the therapists often use. 'You need to build up your resilience,' they say. Easier for some than for others, I guess. But I think Lisette is a good example of what it means.

I used to do the same sometimes, going out of my body. In bed, with Zac, at first his love-making was a heady mix of tenderness and passion. But then it turned into something else; something angry and loveless and oppressive. That's when my mind would leave my body and I would imagine myself somewhere else – anywhere but there, with him.

I could sense his need to dominate, to possess, to control; he would give affection and then withdraw it, until I became confused and frightened. I grew unrelentingly watchful, unable to relax for a second, waiting for the next outburst, or cutting remark, or a glance in my direction that made me freeze, knowing that whatever I said or did next would be a trigger for his anger.

Once I had started the Open University degree course, I didn't feel quite so trapped in the apartment. I had other places to go – even if they were still mainly only in my head. I was doing a degree in English Language and Literature, so although I ventured out of the apartment less and less often, ordering my books and studying online, writers like Charles Dickens, Jane Austen and George Eliot helped me escape into other worlds. I got good marks for my essays, too, and, little by little, I started to believe that I might be able to get a good degree at the end of it.

There were tutorials to attend every now and then, and I could have opted for doing them online, but I saw them as opportunities to escape for the odd evening and told Zac that they were compulsory. Another lie. Another tiny act of defiance. By that time, stepping out of the apartment on my own felt like a terrifying ordeal, but I knew I had to make an effort. Afterwards, though, when the others in my tutorial group, who seemed a friendly lot, suggested going for a coffee, I would make my excuses and hurry home. I knew Zac would be watching the clock and checking my whereabouts on his phone. Any unaccounted-for lateness would mean trouble.

Nonetheless, I'd managed to cut through one or two of the silken threads that bound me to him. And I felt that little flicker of Self inside me rekindle, like a tiny, warm flame.

Eliane: 1942

Waking early the following Saturday, Eliane stacked her jars of honey into baskets ready for Gustave and Yves to load into the truck and drive to the market. Running the stall wasn't at all the same without Francine, but she knew she had to carry on distributing the honey supplies as fairly as possible. Rationing was hitting them all harder than ever.

In Coulliac, the river and surrounding woodland offered useful sources of additional fish and game with which to supplement the meagre allocation they spent so many hours queuing for at the butcher's shop and the bakery. And most people in the local community had at least a patch of garden where they grew what fresh produce they could. But Eliane knew things were harder for those living in the larger towns. Even in Coulliac, strict demands were placed on everyone by their German occupiers: one-third of all produce still had to be delivered to the depot; hoarding was an offence warranting arrest; and, just the other day, a notice had gone up outside the *mairie* declaring that anyone found secretly raising a pig would face a prison sentence and confiscation of the animal.

So the pigsty at the mill stood empty now. However, hidden in the tunnel behind the door, which was still concealed by the empty trough and a casually stacked pile of corrugated-iron sheets, the Martins had a couple of dried hams swathed in muslin, and a stack of pâtés, *rillettes* and *grattons* preserved in glass jars. They eked these out, eating them only sparingly, and occasionally Lisette would share them with her undernourished expectant mothers.

On one of Eliane's dawn walks to gather the wild mushrooms that poked their heads through the leaf mould carpeting the woodland floor, she had come across a makeshift enclosure, sheltered by branches, where a pair of plump black pigs snuffled and muttered contentedly to themselves as they foraged for acorns. She'd smiled and then carefully covered her tracks. Someone would be having roast pork for Christmas that year.

As she helped Gustave and Yves load the baskets of honey into the truck, Eliane was startled to see a group of German soldiers appear among the trees on the far bank of the river. She had to peer over the tangle of barbed wire to make out what they were doing.

One of the men waved at her, cheerfully, perhaps recognising the *mädchen* who worked at the château by the scarlet scarf she wore knotted peasant-style to keep her pretty dark-blonde hair out of her eyes. Then they took off their jackets and set to work with axes and two-man saws.

Eliane gasped. 'What are they doing, Papa?'

'They've been ordered to cut down the trees over there. They're still suspicious that people may be crossing somehow, even with all their damnable wire messing up my river. Jacques told me they're clearing the far bank and mounting regular patrols there now.'

She wondered how Jacques knew such things, but understood it was better not to ask.

She picked up one of the jars of acacia honey that she'd filled so carefully. It was as pale and clear as champagne. Across the river, a tree fell with a crash and a flurry of leaves, which were torn from its branches like confetti. Setting the jar back in the basket, she sighed. There'd be no more acacia flowers there now. But the bees would manage to find other sources of nectar among the wildflowers and the apple blossom: even they would have to make ends meet, just like the rest of the community.

※

Business was slow in the market that day. Few people were able to afford a luxury such as honey, even though there was scarcely any sugar either these days. Many of the stallholders had given up coming to the market now as they had no produce to spare, with so much of it having to be handed over at the depot and rationing so tight. It was all most people could do to feed themselves and their families. One or two tables had neat pyramids of root artichokes, potatoes, courgettes and summer turnips, but they seemed colourless and unappetising compared with how things used to be. Besides, everyone was sick of eating the same things day in, day out.

There were still some surreptitious exchanges: a few people who visited Eliane's stall and hung back until there was no one else waiting to be served, then sidled up to tuck a few eggs or a couple of rabbit skins beneath the gingham stall cover in return for a small jar of honey. More often, people handed over a few coins to buy one of the larger jars of beeswax; polishing the furniture had fallen far down most people's list of priorities now, but lamp oil was also scarce and the wax was useful for making candles to use during the increasingly frequent power cuts.

Two boys, who looked about ten and twelve years old respectively, appeared at the side of the stall. The clothes they wore, which were far too small for them, were patched and darned and the skin was stretched tight over the bones of their thin wrists, which protruded several centimetres beyond the frayed ends of their sleeves. The elder one removed a damp, newspaper-wrapped offering from inside his jacket. 'Would you give us a jar of honey in exchange for these fine perch?' he asked. He unwrapped the parcel to display two small fish that, she knew, would be full of bones.

'We caught them this morning,' added the younger boy. 'We managed to keep it a secret. It's Maman's birthday. We want to give her a present.'

With a smile, Eliane gave them one of the precious jars and then wrapped up the fish again. 'Take these back to your maman as well. They will be a treat for her birthday lunch. And wish her many happy returns from me.'

'Thank you, Honey Lady.' The brothers grinned. The elder one stashed the parcel back under his jacket and they ran for home, the younger boy carrying the jar of honey carefully before him, as if it were a casket of jewels.

Once the last few jars were gone, Eliane began to pack up, tucking the *marché amical* articles into her basket and covering them with the neatly folded gingham cloth.

'Good morning, Mademoiselle Martin.' Oberleutnant Farber's voice startled her, but she quickly composed herself.

'Good morning, monsieur.'

'Alas, I see I am too late to buy a jar of your delicious honey today.'

She nodded. 'I'm afraid so. And there's no jam that I can offer you either, now that there isn't enough sugar to make it. But, you know, there's no need for you to buy honey from me here. I am obliged to provide it for you and your colleagues every morning for breakfast at Château Bellevue.'

'Even so, I like to support local commerce,' he replied. There was a pause. 'How is your mother?' he asked, politely.

'She is better, thank you. Well enough to go back to work now.'

'That's good.' And then, without changing his expression, he said, 'You must miss your friend very much. The one who used to help you run this stall.'

His tone was mild, but when she glanced up at him he was watching her intently.

She nodded briskly. 'Indeed I do. It's twice the work without her. And so, if you'll excuse me, monsieur, I must be getting on.'

He smiled. 'Of course, mademoiselle, I don't wish to delay you when you are so busy. Good day.'

'*Bonne journée, monsieur.*'

Her hands were trembling after this exchange. Why had he mentioned Francine's absence just after he'd enquired after Lisette? Usually, Eliane was an astute judge of character, but she couldn't make out Oberleutnant Farber. He was the enemy, and yet he seemed to want to be a friend. Was he genuine? Or was it simply an attempt to trick her into giving something away? How much did he know? What had he seen? Unconsciously, as she watched him disappear up the steps of the *mairie*, she raised a hand to stroke the silk scarf, which she was wearing knotted about her neck today.

And only then did she realise that someone was watching her from the other side of the square. A young man as big as a bear, with dark, shaggy hair.

Her heart leaped and her eyes filled with tears of joy. 'Mathieu!' she cried and she ran towards him as he strode forward to envelop her in his arms.

They sat at the Café de la Paix, while they waited for Gustave to arrive with the truck, holding tight to each other's hands as their cups of bitter, ersatz coffee grew cold on the table beside them.

Eliane had so many questions to ask him, and so much to tell him.

But there was so much that she couldn't tell him, too, she reminded herself. She couldn't tell him that Blanche wasn't really the daughter of her father's cousin; she couldn't tell him how Jacques Lemaître had appeared across the weir one night, and that he wasn't only the baker's assistant; she couldn't tell him how Yves had forewarned several Jewish neighbours of their imminent deportation, giving them time to escape; she couldn't say what Lisette had done, nor where Francine had gone. And she couldn't tell him about her walks around the château's garden walls. Somehow all these secrets made her feel that there was still a distance between them even though he was there, now, beside her.

'I can't believe you're really here!' She stroked the calloused palm of one of his hands and the softer skin across the back, which was sun-darkened from hours of outdoor labour; this was a hand that felt at once familiar and strange after all this time. 'How did you manage it? How did you get here?'

'I walked across the bridge of course,' he laughed. 'All official. I can assure you, my papers are in order.' He produced a folded travel permit from the breast pocket of his utilitarian cotton jacket. 'I'm on my way to Bordeaux for the week. To be trained for my new job. I've managed to get work on the railways in the *Service de Surveillance des Voies*.'

Eliane looked at him, confused. 'The Rail Surveillance Service? What does that entail?'

He couldn't quite meet her eyes as he replied, 'I'll be part of a team patrolling to make sure there's no subversive action on the line between Brive and Limoges.'

'Subversive action? What do you mean?'

'There's been an increase in Resistance activity lately. That line is part of the strategic rail link between Paris and Toulouse. My job will be to ensure the trains can keep running safely. The training will be in Bordeaux, but I managed to persuade the powers that be that this would be the best route for me to take to get there. I've got this weekend and the next one to spend with you, but then I have to return to Tulle. I tried to send you a postcard to let you know, but it was sent back to me stamped "*Inadmis*" because I'd put the reason for my visit on it and apparently that's not allowed between the occupied and unoccupied zones. But anyway, here I am! Two weekends to spend with you, after all this time: it seems miraculous!'

Just then, Gustave and Yves turned up with the truck to collect Eliane. They were amazed and delighted to see Mathieu, and there was much hugging and manly back-slapping. 'Come,' said Gustave, once Mathieu had briefly explained how he'd managed to get there. 'We mustn't waste a moment of your visit. Let's get you back to the mill. Lisette will be so happy to see you. Tell me, how is your Papa? And Luc . . . ?'

They loaded Eliane's baskets and then scrambled into the truck, heading for home.

That evening, Eliane and Mathieu sat beside the willow tree as they had done so often before. Now, however, because of the barbed wire, they could no longer sit on the riverbank beneath the canopy of its trailing branches, so they spread out a square of canvas taken from the barn and perched higher up the bank, lifting their faces to the warmth of the summer's evening.

Mathieu had whistled when he'd first caught sight of the changes wrought by the Germans at the Moulin de Coulliac: although the brutal-looking tangle of thorny wire partially obscured the view across the river, the butchered stumps of trees were still visible on the far bank beyond another looped barricade of the wire, which had been installed that morning once the soldiers had finished their job of clearing the acacias.

'When did they do that to the trees?' he asked.

'Just today. And they added the wire over there today, too. They're tightening the security.'

He nodded, then turned to face her. 'I tried to come and see you before. One night last year, I managed to get a lift as far as Sainte-Foy. I walked the rest of the way, dodging the patrols on the far side because I had no travel papers then. I knew if I was caught it would be an automatic jail sentence, or deportation to a work camp. But I had to take the risk, to try to see you. I made it this far, but as I stood just over there, I realised someone had closed the sluice gates so the weir was un-crossable. I tried, but I was forced to turn back.'

She leaned closer and kissed his cheek. 'Oh, Mathieu. I always knew you were out there, though. Even when the postcards didn't come and my own ones to you were returned. It didn't matter. I knew you were there.'

'Those damn postcards. Printed boxes to tick and then space for just thirteen lines to try to say what's in your heart, knowing it will be read and may be sent back or destroyed. It's awful that this war has stopped us from being able to speak freely. They've taken our country from us and they've even taken away our voices.'

'But there are some things they can't take,' she replied, gently. 'Our river, for example. They can put it in a cage of wire and cut down the trees, but just look at it.' She gestured with an open palm at the water, which the evening light had once again turned to gold. They watched the dance of the sapphire-blue damselflies for a few moments. 'And they can't take our hopes and our dreams, either. No matter how many rules and regulations they put in place, no matter how they starve us.'

He returned her kiss and they sat, hand in hand, watching the river flow past, carrying those dreams of theirs off into the future.

Then Mathieu said, 'I bumped into a friend in Sainte-Foy, the guy who used to test the wines at Château de la Chapelle. He says the Cortinis are doing okay. But then he also told me a rumour about Resistance activity over here in the occupied zone. He reckons there's a secret network that is able to get messages to and from General de Gaulle's Free French Army, supporting the Allies. They say that people have been smuggled across the line, somehow, and through the unoc-cupied zone to safety. Have you heard about anything like that around these parts?'

Eliane shook her head and shrugged, still keeping her eyes fixed on the river. 'Coulliac is the same quiet place. We're all just trying to find enough to feed ourselves; there's not much time for anything else.'

A sudden image of Monsieur le Comte sitting by the altar in the chapel at Château Bellevue came, unbidden, into her mind. She remembered thinking she'd heard voices, but then finding him there alone . . . Suddenly she knew for certain that her walks were passing on messages from London to the Resistance fighters in the hills above Coulliac, directing their movements, helping them to plan their activities. And she knew that this was another secret that she had to keep from Mathieu. Even as she sat holding his hand in hers, she could feel the wedge of all those secrets being driven in a little deeper, forcing them apart.

On the still evening air, the sound of a train in the far distance gave her a welcome opportunity to change the subject.

'Tell me more about this job you're going to be doing?' she asked him.

'It's quite a new role. The railways are taking on more employees because of the need to keep the lines open. There are more and more acts of sabotage by the Resistance, so my job is to patrol the lines and try to either prevent those acts before they happen or fix the rails afterwards so that the trains can run. For a long time now, I've been trying to find a way to be able to see you and still help my father. His back has been giving him real problems lately – some days he can't stand, he's in so much pain – and Luc can't manage the farm by himself. So I have to be there with them – you understand that?'

Eliane nodded. 'Of course I do . . .' She hesitated before she went on. 'But, Mathieu, the trains that run on those lines . . . What are they carrying?'

He looked down and plucked a stem of grass, which he carefully split with his thumbnail. 'They carry vital supplies to and from Paris.'

Gently, she took his hand. 'They also carry weapons and ammunition that the Germans use to kill more of our people. And sometimes they carry the people themselves. You must have seen with your own eyes the cattle trucks that we've all heard about, carrying our own countrymen away. Those people don't come back, Mathieu.'

'They're going to work camps,' he replied.

She shook her head, sorrowfully. 'Women and children, whole families . . . They're going to prison camps where the conditions are so terrible that they may not survive.'

'How do you know that? Those are just rumours.'

She met his pleading, dark-brown eyes with her own clear grey gaze. And then she repeated, 'Those people don't come back, Mathieu.'

His face flushed – with guilt or anger, it was hard to tell which – and his expression grew wounded.

'I took this job so that I could see you, Eliane. It's been two years. I hate being apart from you. It's just a means to an end to enable me to travel more easily. I'm holding down two jobs now, working on the farm in the daytime and on the railways at night. And I'm doing it for us, as well as trying to put enough food on the table for my family. We're really struggling to make ends meet now that so much is appropriated for the war effort.'

She gazed towards the river again, but the light had shifted and the water was a dull brown once more now. The damselflies had gone and, trapped in its cage of metal thorns, the river seemed suddenly lifeless.

'I know, Mathieu. I understand.'

'We all have to make compromises these days. It doesn't mean I'm on the side of the Germans. I have to do this, for you and my father and Luc.'

She shivered slightly, although the summer air was hot and heavy. 'Time to go in now,' she said, and smiled at him.

But, as they gathered up the piece of canvas they'd been sitting on and returned it to the barn, neither of them could meet the other's eyes.

When he took his leave at the station the next day, on his way to catch the train to Bordeaux, he held her tightly, as if he couldn't ever bear to let her go.

She kissed him, and said with a smile, 'Good luck with the training. See you next weekend.'

He nodded, unable to speak for a moment, and then quickly turned and walked away, not looking back.

Abi: 2017

A storm is brewing, like the one that brought me here. You can feel it approaching – the heat is stifling and the night sky is so black that it's like being inside a cave. Thick, threatening thunderclouds have put out the stars. I've been lying with the shutters wide open, hoping for the night to bring a little coolness into the attic room. But the hot air presses in on me from all sides, making sleep impossible.

Suddenly the room is illuminated starkly by a flash of lightning and a moment or two later thunder rumbles ominously across the blackened sky. I draw the mosquito net aside and go to the window. Another flash of lightning burns an image of the river and the trees beyond it on to my retinas like the film in a camera and I lean out to grab the edges of the shutters and pull them closed – cursing the broken metal catch, which refuses to fit snugly into its notched fastenings. I grab my shirt and use the sleeves to tie the two parts of the catch together, shutting out the next roll of thunder before it shakes the air like a bomb blast.

I scramble back to the bed. Behind the double barrier of the shutters and the netting I feel safe, knowing the storm can't reach me here.

Eliane and Mireille must have lain like this on many occasions when they were growing up, listening to storms, watching the lightning flash and hearing the rain beat down on to the roof of the mill house, knowing that the sky's empty threats couldn't touch them.

To Eliane, the war must have felt a little like this storm, I imagine. At first it was something far off, gathering on the horizon but unable to reach her; but then, as it engulfed them and raged on for all those years, she chose to step out of the safety of the attic room and face it head-on, reaching to help others who'd been caught in it too.

I can feel her presence here tonight, keeping me from harm.

Eventually the gap between lightning flash and thunderclap grows longer as the storm moves off. The rain becomes a soft roar on the roof overhead. As I drift somewhere between wakefulness and sleep, Eliane appears in my mind's eye.

'It's your choice, Abi,' she tells me. 'The world is out here, waiting for you when you're ready. You're stronger than you know.'

She smiles as she goes, leaving the faint scent of beeswax and lavender hanging in the air in her wake.

Eliane: 1942

During the week while Mathieu was in Bordeaux undergoing training for his job in the Rail Surveillance Service, Eliane found it hard to concentrate on her tasks at the château. It was early August and the hot, humid air seemed to drain the energy from her limbs. She felt as though she was walking through a thick soup as she watered the herbs in the garden. Even the bees seemed to move more slowly than usual, drunk on the bounty of summer nectar as they worked to fill the upper frames in the hives. Eliane collected the honey as often as she could, but she was conscious that, in a few weeks' time, as summer turned to autumn, the precious supplies would dwindle. And she would need to take particular care to leave the bees with enough to see them through the winter now that there wasn't enough sugar to supplement the honey supplies should they begin to run low.

But it wasn't just the heat that sapped her strength. The memory of her conversation with Mathieu the previous weekend distracted Eliane. He was right: he was simply taking on a job that would help his family to make ends meet, as well as giving him a little extra freedom to travel from the unoccupied zone across the demarcation line so that they could meet from time to time. Why, then, did it unsettle her so? The thought of those trains carrying people to the camps appalled her. But, as well as that, it felt as though he and she had suddenly found themselves on different sides of an invisible line. It wasn't just the official demarcation line that was keeping them apart now; they were working against one another, being pulled in opposite directions by the currents of the war.

And all the things she couldn't say to him sat between them, as starkly impenetrable as a barricade of barbed wire.

 ⁂

Mathieu appeared in the marketplace in the middle of the morning. He came across to Eliane's stall and enveloped her in a powerful hug. She kissed him and then buried her face against his heart for a moment, breathing in the smell of his cotton jacket. Usually, it smelled of fresh air and hay from the farm but, during his week in Bordeaux, it had absorbed the unfamiliar scents of the railway: diesel fumes and cigarette smoke and engine oil; the scents of a stranger.

'I'll go and sit at the café,' he said, as her next customer appeared.

He crossed the *place* to the Café de la Paix, where he set his canvas holdall down on the cobbles and pulled out a chair at one of the round tin tables.

He sat watching Eliane smiling and chatting as she served the small queue that had formed, but his reverie was quickly interrupted.

'Well, hello, Mathieu! What a pleasure to see *you* here after so long.'

'Stéphanie. Hello. It's good to see you too.' He got to his feet to kiss her on both cheeks.

Without waiting to be invited, she sat down at his table. 'So, tell me,' her eyes were wide and guileless as she laid a hand on his arm. 'What brings you back to Coulliac? Oh, I have so many questions for you; you must tell me all your news. It's so boring here these days, having to scrimp and scratch around to get enough to eat, and I can't tell you how many hours I spend standing in queues every week. I expect it's probably easier for you in Tulle. You don't have German soldiers breathing down your neck every second of the day.'

'We have the police and the civil guards, though, who enforce the rule of the Vichy government,' he replied mildly, when he could get a word in edgewise. 'I suspect it's much the same.'

'Look how thin I've got,' she continued, as if he hadn't spoken. 'I'm sure I must look dreadful?' She smoothed back her long, black hair and simpered, waiting for a compliment from him.

Mathieu glanced across at Eliane's slight figure behind the stall. Her apron strings were knotted tightly around her waist to hold in the looseness of her blouse, and the leather money belt had had a few new holes punched into it so that it didn't slip down over her hips.

'I suppose we've all changed a great deal in the last two years,' he remarked.

Following his gaze, Stéphanie gave his arm a petulant little tap to try to reclaim his attention. 'And just look how threadbare my dress has become. But one simply has to make the best of what one has, I suppose.' Again, she fished for praise.

'You look very nice, as always, Stéphanie,' he replied, politely.

She smiled, her eyelashes fluttering, and then said, 'Aren't you going to order me a coffee, Mathieu?'

Once they'd been served a bitter brew in tiny, thick cups, Stéphanie watched as Jacques Lemaître emerged from the baker's shop for his morning break and walked over to the fountain to chat with Yves Martin, who had arrived on his bike.

'Who is he?' Mathieu asked. 'I don't think I recognise him.'

Stéphanie turned to him, as if surprised. 'Jacques? He's the baker's assistant. He's been here a while. As you can see, he's great friends with the Martin family. Haven't they told you about him? He's often hanging around with Yves. And Eliane, too,' she couldn't resist adding.

'They haven't mentioned him,' Mathieu shrugged. 'But then we've hardly had any time to talk really.'

'So, tell me what's been keeping you so busy?' Stéphanie turned her full attention towards him and leaned closer as she listened to his explanation of his training for the job on the railways.

'Oh, Mathieu, it's so reassuring to know you're looking after the safety of everyone. Not that I ever go anywhere by train these days. Or anywhere at all, really, come to that. Was Bordeaux wonderful?'

He shrugged again. 'If you like that sort of thing, I suppose. It's a city. Too many people for my liking really.'

Increasingly irritated by his inability to play along with her attempts at flirtation, Stéphanie slouched back in her chair again, surveying the market square. Just then, Oberleutnant Farber emerged from the *mairie*. She nudged Mathieu.

'There's another one of her new friends that I bet Eliane hasn't mentioned to you.' A spark of malice glinted in her eyes, but Mathieu didn't notice it as he watched the German approach Eliane's stall.

The officer said something to Eliane and Mathieu saw her smile and nod. Then she reached into a basket beneath her table and placed a jar of honey in front of him. He counted out some money and passed it over and she slipped it into her money belt. But the soldier seemed in no hurry to move off straight away. There were no other customers at the stall and so he stood and chatted with Eliane for a while longer. Mathieu saw her smile again and adjust the bright scarf that was knotted about her neck.

Finally, the oberleutnant picked up his jar of honey and sauntered back to the *mairie*, pausing to speak to one of the German guards on the steps before he disappeared back inside.

'It must be nice to have friends in high places,' Stéphanie commented, with studied insouciance. 'She has an advantage, of course, because she consorts with the Germans every day up at Château Bellevue. It's very useful to have such special dispensations – the Martin family seem to eat much better than the rest of us around these parts. They're forever showing off and handing out scraps to us charity cases.

And, while everyone else has to hand over their produce, Mademoiselle Eliane is allowed to keep her honey and sell it. I've also heard she wangles extra petrol vouchers so that her father can fetch and carry her in that truck of his.'

Mathieu drained his coffee's bitter dregs and set the cup rattling back down on its saucer.

'I don't think that's right, Stéphanie,' he said.

But she could see that her comments were getting a reaction from him, and that spiteful spark danced in her eyes once again. She sighed, as if in great sorrow. 'Oh, Mathieu . . .' She laid her hand gently on his arm once more. 'I hate to have to be the one to tell you . . . I know how close you were to Eliane before you left. But, as a friend, I feel I have to let you know the truth.'

'The truth? What do you mean?' She certainly had his full attention now.

'Look,' she nodded to where Jacques Lemaître was approaching Eliane's stall now. 'See how she flirts with everyone. The baker's assistant, that German officer – she didn't wait long after you left, I can tell you.'

Mathieu's face flushed red with anger. 'That's not true! That's not Eliane.'

'I'm afraid it is, these days, Mathieu. Of course, one has to try not to judge too harshly – war does terrible things to change people. But you see that scarf she's wearing?'

He nodded. She'd been wearing it last weekend, too, he recalled.

'Well, they say it was given to her by her German lover. Where else would she get a scarf like that around here? She shows it off everywhere she goes.'

'But she told me it was a present from her sister, in Paris,' he retorted.

Stéphanie laughed, lightly but scornfully. 'Is that what she said? The only present the Martins have received from Mireille is that baby she appeared with. People say that Eliane's not the only Martin sister to consort with Germans. Mireille dumped her illegitimate child with her family and then hightailed it back to Paris as fast as she could. We all thought it was odd that she should want to get back there so quickly, but of course the lure of the high life, being wined and dined by German officers at the best restaurants, must have been irresistible once she'd offloaded the child. They concocted that story about it belonging to a cousin of Gustave's to try to cover up the family's shame.'

The blood had drained from Mathieu's face now and his skin was beaded with sweat, sallow and clammy despite his farmer's tan.

'I don't believe any of what you say, Stéphanie,' he said, sounding sickened.

She shrugged her narrow shoulders. 'Don't believe me then, Mathieu. I know it must be a terrible shock for you to hear the truth. All I can do is tell you what's really been going on, for your own sake. I hate to see you being made a fool of. But it's all the same to me whether you believe me or not.' She stood and tugged the skirt of her dress into place, then smoothed back her hair. 'Thanks for the coffee, Mathieu. And good luck with the job. Come back and see me sometime if you're passing this way.'

With a glance at Eliane to make sure she'd noticed the company Mathieu was keeping, Stéphanie stooped down and kissed him goodbye.

Mathieu sat, shell-shocked, replaying Stéphanie's words in his head. After a few minutes, Yves appeared, wheeling his bike. '*Salut*, Mathieu! Mind if I join you?'

'Please do. Some sane company would be most welcome.'

Yves grinned at him. 'Yes, I saw Stéphanie making a move on you. That girl never stops trying, I'll give her that!'

'Who's that guy you were chatting with by the fountain?' asked Mathieu.

'Jacques? He's a good mate. Works in the bakery, so I got to know him from delivering the flour.'

Mathieu noticed that Yves, who was usually so open and candid, didn't quite meet his enquiring gaze as he said this.

'Not that there's much flour to deliver these days, of course,' Yves continued. 'We're grinding chestnuts now. Maize and oats as well. Reduced to eating animal feed. But I suppose it's the same on the other side of the line too? Tough times . . .'

And Mathieu realised that the conversation had been well and truly diverted from the subject of Jacques Lemaître. For some reason, Yves didn't want to talk about this great new friend of his.

Mathieu looked across the *place* and Eliane caught his eye and waved. She adjusted the silk scarf so that it lay straighter and then began to pack up the stall.

Instead of going across to help her, as he normally would have done, Mathieu sat, watching her thoughtfully and letting Yves' stream of inconsequential chatter wash past him.

He was quiet in the truck on the short drive back to the mill house and then scarcely touched the lunch Lisette had prepared for them, using vegetables from Eliane's *potager* to make a rich broth that was served with chestnut bread, soft goat's cheese and, in honour of Mathieu's visit, a few slices of precious dried ham from the cave behind the pigsty.

The good food turned to sawdust in Mathieu's mouth, poisoned by the doubts that Stéphanie had sown in his mind.

When they'd finished their meal, he said, 'Come, Eliane, let's go for a walk along the river.'

She took his hand in hers as they set off, and curled her fingers around his broad knuckles, but he barely reciprocated. As they followed the riverbank, picking their way along a narrow, dusty path that skirted the coils of barbed wire, she asked him, 'Mathieu? Is something wrong?'

He stopped and turned to look at her. Then he reached out and touched the rich silk of the scarf that she still wore knotted loosely around her neck. 'Who gave you this?' he asked, his voice barely louder than a whisper.

She dropped her gaze. 'I told you – it was a gift from Mireille.'

'Eliane,' his tone was pleading now. 'Tell me the truth. Where did you get this scarf?'

She looked up, meeting his eyes again. 'I'm sorry, Mathieu. I can't tell you.'

'I see,' he said, quietly. 'And Blanche . . . ? Who are her real parents?'

She frowned slightly, confused at the change of subject. 'I'm sorry, Mathieu, I can't tell you that either. I want to tell you the truth. But the truth is that there are things I cannot tell you.'

He turned to face the river, where the water was incarcerated in its cage of steel wire. He seemed to be struggling to speak and he swallowed several times before saying, 'Oh, Eliane. What has this war done to you?' His voice trembled with the unbearable pain that was tearing his heart in two.

She reached to try to hold him, but he turned away from her. 'Mathieu,' she said, 'look at me, please.'

With an effort, he faced her again. He bit his lip hard, and his eyes were red-rimmed, stung by the tears that he refused to let fall.

'This war has done the same things to me that it has done to you,' she said. Her voice was calm and firm, where his had been so full of emotion. 'I have had to make choices and decisions, just as you have done. All any of us is trying to do is survive.'

'But Eliane, the war can't last forever. So what happens afterwards? When it's over, every one of us will have to live with the things we have done.'

'Yes, Mathieu,' she replied. 'We'll have to live with the things we've done. And every one of us will have to live with the things we *haven't* done, as well.'

They stood in silence for a while and then turned and walked back to the mill, each cocooned in their own thoughts.

'What do you want to do now?' Eliane asked him as they reached the final part of the track to the mill house.

He shrugged. 'I've been away from my father and Luc long enough. If I leave now, there's a train I can catch from Sainte-Foy that will get me home tonight.'

A tear ran down her cheek then and fell on to the scarf, staining the scarlet silk border a dark blood-red. 'Mathieu,' she choked, 'I'm sorry.'

He nodded, unable to speak again for a moment. And then he said, 'Do you remember what I said last weekend? That they've taken our voices, as well as our country.'

She raised her eyes to his. 'They can't silence us forever, though. The day will come, eventually, when the truth can be told.'

He shook his head. 'The truth seems to be such a very complicated thing all of a sudden. Sorry, Eliane, but it's best that I collect my things and go now.'

She went with him as far as the bridge. She watched him show his papers to the guards and then be waved across. And as he walked away, unable to look back at her, the line that separated them seemed to have become more impossible than ever to cross.

PART 3

Eliane: 1943

In November 1942, the occupying German forces took control of the whole of France, moving troops into the previously unoccupied zone. But in Coulliac the removal of the demarcation line made little difference – if anything, there seemed to be more roadblocks than ever and the checkpoints on the bridges remained in place. Movement within the country was still forbidden without the necessary papers, and it was just as hard to obtain an *ausweis* as it had been before.

Day after day, Eliane waited for a postcard to arrive from Mathieu. The cards she sent to him disappeared into a void, unanswered. Any reply, even the officially proscribed thirteen lines of bland, censored news about last season's wheat harvest, would have let her know that he'd forgiven her for not telling him everything and that he trusted her again. But none came. She told herself that perhaps he had written but that delivery had been refused, even though she couldn't quite believe that version of events.

Frost had nipped the night air and mist shrouded the river as Eliane set out for work early one February morning. She could hear voices – Gustave and Yves were doing something alongside the sluice gates – but she could only dimly make out their figures. They seemed to be trying to lift something heavy out of the river, so she walked across to see if she could give them a hand. The mist shifted, swirling and clearing slightly for a moment, and she gasped. At the sound, Gustave turned and shouted at her, 'Stay back! Don't come any closer.'

But she'd already seen the body of a man caught in the entrance to one of the sluice channels. Yves was using his horn-handled penknife to cut the man's clothes free from the barbed wire that had snagged them with its sharp talons.

Together, father and son heaved the body on to the bank. River water flowed from the man's saturated jacket and trousers but then, as Eliane watched, the water began to run pink, quickly darkening to a deep red. His torso was riddled with bullet holes.

Gustave ripped open an empty flour sack and used it to cover the corpse as best he could.

'Who is it, Papa?' Eliane asked. She hadn't got a clear look at the face, which was bleached and bloated from its time underwater. For one terrible moment, she thought it might be Jacques Lemaître.

Gustave shook his head, his expression grim. 'Not someone I recognise. But a *maquisard*, I'm sure. The Germans are intent on stamping out the Resistance. They must have caught him and executed him.'

Yves, who was kneeling alongside the body, lurched suddenly to one side and vomited on the grass. Gustave patted his back, murmuring soothingly, and then, when Yves' retching had stopped, helped him to his feet.

'Eliane, help your brother back to the house and tell Maman what's happened.'

'What do we do now, Papa?'

'I'll wait until nine o'clock and then go and report this at the *mairie*.' His face was almost as pale as Yves'. 'Do you feel strong enough to go to work, Eliane? I think it would be best to try to carry on as normal as much as possible.'

She nodded. 'I'll be okay.'

'And Eliane?'

'Yes, Papa?'

'Have you got your scarf with you? I have a feeling you may need to go for a walk later on today, once this mist clears.'

She pulled the scarf from her apron pocket and showed it to him. Without a word, she tied it firmly over her hair and then took Yves' arm to support him as she led him back to the mill house.

Abi: 2017

As I get ready for bed, I think of the part of Eliane's story that Sara has told me today. I lean out of the window to reach round and pull the shutters closed and in the moonlight the river flows past, making its way quietly onwards towards the sea. I hear the flutter of leather-winged bats in the darkness as they swoop over the black water of the pool above the weir, and I shiver. It's hard to picture the horror of the dead body floating there; Gustave and Yves pulling it from the sluice, Eliane helping her brother back to the house.

I settle the heavy iron catch in place to close the shutters tightly against the image. Jean-Marc has been in today to mend the fixings and now the catch fits snugly, shutting out the bats and the moths and the other winged creatures of the night. He's given me some dried-lime-blossom tea, as well, and I've brought a cup of it up to the attic bedroom to sip. It smells sweetly of summer days.

I stretch my legs out languorously beneath the sheets as I sip my *tisane*. It's a novelty, feeling able to take up so much space. When I shared Zac's bed, I used to lie on my side, right by the edge of the mattress, taking up as little space as possible. I would shrink from inadvertently touching him, not wanting to risk waking him. I made myself smaller and smaller, until I wondered whether I might disappear completely.

I finish my tea and set the cup back on the bedside table, reaching to turn out the lamp. In the darkness beyond the shutters, I hear the faint splash of a fish as it leaps and then dives back into the mysterious depths of the river.

As I begin to drift towards sleep, thoughts and memories swim in and out of my head . . . A dead body looks like it's made out of wax. What's left behind looks unreal once the life has gone out of it. I wonder what it is, that spark of life that is extinguished. What it is that makes up our Self. I came so close to losing it, my own Self. I thought that it had died inside me. But somehow the spark survived . . . Somehow, at the last moment, just as it was about to be extinguished for good, it flared into life again.

Eliane: 1943

Gustave had been right: on the day they'd pulled the body of the *maquisard* from the river, the count had asked her to walk around the walls of the garden again, once the pale winter sun had burned the mist out of the river valley. It had been a longer walk than usual, though – three times around, and in an anticlockwise direction. Beneath the headscarf, her scalp prickled with sweat, despite the chill of the day, and she felt more exposed than ever to the eyes of whoever the unknown watchers were, out there somewhere. She couldn't get out of her mind the image of the man's body caught in the barbed wire and she felt queasy and ill at ease as she walked. Relief flooded her body as she stepped back across the threshold into the château's kitchen afterwards, and she busied herself with tying up bundles of the plants she'd gathered so that they could be hung above the range to dry back at the mill house.

When she arrived home that night, there was no one in the kitchen. 'Papa? Maman? Yves?' she called. She heard the creak of floorboards overhead as quick footsteps walked to and fro. She went upstairs to find Lisette pacing back and forth in Yves' room, taking clothes from his wardrobe and folding them into a canvas duffel bag. From next door, Blanche began to wail from her little bed in the corner of Lisette and Gustave's bedroom.

'What's happening?' asked Eliane, bewildered.

'Yves is leaving,' Lisette replied. Anguish etched lines on to her face and made her look much older, suddenly. 'When your father went to the *mairie* this morning, to report finding the body in the river, the mayor's secretary handed him a notice to give to Yves. It's a new law – the *Service du travail obligatoire*. They've posted an ordinance about this Compulsory Work Service in the square today, too. Instead of sending workers with particular skills, they're now going to send entire age groups to the work camps. Yves has been told to report in a few days' time for transportation.'

'Yves . . .' whispered Eliane. She thought of the trains that rumbled past in the distance. And then another thought occurred to her. 'And Mathieu? It will apply to him too.'

Lisette paused as she folded a woollen jumper. 'Yes, but don't worry; Mathieu won't have to go. The ordinance stated that certain classes of worker are exempt, like the police and the fire service. And those in the Rail Surveillance Service.'

A confusion of emotions buffeted Eliane, making it was hard to think straight. 'But Yves . . . In a work camp . . .'

Lisette pressed her lips together and shook her head. 'Your brother's not going to a work camp.'

'But you're packing his things . . . ?'

'He's decided to go into hiding with the *maquisards*. Tonight. He and your father are just sorting out a few things in the mill to make it easier for Papa to run it singlehanded, so I said I'd pack for him. He can't take much . . .' Lisette broke off, unable to speak as a sob constricted her throat.

Eliane stepped forward and put her arms around her mother, to hold Lisette as she wept into the folds of the jumper she was still holding, her shoulders heaving.

'What can I do?' Eliane asked.

Blanche's cries grew more frantic from the next room and Lisette smiled, wiping her eyes with the back of her hand. 'Go and comfort the little one. Take her down to the kitchen and give her a camomile infusion. I'll be down in a minute. And Eliane – we need to put on a brave face when we say our goodbyes to Yves. Let's give him the memory of our smiles and our love as a leaving present. From here on, he's going to need all the strength we can give him.'

Blanche's dark curls were damp with tears and she reached her arms out when Eliane bent down to pick her up, clasping her hands behind Eliane's neck and hanging on tight, as if she'd never again let go.

Eliane soothed her. 'Hush, *ma petite*, it's alright. Everything's going to be alright.'

'Eyann, where Yves?' Blanche asked. She'd been slow in learning to speak ('And no wonder, after all she's been through,' Lisette had said), but was beginning to make strides with her vocabulary now – although 'Eyann' was the closest she could get to Eliane's name.

'He's coming. He's helping Papa, but he's going to come and give you a big hug. He's got to go away for a little while, but he'll come back to us again.' She fervently hoped that she was telling the truth, for her own sake as much as for Blanche's.

'Yves come back soon?' Blanche asked, the lashes surrounding her big brown eyes still spiky from her tears.

'I hope so.'

'I hope so,' repeated Blanche, nodding emphatically. 'Soon.'

Eliane steeped a few dried camomile flowers in some warm water and then strained the liquid into a little china cup decorated with butterflies, which Blanche loved. She sat and rocked Blanche on her lap, singing softly to the little girl as she sipped her soothing tea.

The door opened, allowing a gust of chill winter air to invade the warmth of the kitchen for a moment, and the men walked in. Gustave was making an effort to appear calm and positive, focusing on practicalities and giving Yves snippets of advice. 'Keep your feet dry, or you'll regret it. I've waxed your boots well for you. Listen to what the others tell you – they're experienced now. And I'm sure there'll be more like you joining soon, who think it's better to have to survive in the wild than to be incarcerated in a work camp.'

Yves was quiet, far more subdued than usual, and he seemed to Eliane both older, suddenly, and frighteningly young. She wanted to weep for him, her little brother, forced to make this choice, forced away from the warmth and love of his family home to live on the run, sleeping rough with a band of strangers. But she reminded herself of Lisette's words and forced herself to smile at him instead. She didn't trust herself to speak, in case she broke down, but she nodded at him and then softly began to sing one of Blanche's favourite songs – to Yves as much as to the little girl in her lap: '*Il y a longtemps que je t'aime . . .*' I've loved you for so long . . .

Yves gripped her shoulder briefly, and her voice faltered for a moment, but she took a deep breath and carried on again as Yves stooped to plant a kiss on Blanche's curls. The little girl reached up and put her arms around Yves' neck, smiling and joining in the words of the song as she hugged him.

He tore himself away as the song ended and left the kitchen abruptly, taking the stairs two at a time with his long, loping strides.

After a few minutes he reappeared, carrying his pack in one hand and with his other arm wrapped around Lisette's waist. She had dried her earlier tears and, like Gustave, was trying to put on a brave face.

There was a soft knock at the door and Eliane swivelled round in her chair to see Jacques Lemaître on the threshold. He nodded at them all and clasped Yves' hand, shaking it firmly.

'All ready?' he asked, without preamble. 'It's time to go.'

Yves nodded, his throat constricting so that he couldn't get the words out to say goodbye to his family. He hugged each of them in turn, holding his mother for several, silent seconds. Over his shoulder,

Eliane saw Lisette's eyes close and a momentary tremor of the intense pain of parting flicker across her features.

Finally, Yves let her go and shouldered his pack. Jacques clapped him on the back and then smiled at the family. 'Don't worry; we'll take good care of him. I'll get a message to you whenever I can to let you know how he's doing.'

'Thank you, Jacques. God be with you.' Lisette extended a hand towards Yves once again, to touch her son one last time, but he had already turned and begun to walk towards the door. So she let it fall, plucking at her apron. Eliane reached out and took it instead, squeezing it tightly to give them both strength.

And then the door closed behind Yves and Jacques and they disappeared into the bitterly cold night.

✻

Since the beginning of the year, a new kind of French police force, the Milice, had been commissioned to work alongside the Gestapo. In the market that weekend, as she set out her few remaining pots of honey and beeswax alongside a couple of jars of apple preserve, to which she'd added nigella seeds to mitigate the sourness of the fruit in the absence of any sugar, Eliane was conscious of a pair of *miliciens* in their brown shirts and blue jackets, who lounged beside the fountain, watching the comings and goings in the marketplace. She vaguely recognised one of them as a local man.

Stéphanie walked past the *miliciens*, carrying her basket, and smiled at them as she flicked her hair over her shoulder. The younger of the two men stood up a little straighter and made a comment that made her stop and turn back towards them, apparently showing them the contents of her basket. She laughed and simpered as they engaged her in conversation for several minutes. As Eliane watched, Stéphanie leaned in closer, as though to share a confidence with the men, and then glanced over her shoulder towards Eliane's stall. The policemen looked up, following the direction of her glance, looking appraisingly at Eliane. After a few more exchanges, Stéphanie continued on her way, casually flicking an imaginary speck of dust off the cuff of her blouse and avoiding meeting Eliane's eye as she passed by the honey stall.

The *miliciens* strolled towards Eliane, taking their time, their breath forming little clouds in the cold morning air.

'Good morning, *messieurs*,' she said, politely, when they reached her stall.

'Mademoiselle Martin, isn't it?' asked the man whose face she'd recognised.

'*Oui, monsieur.*'

'Tell us, mademoiselle,' the man spoke with a low voice, but it held enough malice to make her hands tremble as she adjusted the gingham cloth on her table, 'where might we find your brother these days?'

She looked him straight in the eye and the light of her steady, grey gaze appeared to unsettle him slightly. 'I wish I knew, m'sieur. We haven't seen him for ages.' She held the man's eye contact, refusing to be the first to look away.

At last he blinked and glanced down at the sparse collection of jars on her stall. His colleague's eyes darted to and fro, and the man repeatedly licked his chapped, scaly lips, reminding Eliane of a snake.

'And your boyfriend? Mathieu Dubosq isn't it? Do you ever hear from him?'

Eliane glanced at him, startled. What did Mathieu have to do with Yves? Surely he was busy working to protect the railways. She took a quiet breath to calm herself, reminding herself to be careful not to give anything away. 'I haven't heard from Mathieu since he left Coulliac. I believe he's back home in Tulle. He's not my boyfriend anymore.'

The snake sneered. 'She lies so well this one, doesn't she?'

The first *milicien* frowned. 'Well, if you should happen to hear from either of them, you'll be sure to let us know, won't you, Mademoiselle Martin? We have a few questions we'd like to ask them, regarding certain acts of subterfuge, including the destruction of state property.'

The pair sauntered off, pausing here and there to question the other stallholders. The few inhabitants of Coulliac who'd ventured out early on that chilly morning silently drifted away at the sight of the policemen. The Milice had already gained a reputation for being worse than the Gestapo for their ruthless brutality towards their own countrymen. Their native language and local knowledge – including knowing every informant in the area – made them an even greater threat.

Eliane watched their progress around the market square. The stalls were far fewer in number now, with little produce to spare at the end of another harsh winter. Food was so scarce that almost all families had *jours sans* – 'days without' – when they scarcely ate at all. At the mill, they were eking out the last of their supplies and she had dug up the final few potatoes and turnips from her riverside *potager* only yesterday. Her stomach rumbled and she glanced up at the iron-grey sky, longing for the first signs of spring, when the woods and fields would reawaken, becoming a natural larder once more, and her bees would set to work to create new supplies of honey from the blossom on the fruit trees.

And then she heard the sound, miraculously, as if she had conjured it out of the sky: the rusty creak of the first grey cranes flying overhead. There were only a few, the vanguard of males making their journey of thousands of miles to the northern breeding grounds. The females and the younger birds hatched the previous year would follow later, in vast, trailing skeins of thousands of birds at a time, which would appear over the horizon, filling the blue spring skies with their cries. Her heart beat a little faster. The sign of these first *grues* of the year was a message of hope. Just hang on – spring will come again.

She hoped that, wherever he was, Yves could see the birds too.

And she hoped they had flown over Mathieu as he ploughed the muddy fields of the farm and prepared the ground for that year's crops.

As she watched them disappear to the north, she willed them to take an eastern course, to fly over Paris, creating a line of connection between herself and Mireille. 'We're all still here,' she whispered to herself. 'Just hang on – spring will come again.'

Abi: 2017

How do we find the resilience to hang on? Those years of starvation and isolation from the outside world must have taken such a toll on Eliane and her family. But the Martins had so much to hold on to: they had a community; they had each other.

When I was most alone, when I felt myself withering and dying like a plant deprived of water, light, nutrients, something in me made me reach out. Some deep-seated instinct for survival kicked in, just as I felt the last of my strength leaching away.

It was nothing dramatic. In fact, it probably would have seemed completely insignificant to a casual observer. When Sam, a cheerful, friendly girl in my tutorial group, suggested going for a coffee, instead of making my usual excuses and ducking out, I found myself saying, 'Okay. That'd be great.'

I surprised myself. I hadn't meant to say yes. As the small group of us crossed the road to a local café, my mind whirled. What was I doing? Zac would be furious. What would I tell him? But still, something made me stay with the group; follow them through the door into the bright warmth of the coffee shop, pull up a chair, order a latte. And, for the next forty-five minutes, I remembered what it felt like to talk and laugh easily with a few friendly people, to join in the grumbling about the impossibility of making head or tail of *Ulysses* – let alone writing a coherent essay on the book – and to listen in to snippets of other people's lives.

For those forty-five minutes, I remembered what it felt like to be me.

Of course, there was trouble when I got home. I sensed it the second I turned my key in the door. Zac sat on the sofa facing the entrance to the flat, an almost-empty bottle of red wine on the coffee table in front of him. The television was on, but he wasn't looking at it. He was staring into mid-air and his eyes were as bitterly cold and dark as the winter night beyond the plate-glass window behind him.

He didn't focus on me, just sat there, deliberately waiting for me to make the first move. Cat and mouse.

I hung up my coat, slipped off my boots and then turned to him with a smile that I hoped convincingly camouflaged the fear that flickered behind it. I could feel my shoulders tensing, and I made my hands uncurl when I realised they were clenched into tight fists.

On the way home, I'd considered various excuses. There'd been an 'incident' on the tube (how often had I myself considered stepping off the edge of the platform into that beckoning void, seeking oblivion in the rush of the approaching train?). Or, on a whim, I'd decided to take the bus home ('Big mistake – the traffic was a nightmare!' I could hear myself saying to him). But then that little flicker of Self that had burned a tiny bit more strongly during three-quarters of an hour of coffee and conversation, simply came out with the truth.

'Sorry I'm a bit late. A few of us went for a coffee after the tutorial.' My tone was light and breezy. Maybe I'd get away with it. After all, it's not as if I'd done anything wrong.

But I knew, really, that I wouldn't get away with it. I knew what was going to happen. I knew I wouldn't be going for a cup of coffee after a tutorial again.

Yes, that's definitely the word. Dissociation: when your mind leaves your body – a way of bearing the unbearable.

Eliane: 1943

Despite the long shadow cast by the seemingly interminable war, Monsieur le Comte was as chivalrous as ever to his German 'guests', and they continued to allow the frail old man the use of his library and his chapel each day. In the kitchen, Madame Boin's grumbling occasionally boiled over in frustration at the lack of decent ingredients and the monotony of the food she had to prepare: scraps of horsemeat were often all that was available from the butcher and she swore that once the war was over she would never, ever eat another turnip or *topinambour* again.

With increasing frequency, the count continued to ask Eliane to take her afternoon walks around the garden walls. The silk scarf had faded from wear and grown a little frayed at the corners, even though Eliane washed, ironed and mended it with the utmost care each weekend, but its rich pattern was still clearly distinguishable.

As she walked around the walls these days, though, Eliane's sense of unease was heightened. Whose eyes were on her? She tried to put out of her mind the *miliciens* who had visited her market stall that day so many months ago now, the local man and his colleague with the darting tongue and eyes of a snake, and instead she told herself that Yves and his fellow *maquisards* were watching over her.

Jacques had become a more frequent visitor to the mill after Yves had left. Eliane was grateful to him for the helping hand he lent Gustave when he could, and occasionally he brought word that Yves was fine, doing well with his new band of brothers, and wanted his family to know that he was keeping his feet dry and changing his underwear regularly, as instructed by his *papa* and *maman*. This last bit of news had made Lisette smile broadly – 'That really is Yves all over,' she'd exclaimed. 'His usual cheeky self!'

Eliane also noticed that Jacques seemed in no hurry to leave the mill house after he'd dropped in to deliver his messages or bring them some bread from the bakery. He would often stay on, sipping a *tisane* and asking Eliane about her day. They never seemed to speak of anything very consequential, but she sensed a deepening connection between the two of them and couldn't help noticing that he kissed her goodbye these days and seemed reluctant to walk back to his lonely apartment above the baker's shop.

For her part, she found herself thinking of him now and then as she went about her duties at the château or played with Blanche at the mill. The way his hair flopped over one blue eye; the way his face lit up when he saw her; the way his expression changed from serious and focused to relaxed and laughing in rapid succession: these were the facets of his character that made her feel as if it were a summer's day, even when the sky was overcast. He played his part so well, having been among the local community for some three years now, that she had almost forgotten he was an Englishman who would most certainly disappear back to his homeland one of these days.

As the bitter chill of winter loosened its grip on the land and the first wild daffodils pushed their way through the muddy grass along the riverbank, the Martins breathed a sigh of relief that at least now things would be getting a little easier for Yves in whatever hillside cave or forest clearing he made his home.

In the newspaper there were increasingly frequent reports of Resistance activity – bridges and railway lines had been sabotaged, and the food depot outside Coulliac raided. While such stories described the incidents in the most disapproving terms, they also gave many hope that the tide of the war might be turning. But the subversive acts never went unpunished: people were taken for questioning by the Milice and the Gestapo. Some returned to their homes, beaten and broken, unable to look their neighbours in the eye, having been forced to divulge snippets of information – true or surmised – under torture. Others never returned. Sometimes whole families were rounded up.

And in the distance the trains still rumbled by, ominously, heartlessly, laden with their cargos of human suffering.

That spring, France began to reverberate with rumours of an imminent Allied invasion. The occupying army remained on high alert, forced to remain stationed in France, while the Russians launched concerted attacks on the eastern front. But the weeks wore on and no invasion came. Eliane sensed that the soldiers occupying Château Bellevue were becoming increasingly tense, although they still appreciatively downed bottles of the count's wines from the cellar with the meals that Madame Boin cobbled together from whatever food was available.

The country was starving now, and there were frequent power cuts. Food prices were sky high, but the Martins continued to make ends meet by trapping fish in the sluice channels and foraging in the woods and hedgerows. Soon, though, the relative bounty of spring dried up in the harsh glare of the summer sun. Only Eliane's bees continued, unaffected, as they busily harvested nectar from the wildflowers that were resilient enough to withstand the heat.

'Papa! What are you doing here?' Eliane was surprised to see her father when he appeared at the kitchen door of the château. He was breathing hard, as if he'd been running, and sweating in the heat. A powdering of flour stuck to his clothes, which hung loosely from his once-sturdy frame, and there was a smear of dust across his face.

He leaned against the doorframe for a moment to get his breath back. 'Monsieur le Comte – is he here? I need to speak with him, urgently.'

'Why yes, I think he's in the chapel.'

'Can you go and get him for me? It's safer if I wait here in case anyone's about.'

Eliane presumed that by 'anyone' he meant the Germans, a few of whom were off duty that afternoon and had retired to the shade of the terrace off the drawing room to drowse after lunch.

She nodded and hurried across the yard to the chapel door, knocking and trying the handle, but it was locked. She heard the faint mutter of voices from inside again, and then the scrape of a chair and the count's footsteps coming slowly up the aisle accompanied by the tap of his cane on the ancient flagstones of the chapel floor.

'I'm sorry to disturb you, m'sieur, but my father is here. He says he needs to speak to you urgently.'

The count nodded, pulling the thick wooden door closed behind him and locking it with a heavy iron key, which he replaced in his jacket pocket. 'Lead the way, my dear.'

At the kitchen door, Eliane hesitated, unsure whether she should leave them to talk in private. But the count ushered her in. 'We may need you to walk again, Eliane. And anyway, by now I think you've guessed much of what is going on.' He smiled at her, kindly, and she nodded.

'It's Jacques.' Gustave spoke with no introduction, as if this were a conversation that they were already in the middle of. 'He's compromised.'

The count nodded. 'We knew it was probably only a matter of time. The Milice have been sniffing around for months now and, as we know, their methods of extracting information can be brutally persuasive.'

'We need to get him out of Coulliac immediately.'

'Where is he now?'

Gustave glanced at Eliane. 'Up in the hills today – he had a rendezvous with our friends there. He should be on his way back now, but the Germans are waiting for him at the bakery. I went to deliver flour and saw them. There was a Gestapo officer watching from the window of his apartment, and soldiers in the square.'

'In that case, it's imperative that we let him know. It's not too late for our friends to intercept him. Eliane, would you mind taking a little walk?'

She didn't reply, but simply untied the scarf from around her neck and fastened it over her hair.

'It's going to be a different pattern from the usual today,' the count explained. 'I'd like you to go to the far side of the garden wall and walk back and forth. Please do so continuously until I come and tell you to stop. Can you do that?'

She nodded and picked up her basket. 'If anyone asks, I'll be gathering sweet cicely. It grows along that side of the wall. We could do with some more, in any case.' Madame Boin used the seeds and leaves in place of sugar, to take the edge off the tartness of any fruit they managed to get hold of.

Beside the path that ran alongside the garden wall, the white flower heads of cicely foamed above the fern-like fronds of their leaves. They were just beginning to set seed and the narrow green spears sat proud of the flowers. She walked back and forth, back and forth, hardly pausing as she harvested the plants and placed them in the basket that she carried over her arm. Back and forth she walked again, holding her head high.

The land fell away steeply on that side of the château and the valley below was covered with dense woodland which could conceal . . . What? A band of *maquisards*? Or a couple of *miliciens*? A patrol of German soldiers? Or Jacques Lemaître? She tried not to think about who was watching her. On the far side of the valley, the hillside rose steeply again, the trees giving way to the dry scrub – the *maquis* from which the Resistance fighters took their name. As she walked, she thought she saw a flicker of light from the high ground, as if something had reflected the afternoon sunlight, momentarily, back towards the château. Shortly after that, Monsieur le Comte appeared, leaning on his stick.

'Thank you, Eliane. Have you collected a sufficient harvest to keep Madame Boin happy?'

She showed him her basketful of greenery.

He nodded his approval. 'Take it back to the kitchen now, my dear. Your father has gone home. All is well.'

He walked away from her, towards the chapel again. Despite the heat of the afternoon, a slight shiver of foreboding ran through her as she watched him go; he looked so frail, all of a sudden, such a vulnerable old man to be engaged in untold acts of courage beneath the very noses of the mighty German army.

Nothing appeared out of the ordinary when she walked along the track to the mill house that evening. Beyond the barbed wire, the river flowed quietly on its way and the evening insects floated in the last rays of sunlight above the surface of the water. Every now and then, a fish rose to catch one of the tiny flies, disappearing as quickly as a dream and leaving only a circle of ever-widening concentric ripples as evidence of the act.

But when she entered the kitchen, Gustave was pacing to and fro, in an agitated state.

'Oh, thank goodness, there you are at last, Eliane!' he exclaimed.

'I'm no later than usual, Papa,' she replied, smiling calmly.

'I know. But the Milice are sure to come and pay us a visit this evening. They are trying to trace the whereabouts of Jacques Lemaître, since he didn't return to his apartment above the bakery this afternoon. They will particularly want to speak to me, I'm sure, but they may want to question you and your mother too. It would be better if you weren't here when they arrive.'

'Where is Maman?'

'She's upstairs, putting Blanche to bed.'

'But Papa . . .' Eliane began to protest, and he silenced her.

'No objections, *ma chérie*. In any case, I have another job for you to do. I need you to help hide Jacques.'

'But where? And where is he?'

'He's in the barn. We need to get him out of there, right now.'

'And where can we hide him?'

Gustave smiled, a little grimly. 'We have the perfect place. And it's right under the feet of the Germans.'

'The tunnel?'

He nodded. 'The tunnel. Come, take this basket of food that your mother has prepared. There's a bottle of water in there too. We must go. Now.'

At the barn, he pulled open the door and called softly.

'Hello, Eliane,' said Jacques as he emerged from the dark interior. 'You did well today. I owe you my life.' He was carrying a suitcase that appeared heavy, its weight making him lean slightly to one side.

'You managed to get some of your things out of the apartment?' she asked.

He shook his head. 'No, Eliane. This is a radio transceiver. Fortunately, we were using it to transmit messages to the network this afternoon so I had it with me. They wouldn't have found anything suspicious when they raided the apartment. We've managed to save a valuable resource, as well as to conceal a piece of very incriminating evidence.'

Gustave had already thrown open the rough wooden door of the pigsty and was pulling aside the stack of wooden planks and corrugated-iron sheets that leaned against the back wall. Behind them was the makeshift door, set into the rock wall at the back of the small cave where the pigs used to be housed. He took a key out of his pocket and fitted it into the rusty lock. With a bit of effort, it turned and he pushed the door open, beckoning them to follow him. On lighting an oil lamp that sat on a shelf hewn into the bedrock, they could make out the stores of wine and flour hidden there – sadly depleted now. There was no more ham left in the secret storeroom and the jars of pâté and *grattons* had been finished long ago.

At the back of the small room, a narrow opening led off into the darkness. Gustave handed Eliane the lamp and pointed. 'Follow it upwards. It twists and turns. When you reach a fork, keep to the left. Eventually you will come to the big cavern that sits directly beneath the château. Stay there. There's enough oil in the lamp to last you for a couple of hours and there are matches and spare candles in the basket. We'll come and get you when it's safe again, Eliane. But be prepared to sleep the night there if need be. You know how persistent our friends in the Milice can be.'

He kissed her and held her tight for a moment. She noticed how thin his arms were now; and yet they still had a steely strength, which gave her the courage she needed to take the lamp and lead Jacques into the darkness beneath the rock face.

Before he left them, Gustave pointed to a sturdy bolt on the inside of the storeroom door. 'Lock that behind me,' he told Jacques, shaking his hand.

Jacques nodded. '*Bon courage*, Gustave.'

'And to you too.' He turned abruptly and left them.

Once Jacques had bolted the inner door, they slipped through the opening at the back of the storeroom and entered the tunnel, where the path began to climb steeply. Eliane held the lamp aloft to light the way. The tunnel was narrow here and, behind her, Jacques had to carry the heavy suitcase awkwardly in front of him to squeeze through. But as they climbed, sometimes following a smooth path carved into the limestone millennia ago by flowing water, sometimes negotiating steep, rough steps hewn into the rocks by the hands of men, eventually the tunnel began to widen. The darkness was silent and cool, and they seemed to have travelled a hundred miles from the warmth of the evening outside in just a few hundred steps, but the atmosphere was surprisingly dry. They came to a fork in the tunnel, just as Gustave had described, and went left, carrying on upwards. The tunnel grew wider and the gradient less steep, until they were able to walk almost upright along the limestone path that had been carved and smoothed by an ancient river. Finally, it opened out in front of them and, lit by the light from Eliane's lamp, they found themselves standing in a spacious cavern. The floor was dry, powdered with a fine dust, and the rays of the lantern illuminated a curving, vaulted ceiling several feet above their heads.

'Oof!' Jacques grunted as he set down the radio set, flexing his fingers, and stretching to ease out the stiffness in his back from carrying the heavy case through the tunnel, stooped over for much of the way.

At the far end of the cavern, more rough steps were cut into the bedrock, leading steeply upwards. Eliane walked over to them and lifted her lantern. She smiled as she saw the curved staves of a wine barrel covering the opening at the top of the stairs. She put a finger to her lips, motioning to Jacques to keep his voice down and then pointed upwards.

'The château's wine cellar: the kitchen is just above that – and the Germans, too.'

'Don't worry; they won't be able to hear us. There's several feet of solid rock between us and them, as well as the cellar space.'

The light from the lantern cast shadows across his face as he smiled at her and took her hand. 'What a place! It feels as if we've stepped out of the real world and into another completely separate one. How strange – and how wonderful – it is to be cocooned here. And yes, you're right – underneath the noses of the German army! Are you sure no one else knows about the tunnel?'

Eliane nodded. 'Only the Comte de Bellevue has been down here in living memory, and that would have been many years ago. There's no way he could manage the stairs down to the wine cellar these days, never mind those steep steps in the rock. Papa uses only the first few metres of the tunnel at the end by the mill house and, as you saw, he keeps the entrance well hidden. You'll be safe here until they can get you out.'

'And you?' He caressed her hand with his thumb, trying to comfort her, and she smiled back at him. 'You're okay staying here with me, Eliane? I know it must be difficult but, as you know, the Milice and the Gestapo may well search the mill. It's better that you are not there when they do.'

A look of fear flashed across Eliane's face. 'Papa . . . And Maman . . . It doesn't feel right not to be with them.'

He put a hand on her arm to reassure her. 'If your parents are questioned, don't you think it will help them more to know you are safely out of the way? Your father will come and get you when it's safe, as he said.'

She nodded, reluctantly agreeing that he was right.

Jacques removed his jacket and spread it on the floor of the cavern. 'Don't worry, your parents will be alright. There's no evidence against them. As long as the tunnel remains a secret, we'll all be safe.' He put his arms around her to comfort her and then added, 'I promise I'll keep you safe, Eliane.'

His chest was broad and his shirt smelled of the forest – of fresh air and pine resin and leaf mould – as she pressed her face against it, breathing him in, this familiar stranger who had come to live among them and was risking so much as he worked to help co-ordinate and strengthen France's Resistance.

'Were you with Yves today?' she asked.

When she looked up at him, his blue eyes were gazing down at her, filled with an expression of such tenderness that it made her heart skip a beat. She'd known they were growing closer, but until this moment she hadn't realised fully how much he loved her.

He smiled and whispered, as if someone might overhear him. 'Yes, I was. He's on good form. He's one of the more experienced members of the group now. They're very busy, planning . . . And I can't say any more than that.' He stopped short. She could see that he was annoyed with himself for having already said too much. But perhaps he felt, like she did, that there was something about the otherworldly feel of this place and about being hidden safely together that had made him relax his guard.

'I know,' she said. And then she stood on tiptoes and her lips brushed his. Cocooned from the war for this brief spell, away from the daily grind of danger and deprivation, she, too, had lowered her guard for a moment. But then she stepped back, confused and ashamed at her own uncharacteristic boldness.

With mock formality, to help cover her embarrassment, he gestured to the jacket on the floor and said, 'Mademoiselle Martin, please take a seat and let us dine together. After all, we find ourselves in such a very exclusive restaurant. I believe the food is supposed to be very good here.'

She laughed, relaxing again, and settled herself on the floor, untying the silk scarf and letting her honey-blonde hair fall forwards on to her shoulders. She pulled closer the basket that Lisette had packed for them.

With a lethal-looking commando knife that he pulled from a concealed pocket sewn to the inside of his jacket, Jacques cut slices from a loaf of dense, yellow chestnut bread, and spread them thickly with creamy, herb-flecked goat's cheese. There were two of the huge red tomatoes that had been sun-ripened in Eliane's *potager* beside the river, and he cut slices from these and placed them on top. 'Your *tartine*, mademoiselle. I hope it is to your satisfaction.' He presented it to her with a flourish.

'Delicious,' she pronounced, having taken a large bite. 'But wait a moment, there's something missing.'

She climbed the rough-hewn stairs and carefully pushed on one side of the barrel's stout belly until it rolled over slowly and rested against its neighbour. She climbed up into the cellar and, in the darkness that was lit only faintly by the lamp from the cavern beneath her, felt her way along the wine racks. She took a modest bottle – not one of the count's finest wines, but not one from the despised 1937 vintage either – and climbed carefully back down the steps, pausing to reach for the length of knotted rope attached to the bunghole of the barrel. With a gentle tug, the barrel rolled back into place, covering the stairway once again.

Using Eliane's penknife, they managed to remove the cork.

'Now this really *is* what I call fine dining,' said Jacques. He put his arm around her again. 'I can't think of a more perfect way to spend an evening.'

After they'd finished their meal, they turned out the lamp to conserve the remaining oil for the morning. They lay on his jacket and Jacques held Eliane close to him.

She brought her fingertips to his face, softly tracing his features in the pitch-darkness. 'What is your real name?' she whispered.

He hesitated for a moment. And then whispered back, 'Jack Connelly.' He spoke the words with an English accent, which startled her a little. The French accent of Jacques Lemaître had evaporated, suddenly, and in English he seemed like someone else altogether.

'Jack Connelly,' she repeated, and then she pressed her finger against his lips, as though sealing in his secret again.

He kissed her, seeking her lips with his in the darkness. And then he whispered, in that same pure English accent, 'Jack Connelly loves Eliane Martin.'

Abi: 2017

Sara and I are prepping vegetables for tonight's supper. The guest list for this weekend's wedding includes two vegetarians, a vegan, one person with a severe nut allergy and three people who don't eat fish. Sara has consulted her extensive collection of recipe books and managed to come up with her usual creative and delicious menu suggestions and now I am spiralising enough courgettes to feed a small army.

'So are you telling me Eliane and Jacques spent the night hiding right underneath where we're now standing?' I ask, amazed.

Sara grins. 'Yup. After you've finished that I'll show you if you like.'

As I take a break from my spiralising to chop the ends off the last few courgettes, she washes her hands and then opens the door to the wine cellar. Picking up a torch from a shelf beside the door and glancing back over her shoulder, she smiles at me. 'Well, are you coming to see the cavern or not then?'

It's all just as she's described: the three barrels in the corner of the wine cellar; the steep steps cut into the rock leading down to the cave beneath the kitchen; the light from the torch bouncing off the curved rock above us; the dry, dusty floor, which is scuffed with the smudges of footprints – could some of them even belong to Eliane and Jacques, I wonder.

Sara beckons me over to one side of the cavern and directs the torchlight on to the rock wall. Wordlessly, she points.

'It's them!' I gasp.

A heart is incised into the rock as distinctly as if it was carved only yesterday, protected from the elements in the darkness of the cave. And still clearly legible are the initials within it: E. M. and J. C.

I run my fingertips over it, tracing the outline and trying to imagine what they must have felt as they hid here with the German soldiers living just a few metres above. Fear, perhaps? But Sara has said that they'd felt safe in this other, underground world, away from the challenging reality of the world above them.

So maybe, for that one night, they were able simply to feel love.

Eliane: 1943

She hadn't expected to sleep, lying beside Jack on the dusty cavern floor, but awoke to find she'd done so surprisingly well, nestled against the warmth of his body, with his arms wrapped around her. He was already awake and she wondered how many hours he'd spent watching over her in the darkness. He felt for the matches in the basket and lit the lamp.

'What's the time?' she asked. Usually, she had no need for a watch as she could sense the time of day from the intensity of the light, the length of the shadows and the songs of the insects and birds all about her, which told the time as accurately as any clock. But in the darkness of the cavern she had no sense at all of the hour.

Jack tilted his watch towards the light so that he could read it. 'It's just gone six. At the bakery, I'd already have been up for hours. One of the advantages of being on the run is being able to lounge in bed with a beautiful woman!'

Eliane blushed, thankful that the lamplight wasn't strong enough to give her away. She'd never spent a night alone with a man before – not even Mathieu. At the thought of his name, she felt her cheeks flush even more deeply. She hadn't heard from him for over a year now, but somehow she still felt she was being unfaithful to his memory.

Jack had got up and walked a few metres back down the tunnel to relieve himself. Instead of coming to sit back down beside her again, when he returned he wandered across to the water-smoothed wall of the cavern and pulled out his commando knife. She craned her neck to see what he was doing as he scratched something into the rock. Scrambling to her feet, she brought the lamp over to get a closer look. He'd carved a heart into the bedrock and, with the tip of his knife, was now scratching two sets of initials in its centre: E. M. and J. C.

He turned and kissed her on the top of her head, then stood back to admire his handiwork. 'There,' he said. 'Proof that this wasn't a dream. Proof that we really were here, you and I. And proof that, in the middle of a war filled with fear and hatred, we found love. Let it be a sign to remind anyone who finds their way into this cave in the future that, come what may, to have known love is the most important thing there is.'

She hugged him tightly, not wanting to be reminded of the world outside, wishing that this moment could last forever . . .

But then they both froze. Faint but distinct footsteps could be heard from the cellar overhead.

Jack gripped his knife more tightly and stepped in front of Eliane to shield her. 'Get back into the tunnel,' he whispered, urgently.

The barrel covering the top of the stone steps rumbled as it was rolled back, and Jack tensed, preparing to strike.

A pair of stout, blue-veined calves appeared at the top of the steps, accompanied by a wheezing and a muttered grumbling.

'Madame Boin!' Eliane came forward from the shadows.

The cook bent down, with some difficulty as her ample girth got in the way, and peered at them in the dim lamplight.

'Oh, *mon Dieu*,' she complained. 'I never thought I'd get down those stairs again, at my age. They were nearly the death of me! The things I have to do . . . Eliane, the count says you mustn't go back down to the mill. It's not safe yet. The Milice are there. But you should come up to the kitchen so that you're at work as usual if they come and check the château. That way no one will suspect that you know anything about the whereabouts of Monsieur Lemaître. Good morning, m'sieur,' she added as an afterthought, as if she'd only just noticed Jacques – though she was clearly here to talk to them both. 'The count says you are to stay there until they can send someone up from the mill to get you. It shouldn't be too long – the *miliciens* won't find anything and so they'll soon get bored and go looking to make trouble elsewhere.'

Not for the first time, Eliane was struck by the thought of the network of people secretly working together to get vital messages through. She silently marvelled at Madame Boin's capable manner. She knew, of course, that the cook would likely have been making her own contribution to the covert activities happening around the château, but in three years the two women had never discussed this. As Madame Boin had said, they made an unlikely secret force – but maybe that was what made them so effective. Obediently she began to scramble up the steps out of the cavern towards the wine cellar. As she did so, Madame Boin tutted. 'You will have to help me get back up the cellar steps again. You'd better go first and give me a hand if I get stuck. Heaven only knows, I'll squash you flat if I go in front and have one of my dizzy spells . . .'

Eliane stooped to look back into the cavern. Jack smiled at her and gave her a thumbs-up gesture, then blew her a kiss. She had no idea when she'd see him again, but she fixed her clear-eyed gaze on him for one last, long moment, committing to memory his clean-cut features, his broad shoulders, the strength of his arms, and the way his eyes lit up like the summer sky whenever he looked at her.

Then she rolled the barrel back into its place and climbed the cellar stairs ahead of Madame Boin.

The château's kitchen was bright and warm after the cool darkness of the cavern, and Eliane blinked as she emerged from the cellar. She reached out her hand to Madame Boin to help her up the last few steps.

'Go and give your face a wash if you like, my dear, and I'll get you some breakfast and a hot cup of coffee. Spending the whole night in that dark cave, whatever next?'

As she smoothed back her hair and tied the scarf in place, Eliane smiled to herself, remembering Jack's arms holding her in that other world, beneath their feet; a world where love was something simple, carved in stone; a world so very far removed from the complexities of reality.

Later that day, as Eliane and Madame Boin were preparing dinner, a black car pulled up at the main door of the château. The general climbed out of the back, followed by Oberleutnant Farber, and two other men got out of the front of the car. Unlike the soldiers, they wore black shirts and long overcoats, in spite of the heat, but their caps were emblazoned with the same insignia as the army uniform – an angular, silver eagle with wings outspread – and around the top of their left sleeves they each wore a bright-red armband displaying a black swastika on a white circle.

Madame Boin peered at them from the kitchen window, her eyes narrowing, and then turned to Eliane, drying her hands on the skirt of her apron. 'Looks like the Gestapo are paying us a visit. Keep calm, my girl. Remember, they know nothing. And – more importantly – neither do you and I.'

For a moment, Eliane was anxious that they might head towards the chapel in search of Monsieur le Comte. But a knock on the kitchen door a few minutes later proved that it was his staff that they'd come to see.

Oberleutnant Farber stood there, looking more tense than usual. Eliane could see the muscles in his jaw working as he swallowed, before saying, 'Please, Madame Boin, Mademoiselle Martin, would you be so good as to accompany me to the drawing room? Some gentlemen would like to ask you a few questions.'

The two women untied their aprons, folding them over the back of a chair, and Eliane pulled off her headscarf, smoothing back her hair as she followed the oberleutnant and Madame Boin along the passageway from the kitchen to the main entrance hall. The drawing-room doors stood open, but once the women were inside the oberleutnant closed them with a soft click that made Eliane jump slightly, her nerves on edge.

The general and the two men in their black coats were sitting on the sofas, which faced the vast fireplace at one end of the room. Above the solid-stone mantelpiece, the coat of arms of the Comtes de Bellevue was carved from a slab of limestone the same pale-cream colour as the rock of the cavern walls hidden beneath them. Eliane fixed her eyes on it as she and Madame Boin walked forward, taking strength from the Latin motto, which was chiselled into a banner above the pair of heraldic lions that held a shield between them: *Amor Vincit Omnia*. It was a reminder that love would help her withstand whatever ordeal was ahead: her love for her parents; for Yves out there in the hills somewhere; and for Jack Connelly. Was he still hiding in the cave beneath their feet? Or had someone been able to come up from the mill by that time to spirit him away down the tunnel and off to hide with the Maquis?

Madame Boin and Eliane stood side by side in front of the men, with their backs to the fireplace now, and Oberleutnant Farber perched on an elegant Louis XV chair – and under other circumstances the contrast of this with his grey uniform and sombre expression would have seemed almost comically frivolous.

'Ladies.' The shorter of the two Gestapo officers – a weaselly-looking man with no discernible chin – spoke French, although his accent was harsh and guttural in comparison with that of Oberleutnant Farber. 'It has come to our notice that an enemy agent has been living in the village of Coulliac. Unfortunately, he has disappeared. However, we are sure that all good citizens of the community will wish to do their patriotic duty and help us find him – and indeed any other traitors in our midst, who may have aided and abetted him.'

He paused, waiting for the women to speak.

Madame Boin turned to Eliane with a look of convincing astonishment on her face. 'An enemy agent! Living in Coulliac? Who on earth could that be? Do you have any idea, Eliane?'

Taking her cue from Madame Boin's perfectly executed performance, Eliane shook her head slowly, as if trying to rack her brains. 'I can't think. What a shock to know such a person has been living in the middle of our community, though.'

'Who is this agent, may we ask, *messieurs?*' Madame Boin asked.

The short officer tutted. 'I hope you're not thinking of playing games with us. Either you know already, or you have no business knowing at all. Have you seen or heard anything in the village? Perhaps when you were out shopping there? Or . . .' He turned his narrow-eyed gaze towards Eliane. 'When you were at your market stall? We have received information from a concerned citizen who thinks you may have even consorted with this person.'

Again, Eliane paused, as if considering hard, keeping her expression a blank, trying not to show that his words had unnerved her. Unbidden, a memory of Stéphanie walking past her stall after talking to the *miliciens* that day flashed into her mind, but she immediately dismissed it: right now, she couldn't afford to be distracted by the man's veiled suggestion that someone had denounced her.

She met the man's eyes with her own steady, grey gaze. 'Why no, monsieur. I have fewer and fewer visitors to the stall these days and they are all people I've known for years. Apart from Oberleutnant Farber, of course.' She turned to look straight at him and smiled very slightly. 'He is one of my best customers.'

The officers shifted in their seats to look at the oberleutnant and, surprised at having become so suddenly the centre of attention, the translator dropped his gaze, studying the patterns on the Aubusson carpet beneath his well-polished boots.

The taller Gestapo officer said something in German to the general and his black-coated colleague, in a sneeringly insinuating tone that made them guffaw with laughter. Oberleutnant Farber's face flushed scarlet and he tugged nervously at his shirt collar. Then he looked up at his superiors and shrugged, giving a rueful smile and spreading his hands, as if to say, *Well, what can one do?*

The weaselly-looking officer stared at Eliane, giving her a long, appraising look, which made her feel sick with fear and hatred. 'I see,' he said, at last. 'Well, we are clearly wasting our time here, aren't we, oberleutnant?'

Oberleutnant Farber shrugged again. 'I believe so.' He carefully avoided meeting Eliane's eye.

'Very well. In that case, you may go back to your duties, ladies. After all, the general's dinner must not be delayed.' He fixed Eliane with his beady eyes again, as if assessing potential prey. 'But, a word of warning, mademoiselle. No matter who your friends may or may not be, we are watching you.'

The two Gestapo officers then stood and put their black caps back on, clicking their heels and saluting the general with a brisk '*Heil Hitler!*'

As she and Madame Boin hurried back to the kitchen, Eliane heard the car's engine start up and pull away from the château, and only then did she feel able to breathe again.

'That Oberleutnant Farber is a strange one,' commented Madame Boin, stirring the *blanquette* as it simmered on the stove. 'Thanks to him we were let off very lightly that time.'

Eliane nodded. 'He isn't like the others, that's true. But is he strange, or merely human?'

Madame Boin paused, putting her hands on her hips, and gave Eliane a shrewd glance, her eyebrows raised. She pursed her lips and shook her head.

The sudden thought that Madame Boin might be suspecting her of a real liaison with the officer made Eliane's stomach lurch and an expression of horror flashed across her face.

'Madame, you surely don't believe that I have a relationship with that man on any terms other than the most superficial of friendships, which is all that could ever be possible between enemies?'

Madame Boin smiled and shook her head again. 'Not for one moment, Eliane. I know you. I know what you are prepared to do to protect the people you love – just as I know what you would never be prepared to do. I see your courage and your integrity every day. I'm just surprised at myself, forgetting what it's like to be civilised. Perhaps you're right. This blasted war has gone on for so long that we've forgotten what it is to be human. If there were more men like Oberleutnant Farber and Monsieur le Comte in this world, maybe there'd be no more wars.'

Reassured, Eliane tied her apron around her waist again and resumed peeling the potatoes for dinner. But then she remembered the look in the Gestapo officer's eyes and the spiteful edge to his voice as he'd said that they were watching her. Did he mean that they'd seen her walk around the garden walls? Had they seen her pacing repeatedly backwards and forwards yesterday, issuing the warning to the Maquis that Jacques Lemaître had been discovered and should be intercepted before he returned to his apartment above the bakery in Coulliac? And who was the 'concerned citizen' he had mentioned, who had reported Eliane to them? Was it Stéphanie?

At the thought, her hands trembled and the knife slipped, slicing into her thumb. The water in her bowl turned red – the colour of the silk scarf; the colour of danger – before she was able to staunch the bleeding with the hem of her apron.

Abi: 2017

The coat of arms of the Comtes de Bellevue is still there, above the fireplace in the drawing room. As I polish the inlaid oval table that sits at the opposite end of the room, I imagine Eliane and Madame Boin standing there before the Gestapo. What a formidable pair they were, the elderly cook and the slight young girl, facing down the forces of evil together.

In Sara's telling of the story, she said that Eliane had thought about the network of people secretly collaborating to get messages through. Something occurs to me as I finish rubbing off the excess beeswax from the table's surface, which glows with the patina of age. Mireille had disappeared back to Paris and then seemed to have had very little communication with her family, other than the occasional, standardised thirteen-line postcard that was the only correspondence allowed in occupied France. But Sara had said that, when Mireille left the mill, she'd mentioned something about perhaps being able to help other people like Esther and Blanche. For some reason, Eliane's own thoughts about the covert network have made me think of this.

I tuck my duster into my bucket of cleaning things and hurry back to find Sara in the kitchen. She's just prepared our morning coffee and is setting a cafetière and mugs out on the kitchen table. Karen joins us, setting down her bucket, and Jean-Marc wanders in from the garden. He wipes his feet on the mat by the door and then washes his hands at the sink before pulling up a chair in the space beside mine, removing the cap he wears outside and setting it on the table beside him. I pass him a mug of coffee and he smiles his thanks.

As I pour milk into my cup, I ask Sara about Mireille and she nods as she passes round a plate of biscuits. 'Mireille played her own, very active role back in Paris. The apartment above the *atelier* where she worked, sewing couture for those who could still afford it – and there were still all sorts who could, even during the war years – was used as a safe house. Mireille was a *passeuse* – one of a group of people who helped others escape. Some probably would have been sent through this way from there, moving from one safe house to the next along secret routes that led to the Pyrenees and then through Spain to Portugal. From Lisbon, it was possible to get a passage to America and to safety. Oh yes . . .' She grins at me. 'Mireille played her part, alright. But that's probably another story in its own right.'

Karen downs the last of her coffee and stands up, brushing a few biscuit crumbs from her hands, ready to get back to work.

'So, Sara,' she says. 'When are you going to take Abi to meet them?'

My jaw drops and my coffee cup is frozen in mid-air as I realise what she's just said. Until very recently, Eliane's story has felt like ancient history and I'd assumed that the Martin sisters would be dead by now, if they'd managed to survive the war.

'Eliane's alive?' I ask. 'Mireille too?'

Sara nods. 'Yup. They're both well into their nineties now – in fact, I reckon Mireille must be turning a hundred next year. And Eliane can't be far behind; she's only a couple of years younger.'

'And Yves?' I ask, eagerly.

Sara shakes her head. 'I'm afraid not. Yves had a stroke a few years back and he lived for only a few months after that. But his sisters are still going strong. If you like, I'll see if we can arrange to go over and have tea with them soon.'

I beam. 'I'd love that!'

Sara and Karen leave to resume their duties and Jean-Marc gets to his feet, settling his cap back on his head. Then he looks at me and hesitates, as if plucking up the courage to say something. I meet his gaze, raising my eyebrows questioningly.

'You know, Abi, you look completely different when you smile,' he observes shyly. 'You really should do it more often.'

Eliane: 1943

It was the eve of *Toussaint* and overnight the first frost of autumn had encrusted every twig, every seed head and every blade of grass in a powdering of silver. But now the late-October sunshine was starting to perform its magical disappearing act, drawing the mist from the river and erasing the sparkling chill of the frost, as it cast its spell across the dark land.

Eliane went to open up the chicken shed, accompanied by Blanche, who loved to watch the rooster strut out, stretching his wings with his air of pompous self-importance and announcing that the day could now begin. Then, in a flurry of feathers and cacophonous clucking, the hens tumbled out after him, immediately beginning to scratch in the dust for insects.

Eliane held the basket as Blanche searched the straw-lined nesting boxes in the shed for eggs. The supply was already dwindling noticeably with the change of seasons, and the hens were scrawny these days, having to survive on what they could scavenge in the grass along the riverbank now that there was no longer the plentiful supply of grain that they'd been accustomed to before the war. Their feathers were scrappy and dull and they bickered irritably over the smallest ants and grubs, trying to snatch them from their neighbours and make off with them. Eliane sighed and thought, *Just like people*. It was easier to be neighbourly when food was plentiful and you were plump and contented; these days it was a case of merely surviving and that seemed to bring out the worst, whether you were a chicken or a human being. By and large, the villagers of Coulliac had stuck together. But, as the Gestapo and the Milice tightened their grip in an attempt to control the increasingly frequent acts of sabotage by the *maquisards,* accusations and denunciations were becoming more commonplace. Under the sustained stresses of the war, the bonds of the community were beginning to fracture.

Once the sun had warmed the hives enough for her bees to venture forth, they still worked on indefatigably searching for nectar in the scrubby wild thyme and the last of the clover. They, alone, seemed to remain untouched by the stranglehold of the war.

'Here, Eyann. One, two, three, four.' Blanche showed off her newly acquired counting skills as she took each egg from the hammock of her apron and carefully placed them in the basket.

'Well done, Blanche, that's perfect. One egg for Papa, one for Maman, one for Eliane and – oh, who is the last one for?'

'For me!' Blanche giggled and clapped her hands.

'Of course it's for you, silly me.' Eliane gathered the little girl into a hug and kissed her dark curls. 'And now, shall we go and look for some wild mushrooms too? If we can find a big, fat, juicy *cèpe* then Maman can make a delicious omelette for Princess Blanche's lunch today.'

They were walking back along the narrow path by the riverbank, Eliane holding Blanche's hand to make sure she didn't stray too close to the barbed wire as she danced beside her, when they caught sight of the black car parked outside the door of the mill house.

'Ouch! Eyann, too tight!' Blanche objected as Eliane involuntarily gripped her hand.

'Sorry, Blanche.' She relaxed her hold a little, although a fear that wouldn't let go was gripping her own stomach like a vice.

As they approached the house, the pair of Gestapo officers stepped out of the kitchen, having clearly been watching for their return.

'Mademoiselle Martin.' The smaller of the two men smiled as he greeted her, but his eyes were as cold and weasel-like to her as ever. 'How pleasant it is to see you again.'

'Messieurs.' Eliane kept her tone neutral, trying not to let her voice shake.

'We have a task for you, mademoiselle. You will accompany us in the car, please.' It was a statement, not a question.

Eliane nodded, unable to speak as Lisette and Gustave appeared in the doorway. *They are safe, at least*, she thought. She handed her basket to her mother and ushered Blanche towards Gustave, who was holding his arms out to her.

The larger of the two officers, whose neck overflowed the collar of his shirt and hung in a fleshy fold over the knot of his black tie, said something in German to his colleague, who smiled his cold smile again and nodded.

'*Non*. Bring the little girl, too.'

Eliane froze, horrified. 'But, monsieur, she is only four years old. Please, whatever the task is I will do it for you, but let her stay here with my parents.'

The man shook his head. 'She will be of use as well.'

Lisette began to weep and, for a moment, Eliane thought Gustave might leap forward and attack the officers. She stretched out a hand to stop him and turned to address the man.

'In that case, please at least tell us what the task is. A small child needs to be cared for properly. I have to know . . . Does she need her coat? Can she have something to eat before we go? When will we be coming back?'

The weasel laughed. 'You are brave, mademoiselle. I like that about you. Very well. As you are probably aware, the so-called Resistance has been carrying out many acts of sabotage of late, in a futile attempt to prevent the authorities from undertaking duties essential to the war effort. This evening, a train carrying vital supplies will pass through the region on its way to Bordeaux. We are collecting together some "volunteers" to ensure that this train makes it safely to its destination. You and your little sister, along with a few others, will travel on an open car at the front of the train so that you will be plainly visible to anyone who might be considering trying to stop it. So yes,' he laughed, 'perhaps a coat might be a good idea. After all, the nights are getting a little chilly now.'

Eliane stared at him, aghast. 'Please, monsieur, don't put Blanche through such an ordeal. She's just a little girl.'

His lips compressed into a thin line and anger flickered across his face. 'And that is precisely why she is of use to us. Perhaps those criminals will think twice about murdering a child. We're sick and tired of their interference and have already lost more than enough men and supplies thanks to their acts of treachery. Get her coat. Your own as well.' And then he smiled his cruel smile again and added, as an afterthought, 'Oh, and put on that red headscarf that you're so fond of, Mademoiselle Martin. They'll be sure to recognise you in that.'

As Eliane scrambled to get their coats, her mother hastily made up a greaseproof-paper parcel of chestnut bread and honey, which she tucked it into Eliane's pocket as she embraced her at the door. 'Keep your strength up, *ma fille*,' she whispered. '*Courage.*'

Gustave didn't care whether anyone saw him as he drove the truck up to the tiny cottage where the count stayed. He hammered on the door, but there was no reply. Desperately, Gustave glanced towards the chapel. He would be putting everything at risk if he was seen over there: if anyone was watching him then he didn't want to draw them towards the hidden radio transceiver. If it was discovered, it would be an immediate death sentence for both him and the count. But he had to get word, somehow, to the network to cancel tonight's operation. Eliane . . . And Blanche . . . He couldn't bear to think about it.

He pounded on the cottage door again and finally, to his immense relief, he heard the count's shuffling footsteps making their way down the narrow passageway, accompanied by the tap of his stick on the floorboards. Gustave almost fell across the threshold when the door opened, and the count put out a steadying hand.

'Woah there, Gustave. What is it? Calm yourself and come and tell me.'

Briefly, Gustave explained and the count listened, a frown creasing his brow as he nodded.

'There is no question. The operation must be stopped. Don't worry, Eliane and Blanche will be safe – and whatever other women and children they've rounded up. I'll get word to Jacques. He'll be able to stop them.'

'Oh, thank God!' Tears of relief filled Gustave's eyes. 'If anything happened to them . . . If Yves himself were responsible for their deaths . . . How could he live with that? How could any of us?'

'Wait here. I'll get the message through and be back soon.'

Gustave wiped his eyes and blew his nose on his spotted handkerchief as he watched from the window of the tiny cottage as Monsieur le Comte limped across the courtyard to the chapel. He paused at the door, fumbling in his pocket for the key as if he were in no great hurry. And then he disappeared inside, pulling the heavy oak door shut behind him.

After what seemed like an eternity, but could only have been about half an hour at most, the count re-emerged, carefully locking the door again, and shuffled back to the cottage.

He nodded at Gustave, who had leaped to his feet. 'Jacques has got the message. He understands the full horror of the situation. But he has no transport – the others have already set off to reach the intercept point and set everything up before it gets dark. He says can you bring your truck and meet him in the usual place? You'll need to go right now.'

Gustave took the count's hand in both of his and kissed it. 'I can't thank you enough, monsieur. You are saving my family.'

'Go now,' the Comte de Bellevue replied with more urgency. 'And God be with you.' As he watched Gustave drive away, he sent a prayer heavenwards, that the spirits of all their forebears who would be about on that *Toussaint* eve might conspire to protect all innocents from the evil that was going to be abroad that night. 'And please let there be no roadblocks in the way, either,' he added as an afterthought. 'Every second is going to count.'

The black car pulled up in front of the *mairie* in Coulliac behind a canvas-covered army truck. The *place* was eerily deserted, apart from a huddled group of people who stood on the steps of the *mairie* between two German guards. In the days before the war, at this time on the eve of *la Toussaint*, the shops would usually have been bustling with shoppers buying provisions for tomorrow's extended family lunch – choice cuts of meat, fresh oysters from Arcachon, and exquisitely crafted pâtisseries from the bakery. But such delicacies only existed as distant memories, and the shops were empty of both provisions and customers. Even so, ordinarily there would have been a few people about, queuing in the hope of a scrap of something to break the monotony of their near-starvation diet: a bit of rabbit, perhaps, or a small slice of fatty pork to flavour tomorrow's soup. But, at the appearance of the army truck and the sight of yet more people being rounded up, the inhabitants of Coulliac had melted away, taking refuge behind their shutters and their lace curtains, barricaded in by their fear of being selected to join the little group on the steps of the *mairie*.

The wind was picking up, and it broke the silence as it swirled around the square, scattering drops of water from the fountain on to the cobbles and blowing the dust against the blank faces of the villagers' closed doors.

The Gestapo officers gestured to Eliane and Blanche to get out and join the group in front of the *mairie*. Among the shabby and threadbare clothes that they all wore, Eliane's bright headscarf stood out like a beacon.

The soldiers mounting guard moved the group towards the truck. They dropped the tailgate and lifted the children in first, leaving the adults to scramble up as best they could. Eliane recognised the two little boys who'd offered her the fish in exchange for a jar of honey for their mother's birthday. A thin, careworn woman who seemed to be the boys' mother was there, too, as well as the baker and his wife, Monsieur and Madame Fournier. Monsieur Fournier was so crippled by his arthritis these days that it took the efforts of both of the guards to heave him on to the back of the lorry.

No one spoke as they sat on the slatted wooden benches that ran along each side of the truck, but Eliane reached for Blanche and held her tight on her lap before smiling reassuringly at the two boys.

The guards tied the canvas in place over the back of the truck, shutting them in, and then the engine turned over and they pulled away.

Under cover of the sound of the vehicle, Eliane spoke to the children, keeping her voice as calm and cheerful as she could.

'Does anyone know where we're going? No? Well, I can tell you, we've been chosen to go on a big adventure. We're going to travel on a train, but on a special car right at the front.'

'In front of the engine, even?' asked the elder of the two brothers.

She nodded. 'In front of the engine. It will be cold and noisy, I'm sure, but exciting too because most people don't ever get the opportunity to travel on that special car. It won't be scary, because all of us grown-ups will be there with you.' She glanced around at the rest of the group, whose faces were pale with fear in the gloom, and smiled at them, encouraging them to follow her lead.

Madame Fournier, who sat holding her husband's hand, took her cue from Eliane. 'That's right, we'll stick together. It'll be a bit like going on a ride at the funfair – or like the rollercoaster in Paris. Have you seen pictures of that?'

Monsieur Fournier chuckled. '*Oh là-là*, everyone in Coulliac will be so jealous that we got picked to go on this adventure and they didn't!'

The others nodded, summoning up watery smiles for the sake of the children.

The younger of the two brothers reached for his mother's hand. 'Don't be afraid, Maman. Even if the sound of the train is very loud, we'll be there to look after you.'

The woman surreptitiously wiped away a tear with the frayed cuff of her coat and bent to kiss the top of his head. 'With both my brave sons by my side, how could I ever be scared?'

The truck jolted and swayed. Monsieur Fournier managed to ease the canvas cover apart just a little. 'Looks like we're on the road to Bergerac,' he said.

Eventually, after slowing and swaying as it navigated the narrow streets of the town, the lorry stopped. The soldiers pulled back the canvas and let down the tailgate to allow the group to clamber down. One of the guards stood with them, his gun at the ready to prevent anyone trying to make a run for it, and the other disappeared into the station building.

A few local people hurried past, casting surreptitious glances at the huddled group of women, children and a stooped old man, wondering what crime – real, imagined or fabricated – had resulted in their being assembled in front of Bergerac station at this time on the eve of *la Toussaint*. Fear and guilt, in equal measure, accompanied the locals back to their homes, where, just as the people of Coulliac had done, they too bolted their doors and closed their shutters: here, they'd already witnessed too many deportations, too many people being herded like animals into trains of cattle cars, too much fear and despair.

The guards shepherded the group through the doorway and out on to the platform beyond. As they waited, the cold edge of the wind cut like a knife through their inadequate coats and jackets and they shivered with a mixture of chill and fear. Eliane took the paper-wrapped parcel of sandwiches from her pocket and shared them round, making sure everyone had a scrap or two.

'Give my share to the children,' Madame Fournier demurred.

Eliane shook her head, insisting. '*Non, madame*. Please eat. It's little enough, but we are all going to need strength for this journey.' She turned to the children, trying to distract them from the cold and the nervous anticipation that was now mounting as they stood waiting for the train. 'Do any of you know how my bees made this honey for our sandwiches?'

The younger of the two brothers put up his hand, as if answering a question in class at school. 'They ate it from the flowers and then they pooed it into the honeycomb.'

'Eugh! That doesn't sound very appetising.' His mother looked askance at her crust of bread.

Eliane laughed. 'Almost right, but not exactly. They do collect nectar from flowers by sucking it up with their tongues; but they store it in a special stomach called their honey-stomach, which is separate from the one they use for digesting food. When they have a stomach-full they fly back to the hive. Then they pass the runny nectar, using their tongues, from one bee to the next and they all chew it to make it into sticky honey. It's food for all the bees in the hive really, but luckily they are very generous and they make extra honey, which we can collect and spread on our bread.'

'Sounds like they're really good at working together,' said Madame Fournier.

'They are. Just as we will be on the train. One bee on its own isn't very strong, but when they stick together and become a community they are strong enough to survive the harshest winter and a fearsome enough force to scare away the most determined predators.'

Just then, borne on the wind that blustered along the tracks, they heard the distant rumble of the approaching train. Eliane picked Blanche up and held her tight. 'Ready for our big adventure, *ma princesse*?' Blanche smiled and nodded, but Eliane could feel the little girl's body shivering with a mixture of cold and fear.

A sudden image of Mathieu's face flashed into Eliane's mind. Was he out there, somewhere, protecting the railway? Had he watched this very train go past and been satisfied that he was doing his job well, seeing another transport safely through, little knowing that he was sending it onwards to where she and Blanche waited? Would he have cared if he'd known who the shivering, helpless passengers were who were about to embark on this terrifying journey?

Bile rose in her throat at the thought. And yet, she found herself wishing that he was there; longing for his reassuring touch, his strong, silent presence that would keep them all safe. She shook her head, trying to clear it of these confusing feelings. *Focus*, she told herself. *Mathieu can't help you now. You've got to stay strong and get through this.*

As the train pulled alongside the platform, armed soldiers appeared from the station buildings, stubbing out cigarettes and pulling on greatcoats. Instinctively, the group of civilians huddled a little closer together. They watched in silence as the train pulled up to the platform and then, from a siding, an open flatcar was manoeuvred into position in front of the engine. A handrail had been added to the front of the car, but it was otherwise open-sided.

'*Allez-y!*' One of the soldiers gestured with his rifle that they should climb up the ramp that had been positioned beside the car. 'And don't even think about trying to jump off. I'll be travelling with the driver and I have orders to shoot anyone who tries to escape.'

'Let's organise ourselves a bit,' said Madame Fournier. 'If some of the larger adults stand with their backs against the handrail and we put the children on the inside that will shield them from the worst of the wind.' She reversed so that her ample behind was wedged against the rail and her husband came to stand beside her, taking the hands of the two little boys to steady them on the ride.

Eliane stood in the centre at the front, her back to the tracks that stretched ahead of the train through the hills and the woods and across the wide bridges spanning the rivers between them and Bordeaux, some two hours distant. She held Blanche tight and wrapped the sides of her coat around the little girl to protect her from the chill of the wind and try to make her feel a little safer. In the gathering dusk, the scarlet headscarf stood out like a lantern on the prow of a ship.

With a slamming of carriage doors the soldiers boarded the train, and then the sound of the idling engine began to grow louder and more purposeful. With a hiss, the brakes were released and then, with slow menace, the train began to move.

'Hold on tight,' Madame Fournier called to the children. '*Courage, mes enfants!* Our adventure begins!'

Gustave drummed his fingers impatiently on the steering wheel as he sat in the queue at a roadblock on the bridge at Port Sainte-Foy. It appeared to be no more than a routine delay – the soldiers were simply checking papers and then waving people across – but some drivers seemed to take an inordinate length of time to locate their paperwork. Gustave ground his teeth and muttered, 'Come *on*; you've had ten minutes sitting here to get everything ready.' His own papers were on the passenger seat, waiting to be presented.

When his turn came, the soldier scrutinised the documents and gave Gustave a long, hard look. 'Reason for your journey at this time of day?' he barked.

'Final delivery of flour to the bakers over there. They've run out and need some urgently for *la Toussaint* tomorrow.' The soldier checked the back of the truck and, finding only a couple of sacks of flour, nodded abruptly and waved him across.

He drove slowly across the bridge, careful not to give away the fact that he was in a hurry. But as soon as he got to the other side, he revved the engine and swerved through the darkening streets of Sainte-Foy. On the far side of the town, he took a road through the vineyards that twisted and climbed into the hills, the truck swaying and jolting as he accelerated as hard as he could on the narrow country lane. He pulled up alongside a rough wooden cross, carved with a scallop shell, which marked an intersection on the pilgrim way. From a copse of trees nearby, a shadowy figure emerged and ran towards the truck.

'Sorry it took me so long. I was held up at the roadblock on the bridge,' Gustave said.

'You did well, considering,' Jacques replied as he climbed into the passenger seat. 'I was worried that you might not make it. We should still have time. But we need to go as fast as possible.'

'Where to?' Gustave asked.

'The railway bridge across the river, just before Le Pont de la Beauze.'

Gustave nodded grimly, put the truck in gear and accelerated along the lane again.

'Cut through the vineyard here,' Jacques pointed, and Gustave hauled on the steering wheel, swerving into a rough farm track. They bounced along the tractor-rutted clay, passing between the recently harvested vines, and rejoined the country road on the other side. The river glinted ahead of them as a harvest moon began to rise, impossibly large and honey-gold. Ragged clouds, frayed and ripped by the blustering wind, scudded across its face. It was easy to imagine that the souls of the dead could be abroad tonight.

'Pull in here.' Jacques gestured to a partially concealed track that disappeared into the woods at the side of the road.

Gustave killed the engine and the two men leaped from the truck; Jacques then led the way through the trees to where the railway line ran on an embankment as it led up to the brick arches of the bridge that spanned the Dordogne river. At first, the tracks were silent. But then they began to resonate with a faint hum. A train was approaching.

Up ahead, Gustave thought he glimpsed the brief flicker of a torch, which was immediately extinguished. They ran, crashing through the undergrowth, too late for caution now.

Gustave panted behind Jacques, a stitch stabbing at his side; the thought of Eliane and Blanche on the train and Yves beneath the bridge carried his feet onwards in a headlong dash.

A shot rang out. And, almost simultaneously, Jacques shouted something. And then he tripped, falling forward, his momentum carrying him into the arms of Yves, who had emerged from the group of men hiding beneath the arch and begun to run towards them through the trees.

The railway tracks hummed louder now, and the distinct rumble of the train was carried to them on a gust of wind.

'Stop!' shouted Gustave, with the last of his breath. 'Eliane and Blanche – they're on that train. Stop!'

There seemed to be a flurry of activity beneath the bridge and then he found himself alongside Yves and Jacques on the damp leaf mould of the woodland floor.

He huddled beside them, gasping, as the rumbling of the tracks grew to a roar.

Just then, the clouds parted and the moon's face shone through, illuminating the train.

The group of men crouching beside the bridge caught a glimpse of a red silk headscarf, fluttering in the wind, and a child's pale face, pinched with fear and cold. And then, with a furious rush of wind and noise, the train flashed by and rumbled on, across the river towards Bordeaux.

'*Mon Dieu*, that was close!' Gustave turned to Yves and Jacques with relief.

But Yves didn't look up. He was holding Jacques, leaning over him to undo the buttons of his coat. As he pulled aside the coarse serge, a dark stain spread across the front of Jacques' shirt.

And where the moonlight shone on it, Gustave could see it was the same vivid scarlet as Eliane's silk scarf.

At last, the train began to slow as it wound its way across the broad expanse of the Gironde estuary. The city of Bordeaux was dark in the blackout, but the moon shimmered and danced on the wide waters, illuminating the pale façade of the city's sweep of waterfront buildings as well as the white faces of the group on the flatcar.

'Nearly there now,' Eliane called to the others. The rushing wind and deafening noise of the engine obscured her words, but they saw her smile and it gave them the strength they needed to hang on for the last few minutes with their frozen fingers and aching arms.

When the train pulled in to the Gare Saint-Jacques at Bordeaux, the carriage doors opened and German soldiers streamed out on to the platform. They busied themselves unloading wooden crates of ammunition and weapons from the freight cars, piling up the arms and equipment ready for reloading onto waiting army trucks.

The little group from Coulliac hesitated where they stood on the flatcar, frozen with the combination of their fear, cold and noise-numbed nerves, unsure what to do next.

Amid the shouts and clangs that echoed around the station, the elder of the two brothers asked, 'Do we have to do the journey in the opposite direction too?' Silent tears began to roll down Blanche's chilled, wind-roughened cheeks at the thought of having to repeat the ordeal.

Eliane looked around, rubbing the child's arms to comfort her and to try to get the circulation going again as she searched for someone she could ask. And then, in the middle of all the chaos and din, she caught sight of a familiar face.

'Oberleutnant Farber!' she called.

He picked his way towards them, his eyes fixed on the scarlet beacon of Eliane's headscarf as he stepped around groups of soldiers and stacks of wooden crates.

He held out his arms to take Blanche from her. 'Come,' he said. 'It's time to take you home.'

He helped the group down from the flatcar and led them out of a side exit to where an army truck, similar to the one that had transported them to Bergerac, stood waiting. The driver hopped down from his cab, grinding his cigarette out on the cobbles with the heel of his boot, and helped lift the children into the back. Once again, it took the assistance of both men for Monsieur Fournier to manage to clamber up, so stiff and painful were his arthritic limbs after the ordeal of the journey. Taking her seat beside him in the back of the truck, his wife tried to warm his gnarled hands, rubbing them between her own to ease his suffering.

He smiled at her and kissed her cheek, saying, 'We made it, thank God.'

Exhausted, and lulled by the swaying of the truck as they were driven past the vineyards of Bordeaux back towards Coulliac, some members of the group fell asleep. But Eliane sat watching over them, her nerves still too frayed to be able to relax her guard until they were back safely.

At last, the truck jolted to a halt and Oberleutnant Farber opened the canvas flap at the rear of the truck. 'Eliane, you're home. We're at the *moulin*.' He smiled at the others, his teeth gleaming faintly in the moonlit darkness. 'Not long for the rest of you now. We'll be at Coulliac in a few minutes.'

He took Eliane's hand to help her descend. She took off her headscarf and stuffed it into the pocket of her coat, shaking her hair free so that it fell in a sheet of pale gold over her shoulders where the moonlight caught it. Then the officer reached for Blanche, lifting the sleeping child down into Eliane's arms.

They didn't speak, but he squeezed her arm before he turned to get back into the cab of the truck beside the driver.

She carried Blanche along the track towards the mill house, limping slightly on her aching, stiffened legs. Blanche whimpered in her sleep and Eliane hushed her, saying softly, 'It's alright, *ma princesse*. We're home now.'

As they approached, a gleam of light escaped from a corner of the blacked-out kitchen window. She'd lost track of the time, but knew it must have been well past midnight, and the tightness of fear that had constricted her heart for the past few hours eased a little at the thought of her parents sitting up, waiting for them to return.

She tried to push open the door but, unusually, it was bolted from the inside. 'Maman! Papa!' she called as she knocked. 'It's me, Eliane.'

There was a flurry of activity from inside the kitchen and Gustave flung the door open. 'Eliane! Blanche! Oh, thank God you are both safe.' He enfolded them in his arms, which were still strong, despite being wasted with hunger, and she allowed herself to relax against the comforting solidity of her father, closing her eyes for a moment as she gave thanks.

But then she sensed that there was something different about the air in the room. Instead of the comforting smells of home-cooking and drying herbs, she breathed in a strange scent: the fug of dried sweat, underlain by the scents of wild thyme and pine needles; and she looked past Gustave to find that the kitchen was filled with people.

It took a moment or two for her to make sense of the scene before her. Three heavily bearded men stood by the range, their clothes ragged and dirty. Three rifles were piled haphazardly on the kitchen table. At the sight of Eliane, one of the men took a step forward, an expression of anguish crumpling his weather-beaten features. He reached out a hand towards her. 'I'm sorry,' he said, and his voice cracked. 'I thought it was the Nazis . . .' He dropped his hand again and stood, silent, alongside his companions, the three men forming a tableau of sorrow. And then she realised that they were watching another tableau before them on the floor of the kitchen.

Lisette and Yves knelt on the hard stone flags and they both turned their faces towards Eliane. Instead of smiles of relief, though, their expressions were pale masks of horrified helplessness.

And then she saw that they were kneeling beside a prone body, bloody cloths in their hands, as they tried desperately to staunch the flow of lifeblood from Jacques Lemaître's abdomen.

She thrust Blanche into Gustave's arms and sank to her knees beside her mother and her brother. They both reached out their arms to try to comfort her.

'Jack,' she whispered, reaching for the lifeless-looking fingers of his hand, the skin already becoming waxy in the light of the oil lamp.

His eyes flickered for a moment and then opened, clouded at first, but slowly clearing to the blue of a summer sky as they focused on her face and he smiled.

He tried to speak, but instead his throat rattled and he coughed, his face contorting with pain.

'Sssh,' she soothed him, 'don't try to talk. Everything's alright.' She pressed his hand to her heart, willing the life to stop ebbing from him so remorselessly, praying that the ooze of dark-red blood would cease. But she knew it was already too late.

She placed her other hand gently on his cheek and his eyes closed again. His lips struggled to form words and she bent closer to hear him.

With an effort he managed to whisper, 'You smell of honey and sunshine. Even after all that. The darkness of this world can't dim the light that shines from you, Eliane.'

She bent lower and kissed his forehead.

And so the last breath he took was perfumed with beeswax, and the breeze that blows across the river. And, even as it slowed, faltered, and then stopped, his heart was filled with love.

They buried Jack's body beneath a young oak tree on the edge of a small copse. The grave was unmarked, but one of the *maquisards* carved a long vertical line crossed by two shorter horizontals into the bark of the tree, forming the Croix de Lorraine – the symbol of the Free French Army – so that as the trunk grew the markings would expand. Eliane stood by the grave long after everyone else had left, lost in her memories of Jack. She remembered the look in his eyes when he saw her, and the way he would smile at her shyly when they were alone, in a way that was in marked contrast to his usual confidence around others. She remembered every moment of the night they'd spent in the cavern beneath Château Bellevue, the wine they'd drunk and the confidences they'd exchanged, how warm and safe she'd felt lying in his arms in that underground world where, for those few, precious hours, the war had seemed so far away.

Finally, she roused herself and gathered a bunch of autumn seed heads and berries, which she laid on the rough turfs that had been heeled in to cover the freshly dug earth of Jack's grave. At a glance, the field margin looked undisturbed, apart from the single, forlorn posy lying in the grass. She took one last, long look, etching the spot into her memory so that she'd be able to find the young oak tree marked with the carved cross when she came to visit his grave again.

From the valley below, she heard a church bell ring. It was *la Toussaint* and families were filing into the churchyard at Coulliac to place flowers on the graves of their forebears. Eliane wondered, *What about Jack's family? Are his parents alive? Does he have brothers and sisters? Who will tell them of his death in a foreign land and his burial in an unmarked grave?* She wanted them to know that he'd been among friends when he died. That he'd been admired and respected, as he deserved, for his courage and his selflessness. That he'd died saving her life, saving Blanche, saving Yves from a living hell. She wanted them to know that he'd been loved. But there was no way of telling them.

She was startled, suddenly, by the sight of a figure standing stock-still among the trees. It was Yves, who must have remained behind when his brothers-in-arms had slipped away from the graveside. He stepped forward and put an arm around her. Burying her face against his shoulder, she sobbed.

He stood there silently, letting her cry. And then, when her sobs began to slow and quieten, he pushed back a strand of her hair from her tear-soaked face. 'Eliane,' he said. 'Listen to me. You think you have lost both the men you love. But you haven't. Mathieu is still there. And when this war is over, you will know that you never really lost him. That he was always there.'

She pulled back, looking into Yves' face. 'What do you mean? How could I ever love Mathieu again? He's on the other side now. He was working against Jacques. He's working against you.'

Yves shook his head. 'He's not, Eliane. That's all I can tell you. But you have to believe me: he's not.'

He hugged her again and then slipped away into the trees without a backwards glance.

As she turned away from the grave and walked slowly back down the hill, her tears fell like raindrops on to the dry meadow grasses, which bowed their heads and sighed in the chill November wind.

Abi: 2017

On my next day off, Sara gives me the directions and I climb up through the fields above Coulliac to where the tree line begins. It takes a little bit of finding, but eventually I spot it: an oak tree with the Cross of Lorraine carved into the trunk.

I know that Jack's body no longer lies here. At the end of the war, his parents were notified of his death and of the location of his make-shift grave, and so they were able to bring their son home, to lie in the local churchyard close to his family home. But I sense that a part of him will always be here, in the hills above Coulliac, watching over the land he helped to liberate.

As I stand gazing out across the valley, I can't help comparing Jack Connelly's funeral with the service that was held in the grand London church for Zac. I sat in the front pew beside his mother, though I could feel the waves of loathing coming off her as she angled her body slightly away from me, keeping her eyes focused on the coffin. She'd arranged it all, from the venue and the guest list to the bouquet of lilies on the fine-grained lid of the beechwood coffin. I could only imagine how desperate it must have felt for her, to have lost her beloved only son. And worse, for him to have been survived by the silly young wife whom she so hated. I could hear her thinking it, as the vicar began the service: *Why is she still here when he is gone? Why couldn't it have been Abi who died in the accident, not my Zac?*

And I could feel my own guilt radiating in waves through the fabric of my black coat. It'd been weeks since the accident – long enough for my swollen, blackened knee to have begun to heal and for the bones of my arm to begin to knit themselves back together. It had taken that long for the police to complete the enquiry into the circumstances of the accident, to conduct their interviews with me and the other witnesses, and for the autopsy report to be issued. Loss of control while driving under the influence of excessive alcohol in the bloodstream – that was the official verdict.

Even though I'd told the police how I'd grabbed the wheel. Even though I knew I'd killed him as he'd tried to kill me.

The service was bad enough, although at least in the church Zac's mother had managed to keep up some semblance of civility towards me, even if only for appearances' sake. But after the service, in private at the crematorium, she made no pretence at all. After the coffin had glided silently away as the curtains had fallen back into place, she turned towards me as we sat on the stiffly upholstered chairs. Instinctively, I'd reached out a hand to her, hoping, I suppose, for some small gesture of reconciliation or mutual support at the very end. But she'd just looked at me with utter hatred, her eyes hard and cold, and she'd recoiled from my touch. I'd let my hand fall to my side and she'd walked off, leaving one of the funeral director's men to help me to my feet and hand me the crutch that helped to take the weight off my knee when I walked. He'd been kind, a fatherly-looking man, and had driven me back to the apartment. As he'd helped me from the back of the black saloon car and seen me safely into the building, he'd patted my hand where it protruded from the cast on my arm. 'Don't worry about her, love. Grief does strange things. I've seen enough funerals to know they either bring out the very best or the worst in people. Everyone needs space and time to grieve.'

That was the only moment, on the day of Zac's funeral, that tears came into my eyes. A few words of kindness offered by a stranger were the only comfort I received that day.

The accident. I haven't thought about it for a long time. 'Accident' is a useful word, but I still wonder just how accurately it describes what happened. Because, in a way, it was inevitable. Not some haphazard fluke of fate but rather an unavoidable conclusion to the path we'd been set on ever since that day he first saw me, and targeted me as his prey.

We were in his car, driving back from Sunday lunch at his mother's. He'd had a few glasses of wine, as usual, despite my anxious glances and my tentative suggestion that maybe the glass of port at the end of the meal was a drink too many.

'Nonsense, Abigail, Zac knows his limits. I always think a nagging wife is one of the most unattractive things there is,' his mother had retorted, pouring him a glass from the crystal decanter that sat on the polished sideboard in the dining room.

'Are you sure you wouldn't like me to drive?' I'd asked him as we walked to the car. He'd taunted me then, leering at me, dangling the keys in front of my face and pretending to stagger drunkenly down the path.

'Come on, Zac, please. Let me drive,' I'd said more forcefully.

A mistake.

His expression immediately grew cold, his eyes frosting over with anger. Most people describe anger as hot and fiery, but Zac's was always as cold as ice.

'Get in,' he snapped. 'Or would you rather walk home?'

I should have refused to get in.

I should have walked.

I shouldn't have gone home.

I should have left him, then and there.

In the car, he was silent. I tried to make things better, to soothe his anger by talking about inconsequential things: how nice the lunch had been (it hadn't, though – it had been the usual grey, tasteless cut of meat served with overcooked vegetables); how well his mother was looking now she'd got over that nasty cold she'd had; how the weather seemed to be brightening up for the week ahead.

He hadn't replied. He'd just pulled away from the kerb and driven, too fast, through the village, the speed-limit signs lighting up in warning as the car approached and then flashed past them. I'd pulled out my phone, to check the weather forecast and see whether the week ahead was indeed going to be warm and sunny. I'd had the phone turned off during lunch – a formality, really, as I never expected anyone other than Zac to phone me or text me on it. As I switched it back on, it beeped. I glanced at the screen and then swiped the message out of the way.

'Aren't you going to tell me who it's from then?' Zac had said, his tone dripping acid.

'It's a message from one of the people in my tutorial group. She's just saying they haven't seen me for a while and wondering if I'm okay.'

'Let me see,' he said, taking his left hand off the steering wheel. The car, which was travelling far too fast now on the twisting country road, swerved a little and an oncoming motorcyclist flashed his lights and gesticulated angrily.

'Zac, no, be careful.'

'Give me the phone, Abi,' he said, his tone unnaturally calm. In that moment, his voice sounded almost reasonable.

'Here, look,' I turned the phone so that he could see the message.

'Sam?' he said. 'Who the hell is Sam?' A muscle flickered in his jaw.

'Sam is a girl. Just a girl in my tutor group. I told you.'

'Give me the phone, Abi.'

'When we get home, I will. You can look at it then and you'll see. There are no other messages. It's just that I missed the last two meetings and caught up online.'

And then he lost it. 'I said, give me the fucking phone!' He screamed the words and I flinched as if they were blows raining down on my head and arms.

I realised, then, that he was steering straight towards one of the trees growing on the raised verge along the side of the road. Terrified, I reached across with my right hand to grab the wheel, to try to put the car back on course, and he brought the edge of his left hand down hard on my forearm, with such force that I felt the bones snap. I screamed in pain and terror, my hand dangling at an agonising, useless angle. We'd avoided the tree, but the car lurched and swerved again and the engine roared as he stood hard on the accelerator, deliberately steering towards the next one.

In that moment, I realised that he was trying to kill me. Perhaps to kill himself while he was at it, too, but he was going to crush the passenger's side of the car against the tree at full speed, obliterating me.

Where did it come from, that surge of strength through my body? I know, now, that the terror and the pain must have made adrenaline shoot through my veins and that my next movement was reflexive. But I think it was something more than that, too. It was anger at the damage he'd done to me, it was the spark of my Self, suddenly reawakening; it was the resilience of the human spirit. It was resistance.

Because he had the accelerator forced to the floor, my seatbelt didn't restrain me as I twisted round and reached across with my good, left arm. I grabbed the wheel and forced it to turn, resisting his strength, finding my own power at last. I felt the car rise up as it hit the grass verge, missing the solid grey trunk of the tree by a few millimetres, and then it flipped, an almost graceful arc of car-shaped metal flying through the air into the path of the oncoming lorry.

Braced for the impact, I felt my knee twist with a searing pain that brought a red mist down over my eyes and made my stomach heave.

And then I felt nothing. Just a strange, unearthly calm as the car imploded around the two of us. Zac and me.

And when everything finally stopped, I looked over at him. His eyes were wide, surprised, as cold and blue as ice. He opened his mouth, as if to say something, and then his eyes rolled back in his head and the waxy tinge of death suffused his face.

I remember very clearly what I felt in that moment. Relief. Nothing else. Before the pain made me pass out.

Later, when I came to and I saw Zac's face as they cut his body out of the car, I still felt very little. I was deep in shock, of course; but even so I can remember how it was to see his familiar features in his bloodless face and have the sense that this wasn't him.

His body was a lot less cut up than mine was. He had suffered massive internal injuries where the steering wheel crushed his ribcage, splintering the bones and driving them into his heart and lungs.

My injuries were more visible, but not fatal: lacerations to my arms, the lower part of the right one hanging at a useless angle where the bones had been sheared through; a dislocated knee and more lacerations to my thighs. All outwardly mendable, given time. It was the trauma that went so much deeper, though; that crippled me more than my damaged limbs.

But even through the shock and the chaos, and despite the fact that the paramedics were trying to shield me from the sight of him, I can still remember it clearly. His frozen, waxen features; and my sense of stunned relief.

'Little Abi, how perfect you are . . .' I can hear his words now, the words he spoke at the end of our first date, as if they were blown on the wind that stirs the meadow grasses at my feet. And I know, now, exactly what those words meant. To him, I was blank piece of paper on which he could write what he wanted. I was already isolated – it would be easy to control me. I was desperate for affection, but I didn't know what real love was. My mother's love for me had dissolved long ago in a sea of cheap vodka and since then I'd made do with the love offered up by the children I'd cared for, knowing that they would grow up and I would be forgotten as I moved on to another family. What a little mouse I was, naïve enough to be flattered, to mistake the attention he bestowed on me for love. I wanted it to be, and so I made myself believe that it was something it wasn't.

With my fingertips, I trace the lines of the cross scored into the oak tree once more. Almost seventy-five years on, the long, vertical cut with its two cross bars has widened as the tree has grown. But, at the same time, the oak has managed to heal the scar, sealing closed the wound.

I run my hands over the sleeves of my shirt, feeling the faint ridges beneath the thin cotton and I marvel at the way my body has healed itself, just as the tree has done.

The cross is just as much a part of the oak as its branches and its roots, just as my scars are now a part of me, for ever more. And yet, there is resilience. The body finds a way to close the wounds, to live with the scars. To heal.

And, yes, even to grow.

Eliane: 1944

The winter had seemed interminably long. Eliane's heart was frozen with grief and loss, which even the first warm day of spring couldn't thaw. Despite what Yves had said, she felt she'd lost both of the men she'd loved. And the war dragged on, sapping France, bleeding the country dry. The tide had turned against the German army now – that much was evident from the preoccupied air and low spirits of the soldiers occupying the château as they passed more long months away from their homes and families in a strange, starved land where they were hated and feared. Official reports in the newspapers were heavily censored, glossing over the setbacks for the occupying army. But Monsieur le Comte would come into the kitchen on the winter evenings to sit by the warmth of the range and sip his night-time *tisane*, and he would whisper news to Eliane and Madame Boin of the growing groundswell of action, of Allied air-raids, of Soviet victories and of German defeats. As spring arrived and his reports told of a definite, sustained shift in the momentum of the war against Hitler's Wehrmacht, a few fragile shoots of hope began to stir in their hearts.

One morning towards the end of May, Eliane and Madame Boin were in the kitchen preparing the first of the early cherries, which Eliane had picked from a tree that was tucked into a corner behind the barn, where it caught the sun and was protected from the frost and wind so always bore its fruit before any of the other trees. The tips of her fingers were stained pink by the tangy juice as she cut the stones out of the fruit.

As Oberleutnant Farber and the general entered the kitchen, the women set down their knives and wiped their hands on damp cloths, turning to face the soldiers respectfully. Visits to the kitchen by the general were rare – more often it was Oberleutnant Farber alone who came to relay any official orders, or Monsieur le Comte who occasionally passed on requests from the Germans for a particular dish to be served at dinner that night.

The oberleutnant translated as the general spoke. 'Ladies, our units have been ordered to move north. We thank you for your work to make our stay at Château Bellevue as pleasant as possible for all concerned. However, the château will not be empty for long. We leave tomorrow and you will have approximately two days to prepare for your next visitors. Another unit will be coming through the region on its way north also. The château will be used by them as a base for a few days – perhaps longer – until they receive further orders. The situation is a little uncertain right now. Oberleutnant Farber will be staying on here as a liaison officer to assist the new unit, as he knows the ropes. So it is *auf wiedersehen* from the rest of us for now. But, who knows, perhaps we'll be back before too long if the rumours of an invasion attempt turn out to be yet another false alarm.'

With a click of his boot heels he turned and left, the oberleutnant following in his wake.

The next twenty-four hours were a flurry of noise and activity as the soldiers packed up and prepared for deployment. A couple of hours after the last of them had gone, setting off to the station with a final revving of truck engines, Eliane paused at her tasks with the beehives, raising her head as she heard the distant rhythmic beat of a train. This one, she assumed, would be filled with soldiers instead of civilian deportees.

But perhaps it was carrying those soldiers to another place of horror and death. She sensed that the paths of the war were converging as it reached a climactic turning point. Would it be an ending, or just the beginning of something even worse for France?

As the sound of the train faded into the distance, she closed up the hive she'd been working on, picked up her pails of honey frames and carried them back to the château.

The new 'guests' at Château Bellevue were quite different to the soldiers who'd occupied the château for the past four years. The soldiers of the Panzer regiment, who arrived just as Eliane and Madame Boin were remaking the last few beds, were battle hardened from their previous experience of fighting on the Russian front, with eyes that were deadened by the things that they'd seen and souls that were numbed by the things that they'd done. Their tanks rumbled up the track to Château Bellevue, crushing stones and pulverising pebbles into a cloud of thick dust that hung in the air long after the throbbing roar of the engines had ceased.

Eliane hurried about her duties with her head lowered and her eyes downcast. In their black and silver uniforms, these soldiers brought with them a new darkness and she had to swallow the sour taste of fear that rose in her throat whenever she encountered one of them.

When not helping Madame Boin, she spent as much time as possible in the garden, watering the new season's crops, pruning dead branches that had been touched by last winter's frosted fingers, and hoeing the weeds from the beds of the *potager*. She immersed herself in her work, thankful that it distracted her from the heaviness of her heart. She still grieved for Jack, and often walked up through the fields to the young oak tree on the edge of the copse to visit his grave. The grass was well established again there now and wildflowers made a coverlet for his body. Throughout the winter months, the slender branches of the oak tree had been lifeless-looking twigs, with a few dry, crumpled brown leaves clinging on here and there despite the winter storms; but then, early one spring morning, she'd noticed the first of the new growth beginning to open at the end of each twig, tentatively unfurling into tender flourishes of green. That day, she'd turned her face towards the rising sun and gazed eastwards in the direction of Tulle. She wondered what Mathieu was doing at that moment. *Does he ever think of me? How is he managing to survive the despair and deprivation that this war has brought upon us?* In some ways, she thought, it was easier to grieve for the loss of Jack than for the loss of Mathieu. Death brought a sense of conclusion that abandonment did not. Her heart still longed for Mathieu – Yves' words at the graveside had lodged themselves in her head, a flicker of hope like a candle flame in the darkness – even though she still tried to tell herself firmly that she had to accept that he'd made his choice and gone. And even if Yves was right and Mathieu did deserve forgiveness, so much time had passed now – and so much had happened – that neither of them could be the same carefree young people that they had been before war broke out.

***

'Where is Monsieur le Comte?' Madame Boin grumbled. 'His supper is going to be completely spoiled.'

Eliane, washing pots and pans at the sink, looked out of the window and across the courtyard. It was a beautiful June evening and the swallows swooped and soared around the stone cross above the chapel, slicing effortlessly through the stillness of the summer air. 'He must still be at his devotions, I think. He's later than usual.'

As she watched, the count emerged from the chapel, fumbling with the keys as he hastily locked the door behind him. He hobbled across the courtyard almost at a run, moving faster than she'd ever seen him move before. Quickly, she dried her hands on her apron as she went to meet him.

As he crossed the threshold, his eyes blazed with something even greater than hope: it was the light of triumph that she saw there.

'Eliane! Madame Boin! It's happened. The day has arrived. The Allies have landed on the beaches of Normandy! I've just heard General de Gaulle broadcasting from London. He's issued a call to us all: "The duty of the sons of France is to fight with all the means at their disposal." Will you walk for me, Eliane? One last dance to tell our brothers in the hills that the hour has come to rise up and take back our country?'

Hurriedly, she pulled the silk scarf from the pocket of her apron. 'Of course, monsieur.' Her fingers shook as she knotted it behind her head at the nape of her neck. 'What would you like me to do?'

To her surprise, he stepped towards her and gently pulled the scarf from her hair, pressing it into her hand. Then he hugged her tightly for a second before stepping back and saying 'Walk back and forth along the outside of the far wall, as you did once before. Only this time, Eliane, hold that silk square high, so that everyone can see it and know that France's hour has come.'

Madame Boin tutted and shook her head. 'Just make sure that none of our "guests" see you, my girl . . .'

Monsieur le Comte turned and hugged her too, a gesture so astounding that she was instantly silenced.

'Don't worry, Madame Boin, they will be far too concerned with their own orders to worry about what a handful of helpless civilians are up to.' As if in confirmation, they heard the pounding of heavy boots running down the château's main staircase and the sounds of harshly barked commands. 'Come, Eliane.' He smiled. 'It's time to dance.'

'But, monsieur, your supper . . .' Madame Boin protested, trying to regain her composure.

'I'll have it later. Now I must get back to the chapel. As soon as our friends in the Maquis see Eliane's signal, they'll get on to the radio so that I can tell them the news.'

He hurried back outside, his cane tapping briskly across the dusty yard.

She felt more exposed than ever as she paced along the narrow pathway outside the garden wall. Hesitantly at first, she held the frayed square of red silk in the air. She jumped with fright as a squadron of swifts swooped past her, their wings slicing the air before soaring off across the steep rock face that fell away to the valley below. But she regained her poise, and the surge of adrenalin through her veins made her feel braver, and she held the scarf high and waved it as she walked. Back and forth she went, sending out the message of hope, at last, to the *maquisards* watching from the hills, scarcely caring, now, whether the Milice or the Gestapo saw her as well.

But then, hearing a flurry of activity from the far side of the walled garden – the crunch of boots running across the courtyard, shouts, the slamming of truck doors – she instinctively shrank back against the wall. Shortly, the evening air began to hum with the throb of engines as the tanks parked in the field below the château started up. She began to walk again, feeling a little safer in the knowledge that what the count had said seemed to be true – if the soldiers were so busy preparing to dash north to try to repel the invasion in Normandy, perhaps they wouldn't have time to take any notice of the kitchen maid out on an evening walk.

But just then, as the sound of the tanks' engines grew to a throbbing crescendo, a series of shots rang out suddenly from the direction of the courtyard. The crack of rifle fire was followed by a rattling burst from a machine gun, which made her heart pound in her ears even more loudly than the noise of the revving tanks.

She looked around, frantically. What should she do? Keep walking until the count appeared and told her that she could stop, or go and see what had happened?

She forced herself to keep walking: *Three more times along the length of the wall*, she told herself, *and then I'll go and find Monsieur le Comte and ask him if I should continue . . . Surely they'll have seen me by now.*

Her heart leaped with relief when she turned back for the final time, as a figure appeared around the corner at the far end of the wall. She stopped short, though, when she realised it wasn't the Comte de Bellevue coming to release her from her duty but Oberleutnant Farber.

She thrust the silk scarf into her pocket, hoping he would think she had simply stepped out for a breath of air, her excuses at the ready.

But he didn't ask for any explanation. He sprinted towards her, heedless of the narrowness of the path and the steepness of the ground that fell away sharply just beyond it.

Fear gripped her belly and she froze, waiting for him to draw his pistol and fire. She knew that, even if she tried to turn and run, she would still be an easy target, trapped as she was between the garden wall on one side and the steep drop on the other.

He was calling to her as he approached, although she couldn't make out what he was saying above the roar of the tanks. He reached her, panting, and seized her arm. 'Quick, mademoiselle, there is no time to lose. The soldiers are leaving, but they are destroying everything as they go. You and Madame Boin must hide yourselves. I won't be able to protect you.'

'I heard shooting,' she said. 'From the courtyard.'

'There's no time to explain,' he insisted. 'You must come now and hide with Madame Boin.'

'And Monsieur le Comte, too. We must get him.'

A look of anguish distorted the officer's face into a mask of anger and grief, and he shook his head, pulling her along the path towards the kitchen.

'Eliane, it's too late. They found him. Those shots – they came from the chapel.'

Eliane gasped, shock stopping her in her tracks. 'No!' she cried. 'We must go to him!'

'Eliane,' he repeated, although his voice was gentler this time. 'It's too late.' He pulled at her arms again, his grip tightening. 'There's nothing we can do for him now. The count would want you to save yourself.'

Numbly, she allowed him to lead her to the kitchen, staying as close to the shelter of the garden walls as they could. The courtyard was a scene of utter chaos. Behind the frantically manoeuvring vehicles and the running soldiers, some of the château's windows had been broken. The formal beds of clipped box that flanked the front door had been flattened. She craned her neck to try to see the chapel and caught a glimpse of the heavy door wrenched off its hinges, leaning at a drunken angle. Beyond it, two black-uniformed soldiers emerged from the gloom of the chapel's interior, carrying what looked like bits of equipment and a tangled roll of wire, which they flung into the back of a jeep before driving off at high speed.

She longed, desperately, to run across the open expanse of the yard to find out what had happened to Monsieur le Comte, but Oberleutnant Farber pushed her ahead of him into the kitchen. Madame Boin stood with her back to the cellar door, her biggest carving knife in her hand. Her distraught expression turned to one of relief when she saw Eliane. 'Oh, thank God they didn't get you.'

'Hide yourselves, quickly,' Oberleutnant Farber ordered, pointing to the cellar door. With panicked speed, Madame Boin managed to descend the steep steps. Eliane hesitated for a moment. She reached out her hand to Oberleutnant Farber and grasped his. Her warm, grey-eyed gaze met his for a second and she said, 'Thank you, monsieur.'

He smiled at her and nodded. 'Bolt the door and stay down there. Don't come out until morning. It'll be safe then. We'll all be gone.'

She held his gaze for another moment and it felt as if the noise and confusion outside faded away as they stood there, two human beings, understanding one another in the midst of all that inhumanity.

'*Adieu*, Oberleutnant Farber.'

'*Adieu*, Eliane.'

She shut the door behind her and pushed the heavy iron bolts at the top and bottom into place, before following Madame Boin into the cellar. The cook had found the end of a candle and lit it, casting a flickering, feeble light onto the curved stone walls.

'We can escape!' Eliane said, leading the way to the barrels resting on their sides in the corner. 'Down the tunnel to the mill. Then we can raise the alert and come back to find Monsieur le Comte.'

Madame Boin shrank back against the rough wall, looking unusually vulnerable and frightened. 'I can't make it, Eliane. Even if I managed to climb down into the cavern, I'd get stuck in the tunnel. You go, if you must, but I'll have to stay here.'

Eliane realised Madame Boin was right. There were parts of the tunnel, especially towards the steep, lower end, that she and Jack had scarcely been able to squeeze through.

'Don't worry,' she said, 'I'm not going to leave you.' She knew, too, that getting her father involved would only put his life at risk as well. 'We'll do as the Oberleutnant Farber said, and wait here until morning.'

Madame Boin nodded, slumping to the floor with tears rolling down her ruddy cheeks in the candlelight. 'Do you think they've killed him?' she asked.

Eliane didn't need to ask to whom she was referring. 'I don't know,' she replied slowly. 'But they found the wireless set. And he must have been using it when they did.'

The two women wept together then, tears of despair and helplessness, tears of frustration and anger, releasing the pent-up emotions of the past four years at last as they huddled on the flagstones of the cellar.

The stub of candle guttered and then flickered out and they were left in darkness.

It was impossible to sleep. There was silence from above them, but Eliane couldn't be sure whether or not the soldiers had departed. The solid rock above and beneath them shut out all sounds from the outside world. They sat side by side in the blackness, glad to have the reassurance of each other's presence as the hours passed.

They had lost track of time. 'Is it morning yet, do you think?' Madame Boin whispered, trying pointlessly to squint at the face of her wristwatch, which was unreadable in the pitch-darkness.

'No, I don't think so. Probably around midnight. We should wait a bit longer.'

'Sssh! What's that?'

They both tensed at the faint sound of footsteps crossing the kitchen floor above them. Someone tried the cellar door, the latch clicking as it rose and then fell back into place. There was a tapping on the door then and a voice called out 'Eliane? Are you down there?'

'Yves!' she exclaimed, and scrambled up the steps to unbolt the door. She fell into her brother's arms and sobbed on his shoulder. 'Oh, Yves, have they gone? The soldiers? Monsieur le Comte . . .' But she couldn't get the words out coherently.

He pulled her to one side and called over his shoulder, 'She's here, Papa. Madame Boin, too. They're alright. Come and give me a hand.'

Gustave hurried in from outside and took Eliane into his strong embrace while Yves reached down to help Madame Boin up the stairs.

She collapsed into a chair, fanning herself with one meaty hand as she tried to get her breath back.

In the open doorway, Eliane could see the pinpricks of stars in the night sky far above them, but a strange orange light illuminated the yard, throwing flickering shadows across the dust. She moved towards it, but Gustave held out a hand to stop her, grabbing her by the arm.

'Wait, Eliane! Before you go out there, there's something I have to tell you . . .'

She turned to look at him, taking in the pained expression on his face in the sickly light. 'What is it, Papa?'

'We found Monsieur le Comte in the chapel,' he said, slowly shaking his head.

'They killed him.' Eliane said what she had already known to be true.

Gustave nodded, miserably. 'He's lying beside the altar. His body must have been there for some hours.'

'He was using the radio to spread the news. I saw them take it away.'

The ominous orange light flickered and danced, and then she sniffed the air. There was an acrid smell of smoke, but it was underlain by something else. It reminded her of something . . . Something sweet . . . Caramel, or the pralines that Lisette used to make at Christmastime.

And then she realised what was burning and she wrenched herself free of her father's grasp and ran towards the walled garden.

A sheet of flames leaped and crackled, illuminating the *potager* beds and the branches of the pear tree in the corner, sending showers of sparks like shooting stars into the night sky.

Desperately, she tried to douse the flames with a half-filled watering can, but the fire had already gained a stranglehold on the hives.

'*Non! Non! Non!*' she screamed, beating at the burning wood, first with her apron and then with her bare hands. The blazing wax burned her skin and the boiling honey seared itself on to her flesh, as sparks from the burning carcasses of the hives flew around her, threatening to draw her into the murderous dance of the flames as well.

And then her father caught up with her and wrapped his sinewy arms about her, pulling her away to safety.

He held her tight as she stood and watched, sobbing helplessly, as her beehives collapsed into a heap of burning embers and the acrid scent of burned honey filled their lungs. 'But why?' she whispered. 'Why would they do that?'

'To starve us further,' her father replied grimly. 'Or to punish you, perhaps, as they couldn't find you in person. Or maybe it was just one last act of senseless destruction before they left. Is there any point looking for reasons in this war?'

He held her up, supporting her as she seemed about to collapse. 'Stand tall, Eliane,' he said. His voice wavered, but then he said more firmly, 'Don't let them destroy you, too. Promise yourself. We will survive this. We won't let them beat us. *Courage, ma fille, courage.*'

Madame Boin and Eliane did their best to tidy the château, which had been left in a sorry state by the departing soldiers. They swept up broken glass, scrubbed graffiti off the walls in the *salon* and tidied away stray belongings and items of uniform that had been left behind in the rush to leave. 'What shall we do with this?' Eliane asked, holding up a black serge jacket belonging to one of the soldiers of the Panzer regiment. Its silver insignia glinted dully in the light that streamed in through a broken bedroom window, which Gustave was measuring in order to board it up.

Madame Boin snorted. 'Burning would be too good for it.'

Gustave glanced over his shoulder at the garment. 'Best put everything in the attic, just in case they come back looking for it. Make a pile of things on the landing and I'll get the ladder and put them up in the roof for you.'

Cleaning the chapel had been the most harrowing of their tasks. Gustave and Yves had carried the count's body back to the château to be prepared for his funeral. While Madame Boin washed him and dressed him in a once-fine suit of clothes, Eliane had scrubbed the stone flags beside the altar. It took several buckets of water and a whole bar of the soft, ineffectual soap – which was all they had to clean with these days – to wash the blood from the floor. She'd done her best, but a dark stain remained where Monsieur le Comte's lifeblood had drained from his wounds, seeping into the stones of the chapel as he'd manned his wireless set for the last time; as he'd urged his countrymen to rise up and join the fight to rid France of its enemy.

And yet, it felt strange having the German soldiers gone, so suddenly and so completely. The first thing the mayor had done, once the guards left Coulliac, was to announce that Monsieur le Comte's body would lie in state for two days so that everyone who wanted to could come and pay their respects. The people who filed past the plain pine coffin were threadbare and shabby, bony wrists protruding from frayed cuffs as each in turn removed a shapeless cap or worn beret, but they held their heads high, each person waiting their turn with a quiet dignity, ready now to take back responsibility for their *patrimoine,* for which the count had made the ultimate sacrifice. At long last, the French tricolour flew from the flagpole in front of the *mairie* again.

A news blackout had been declared, but rumours of the upsurge in Resistance activity circulated on every street corner, in the cafés and the queues outside the shops; telephone lines had been sabotaged, and railway lines and bridges destroyed so that the progress of the Germans in their headlong dash northwards was frustrated at every possible turn. Madame Fournier had heard from the mayor's secretary, who seemed to know about such things via who-knew-what secret and tortuous route, that the Panzer divisions from Montauban to the south were moving slowly up the road towards Limoges but had been repeatedly delayed by disruptive action and even fighting in the streets of some of the towns along the way. Eliane wondered where Mathieu was and what he was doing in the midst of this chaos and confusion. Surely he wasn't working against *la Résistance*, still trying to protect the railways? Wherever he was, and whatever he was doing, Eliane sent up a silent prayer that he and his family were safe: the route the southern-based Panzer divisions were taking must run very close to Tulle, she supposed.

As the last few people filed past the count's coffin, the mayor's secretary came to lock up the *mairie* for the night. Tomorrow, the funeral would take place in the church in Coulliac – which was large enough to accommodate all the mourners who would be there – before Charles Montfort, Comte de Bellevue's body was laid to rest beneath the flagstones of the little chapel up at the château. Eliane and Madame Boin, who had been sitting on chairs against the wall, watching over the count for the final time, got to their feet.

'I'm hearing that there's been some serious fighting going on over your young man's way,' Madame la Secrétaire said to Eliane.

'He's not my young man anymore,' said Eliane, but her heart still leaped with dread.

The mayor's secretary shot her an astute look. 'If you say so, Eliane. Anyway, I've heard they've done a good job of holding up *les Boches*. Where's that brother of yours these days?'

Eliane shrugged. 'Your guess is as good as mine. I haven't seen him since he came to find us at the château after the Germans had gone.'

'Keeping himself busy, I'm sure.' The secretary patted Eliane's hand sympathetically, noticing that the colour had drained from the girl's face at the thought of the peril her loved ones might be facing. 'Don't worry; it will soon be over and those we love will come home safely, God willing. Go home now and get some sleep. You will need your strength for tomorrow.'

Yves woke her from a troubled sleep just after dawn. For a few moments, she was disorientated. She'd been dreaming that she was in the cavern beneath Château Bellevue again, and Mathieu had been there with her. She was trying to comfort him, because she could see he was in great pain, but as she did so she heard great rocks being rolled over the trapdoor above them and then the entrance to the tunnel collapsed. She realised that there was no way out. Frantically, she'd tried to claw at the stones that blocked the tunnel, her hands torn and bloody. Mathieu had watched her, helpless, and then in her dream the ground had begun to shake. Terrified that the cavern was collapsing in on them, she'd fought her way back to Mathieu and held him as he dissolved into the pale light that crept in through the windows of her attic room and she found her brother shaking her.

'Wake up, Eliane, wake up!'

'Yves? What is it? Are you alright?'

He nodded. 'Something's happened. In Tulle. I'm going over there to look for Mathieu. Will you come too? There may be some people in need of help. Bring Maman's basket.'

'Papa? And Maman?'

'Leave them here. I don't know what we'll find; maybe it's nothing, just rumours. Let them stay and look after Blanche. We'll leave them a note to say where we've gone.'

They climbed into the truck and Yves accelerated along the track, swinging out into the road and turning east as the sun began to rise.

'What have you heard?' Eliane asked him, squinting into the light as the truck swayed around a bend in the road, its tyres skidding slightly in the dust.

With his eyes fixed grimly on the road ahead, Yves said, 'There was fighting in the streets of Tulle. The *maquisards* almost managed to take the town from the occupying forces. But the Germans sent an armoured detachment from Brive as reinforcements. The boys were no match for them and in the end they fled.'

Eliane nodded, digesting this. 'Did they get away?'

Yves pressed his lips together in a hard line and swallowed before he was able to reply. 'Most did, I think. But the Germans rounded up everyone they could find, whether or not they'd been involved in the fighting. There have been reprisals.' He stopped, apparently concentrating on steering across the narrow bridge over the river at Coulliac, one of the few that still remained intact after the carnage of the last few days.

Eliane's blood seemed to freeze in her veins. 'What sort of reprisals?'

Yves shrugged. 'I can't be sure. These are only rumours . . . There's been no official word.'

She turned to look at his profile. He seemed so much older, all of a sudden, a stranger, his features no longer those of the carefree boy he'd once been. All the things he had seen and all the things he had done had etched lines into his face that appeared as pale as marble in the morning light, carved into something harder than it had ever been before. And, despite all he had seen and all he had done, he was still struggling to speak of what he had heard had happened in Tulle. His jaw was clenched and she saw the sinews in his throat tighten as he swallowed again, hard. And then he spoke.

'There have been hangings.'

The silence was loud for a moment, ringing in her ears, making her dizzy.

'Mathieu . . . ?' She almost choked as she said his name.

'I don't know, Eliane.' He shook his head, as if trying to shake off the images that had lodged themselves there. 'I just don't know.'

❈

The most noticeable thing, as they entered Tulle, was the silence. It was a Saturday morning and the town should have been bustling with activity as its inhabitants congregated in cafés and outside shops. But instead an eerie atmosphere of stillness engulfed them as the truck negotiated the streets. And then, as they came around the last corner and reached the centre of the town, Yves stood hard on the brakes.

When they turned on to the main street, the scene was so surreal that it took them a few moments to register it. From each of the lampposts, as far as they could see along the road, a body was suspended, hanging heavy and motionless. From a distance, the figures looked almost peaceful, their hands appearing to be clasped behind their backs and their heads bowed as if in prayer.

At the sound of the truck's engine, one or two curtains stirred in the windows of apartments above the shops. Yves switched it off and the silence was far louder than the noise of the truck had been, pounding in their ears, making Eliane feel even more dizzy. Bile rose in her throat and she had to swallow hard as nausea threatened to overwhelm her. She took a deep breath and turned to reach for Lisette's basket of medicaments. It was a small comfort to hold the wicker handle, even though she knew that the contents of the basket would be of no use to the figures hanging from the lampposts.

They climbed out, cautiously, and Yves slammed shut the driver's door. The sound seemed to trigger something, as if it were an order releasing the people who were trapped in their homes, terrified and traumatised by what they had witnessed. One by one, doors opened and the inhabitants stumbled out into the street.

Yves opened his arms to catch a woman who seemed to be falling towards them, her body shaking uncontrollably. 'It's alright. You're alright now,' he said to her, trying to soothe her with words that felt meaningless. He turned to Eliane. 'Take her,' he said. 'Look after her.'

He stopped a boy – no more than twelve years old – who was running up the street towards them. 'Wait!' Yves said. 'Help me with these ladders. We need to get them down.'

A pair of ladders lay on their sides against the railings at the end of the street, tossed there casually after they'd been used for their murderous purpose.

'My brother . . .' the boy gasped, his face a mask of shock.

'Which one is he?' Yves asked, grimly.

'Over there.' The boy pointed to the third lamppost along, where the body of a skinny teenager was suspended.

Yves nodded. 'We'll get him down. You wait here with my sister.'

Several women – and one or two elderly men – had appeared now, and Yves directed them to help him place the pair of ladders against the first lamppost. 'We need to work together, to bring them down gently,' he said. 'If you can help, then come and stand beneath me. Two people should steady the ladders; the others need to be ready to take the weight as we untie the ropes.' A sturdy woman climbed one of the ladders and Yves the other. 'I'll take the weight off the line if you can untie the knots?' he asked her. She nodded, intent on her task.

One by one, they brought down the bodies. There were more than ninety in all, men and boys.

Eliane did her best to try to bring comfort to those who stood, watching, waiting for their father or their husband or their brother to be released from the rope that bound him by the neck. Outstretched arms received the bodies as they were passed down gently, and laid them out on the pavement. People brought blankets and sheets to cover the bodies, wrapping them tenderly in their makeshift shrouds.

As Yves worked, others arrived to help, bringing more ladders, offering supporting shoulders to those who were destroyed by grief.

It was harrowing work, but they didn't pause for a second, moving methodically from one lamppost to the next. Eliane was about half-way along the street, crouching alongside a woman whose stomach was swollen in pregnancy as she knelt over the body of her husband, when she caught sight of a tall figure, weaving his way through the gathered mass of people and picking his way around the bodies stretched out on the ground.

She didn't recognise him at first; his hair was so wild and his face concealed by a thick growth of beard, a typical *maquisard*. But something in the way he moved – a bear of a man but with a natural grace to his limbs – made her look more closely.

'Mathieu!' At first her voice was a whisper, her throat constricting so tightly that his name couldn't escape. But then she found her strength and called out more loudly.

He turned his shaggy head towards the woman who was calling his name and, as he did so, she saw that his eyes were wild, filled with a terror that she'd never seen in him before.

Eliane straightened up and moved towards him, but even as she reached for him he looked past her in horror at the bodies still hanging in mid-air. She turned to follow his gaze, just in time to see Yves tenderly handing down the body of a young man into the arms of those waiting below to help. Tears were streaming down her brother's face. And then she realised that it was the body of Luc that was being laid out at the edge of the road.

There were no words. Just a keening, like the cry of a wild animal in pain, as Mathieu knelt beside his brother's body. Eliane stood next to him and watched, helplessly, her heart breaking as Yves moved his ladder to the next lamppost and helped bring down the body of Mathieu's father to lay it beside Luc's.

At such a time, when there was nothing that could be said, all she could think of were Gustave's words as they had stood watching the beehives burn: 'Stand tall, Eliane. Don't let them destroy you, too. We will survive this. We won't let them beat us. *Courage*.' She crouched down, reached out and gathered Mathieu into her arms, holding him as tightly as she could manage, with the last of her remaining strength.

The bodies were buried in the graveyard: ninety-seven graves were dug; ninety-seven men and boys of Tulle laid to rest there. There were more rumours of the terrible retribution and devastation wrought by the

German divisions as they moved on northwards to fight what would become their final battles on French soil. But the inhabitants of the little town of Tulle were so overwhelmed with the struggle to cope with their own personal grief that the stories from further afield didn't make much of an impression on them at the time. It was simply impossible to come to terms with what had happened – an impossibility that the community would have to learn to live with, somehow.

Once the funerals were over, Eliane and Yves helped Mathieu into the truck and took him back to the mill house at Coulliac. He had no other family in Tulle and so the Martins opened their arms wide and drew him into theirs.

But the hanging of his father and his brother had been too much for him to bear; he had lost the ability to speak, struck dumb by grief and the trauma of what he'd seen. Lost deep within his shock, he didn't shed a tear. He seemed frozen, uncomprehending, distant, locked away in the silent prison of his mind, and Eliane began to despair of ever being able to reach him again. Day after day, she sat with him beside the river, talking to him softly, speaking words of hope and love that she thought might unlock the prison of silence in which he was held.

News began to trickle through again – not just rumours now, but reports in the newssheets and voices over the airwaves: there was a bitter battle raging in the north; the Germans were fighting for survival along every front, but thanks to the Allied Forces, supported by the determined efforts of the Resistance fighters across France, the tide of the war had turned, irreversibly.

On a grey morning, when storm-clouds bruised the summer sky, Mathieu sat beneath the willow's weeping branches, hands clasped around his knees, head bent forward, gazing dully at the river flowing by. Eliane stood watching him for a few moments, her heart bleeding with grief for the man she loved, who was surely still somewhere within that empty-eyed shell, if she could only find the key to unlock his pain, if only she could reach him. A shaft of sunlight pierced the clouds suddenly, and the light glinted on the steel coils of the barbed wire that still clad the riverbank. Beyond the wire, as the clouds parted, the sunshine fell on to the weir, making the water sparkle with a million dancing lights.

All at once, Eliane knew what she had to do.

She ran to the barn and pulled a pair of rusty shears from beneath a pile of disused tools. Without looking at Mathieu, she strode down the riverbank to where the tangle of wire barricaded the weir. The shears were stiff to open, but she managed to prise apart the jaws. She placed them around a strand of the wire, gathered all her strength into her thin arms and jerked the blades closed. It took a few, frantic chops, but eventually the strand bent and then snapped, springing apart as it recoiled. She started on the next strand. And then a pair of strong hands took the shears from her and she stood aside to let Mathieu hack at the wire. He made short work of it, pulling away the severed coils, ignoring the cuts where the barbs snagged his hands, breathing heavily as he forced the blunted, rusted blades of the shears to close again and again. The last strand sprang apart and he threw the shears down. Eliane stepped out on to the weir, not bothering to kick off her shoes, and stretched out a hand to him.

At last, he looked her in the eye. Her steady, grey gaze seemed to cut through the wire that had trapped his mind and her smile melted the ice that had gripped his heart. The two of them walked out into the middle of the river and then she turned to face him. The storm clouds were moving off now, rolling back to reveal the blue of the summer sky behind them. And as they did so, she saw that same clarity reveal itself in his dark eyes as they were washed clean by the tears that began to pour from them.

She took both his hands in hers and they stood there in the middle of the river with the water foaming about their ankles, the sound of it carrying off the gut-wrenching sobs that were wrung from him as his tears dropped into the frothing veil that covered the weir.

When he grew calm again at last, she leaned close to him and kissed his face, tasting the salt of his tears. 'I love you, Mathieu,' she said.

He drew back to look at her face again, the face that he had missed for so long. And his voice was cracked and hoarse, but it was his own voice, returned at last.

'I love you, Eliane,' he replied.

Abi: 2017

Eliane's house is located a couple of valleys across from Château Bellevue, halfway up a hillside whose sun-baked, south-facing slopes, clad with still more vines, stretch up behind her little stone cottage to the high-lying woodlands beyond. Just as Eliane foresaw, it seems that Mathieu eventually managed to find a position as winemaker at a local château so that they could marry and have a home of their own.

I feel nervous as Sara parks the car on the verge outside the cottage door. We've been invited to morning coffee with Eliane and Mireille. I've already developed such a clear picture of the Martin sisters in my head, through hearing the story of their lives during the war years, and I wonder whether I'll be disappointed if they turn out to be completely different. Of course, I'm not expecting to see the young women they were back then, Mireille with her head of dancing, dark curls and Eliane with her straight, honey-blonde hair – in fact I probably won't recognise them at all on the basis of the images of them that I've imagined, now that they're both not so far off their hundredth birthdays.

Sara leads me past the front door, where pale-pink roses scramble in an exuberant profusion, and make our way round to the back, following a driveway that leads on up the hill to a much larger house – presumably the vineyard's château – that is just visible among the trees above us.

The back door of the cottage stands ajar, and as Sara knocks on it I turn to look around at Eliane's garden.

Held within the embrace of the hillside, three neat vegetable beds have been cut into the rich brown earth: I can identify the scarlet flowers of runner beans, which climb up a row of wigwam-shaped poles, and at the end of the row, bright-yellow sunflowers, taller than my head, turn their faces to follow the sun as it makes its daily procession across the sky. In the nearest bed, juicy-looking tomatoes hang in tempting clusters and courgettes nestle beneath them among the thick leaves of their own sprawling vines. Terracotta pots are planted with an array of herbs that exude their potent, medicinal-smelling perfume into the air around us. A little further up the hill, where the garden meets the vines, several trees form a line of shelter. And beneath the trees there are three white beehives. The sight of them makes me smile.

Higher still, up towards the top of the slope, where the vines meet the woodland, there is a whitewashed wall enclosing a square of the land. Sara notices me looking at it. 'That's the graveyard of the family who own this château,' she says. 'Mathieu is buried there.'

The back door opens wide and a woman steps out who is too young to be either Eliane or Mireille. She envelops Sara in a warm embrace, kissing her on both cheeks before turning to me.

'Hello, Abi,' she says. 'I've heard a lot about you.'

Beaming broadly, Sara puts an arm around the woman's shoulders. 'This is your additional surprise!'

I look at the woman, with a bemused but still (I hope) polite smile fixed to my face. She has rosy cheeks and sparkling brown eyes and she wears her pepper-and-salt-flecked hair tied back in a somewhat unruly bun.

'I'm very pleased to meet you,' she says. 'I'm Blanche. Blanche Dabrowski-Martin.'

I can't speak. And when I can get any words out at all, I blurt, 'Blanche! You're still here!'

She laughs. 'I am. Or, more accurately, I've come back. When we lost Mathieu last year, I decided to move from Paris and keep Eliane company. And it's so lovely to be home again.'

'Paris?' I echo. 'But how . . . ? When . . . ?' The questions crowd into my head so fast that I can't formulate them clearly.

Blanche takes my hand and leads me to a little white wrought-iron table and chairs set beside the back door under a shaded pergola. Trumpet-shaped flowers, the colour of bright flames, hang in clusters around us, their thick canopy of leaves forming a roof above our heads. Bees bury their heads in the scarlet blooms, busily mining the nectar from them to carry it back to the hives.

'I know, there's so much to ask, so much to tell. Sara has said how interested you have been in hearing Eliane's story.' Blanche smiles. 'After the war, my father, who had been fighting with the Allied Forces, came back to Paris to try to find my mother and me. There'd been no way of telling him that Esther had died, and that the Martins had taken me in. But he tracked down Mireille, through the *atelier* where Esther had worked. She brought him here, to the mill. You can imagine how he wept when he saw me and when Lisette produced my birth certificate from between the pages of her book of herbal remedies, where it had been hidden for so long. And so we were reunited. He and I made our home in Paris, but I've always been a frequent visitor to my other family down here in the *Sud-Ouest*.

'Now,' she continues, 'you two sit there while I make the coffee. Eliane will be out in a moment. Mireille isn't here yet, but I think one of her grandsons will be bringing her shortly.'

As Blanche bustles back indoors, we hear the sound of a car engine and a battered blue pickup truck pulls up the drive, stopping alongside the cottage. A cheerful-looking young man jumps down from the driver's cab, waves to us and goes around to help someone else out of the passenger seat.

Leaning on his arm, a tiny, hunched old woman makes her way slowly towards us and we scramble to our feet. Her curls are as white as winter frost, but when she reaches me she gives me an appraising look with eyes that are as bright and sharp-sighted as those of a bird. '*Bonjour*, Abi. I am Mireille Thibaud.' She shakes my hand and I realise her fingers are gnarled and lumpy with arthritis. 'And this is one of my grandsons, Luc. He's just passed his driving test and so his father has let him borrow his old truck. Quite an adventure, the two of us allowed out on our own for once, eh Luc?'

He grins. '*Oui, Mamie.*' Turning to us, he, too, shakes our hands and then says, 'And the price I have to pay for the privilege is going to do the shopping too. I'll be back in about an hour.'

'Don't forget to drive safely like they told you to!' Mireille calls after him, her tone fondly teasing. Despite her great age, I recognise her lively expression and her sense of humour from Sara's descriptions of her.

Blanche reappears carrying a tray, which she sets down on the little table. Pretty china cups and saucers, decorated with butterflies, sit alongside a plate of little buttery biscuits.

And then she's there: Eliane. I would recognise her anywhere. She's taller and stands more erect than her elder sister; her straight, white hair is tied up in a chignon and her face is a perfect oval shape, the bone structure still visible beneath her age-softened skin. But it is her eyes that strike me the most. She fixes me with her gaze and it is the clear, calm grey of a summer's dawn.

I'm expecting a formal handshake, but am taken aback when she steps forward and envelops me in a warm embrace before kissing my cheeks. 'So you are Abi,' she says. She holds me at arm's length to get a better look, and then nods as if she recognises me too. And then she says, 'I'm pleased to meet you at last,' as if she's been expecting me. As if she knew that we would meet one day.

'And I'm pleased to see you still have bees,' I say and then blush, realising that this is hardly an appropriate conversation-opener with these two old ladies whom I have never met before.

She smiles. And then, as if she, too, is continuing a conversation that we'd already begun, she says, 'And you know, Abi, they are the descendants of the bees I kept at Château Bellevue.'

'But how? I thought they were destroyed by the Germans?'

Her eyes cloud slightly, like a mist on the river, as she remembers. 'You're right, the hives were burned. But when Mathieu and I went back to the walled garden to start clearing away the devastation that the soldiers had left behind them, we noticed something. In the silence, up there, a bee began to buzz among the camomile and the peppermint. And then another, and another. And, as we watched, they flew back to a hole in the wall. You see, some of the bees had escaped the fire, enough to begin a new colony. And the next year, when they swarmed, I was able to fill a new hive. And so they have continued, down the years.' She looks up the hill towards the hives beneath the lace-leaved trees. 'Acacia,' she nods. 'The champagne of honey.'

We sit and talk for almost two hours. And, as we do, it seems to me that the Martin sisters grow younger, becoming once again the girls they were all those years ago.

Eliane shows me a photograph of a smiling family – a woman standing between her husband and three pretty, dark-haired daughters. 'Can you guess who this is?' she asks, pointing.

It takes me only a moment to realise. 'Is it Francine?' I ask, with wonderment.

She nods. 'I always knew I'd see her again one day. She lives in Montreal. Her daughters are named Eliane, Lisette and Mireille.'

By the time Luc pulls up in the blue truck again, to take Mireille home, I can see that both the sisters are beginning to tire.

As we leave, Eliane walks us to the car parked in front of the cottage, her arms linked with mine and Sara's. I turn to her.

'Thank you for having us here today, Eliane. And thank you for so much more, too. You see, your story has helped me understand my own power – the strength of human resistance in the face of fear and abuse.'

She nods, considering me with that steady grey gaze of hers, and I feel that she is reading my own story, taking in the scars on my arms, seeing what lies beneath the surface. 'You are stronger than you know, Abi.' Her words are an echo of those she's already spoken to me in my dreams.

'You know,' she says, 'France chose to try to forget what happened in the war; it was too much, too devastating. We had to make the choice to bury it with our dead and move on with our lives. But, all the same, the truth of it is still with us.'

And then she reaches into the pocket of her skirt and brings out a folded square of scarlet silk.

'Your scarf!' I exclaim. 'You still have it!'

'Yes,' she smiles. 'A little faded and worn with time, like the rest of us, but I've always kept it safe. I thought you might like to see it. I always felt brave when I wore it. And, of course, it helped me to communicate things that couldn't be said at the time.'

I'm speechless as she places the soft silk square in my hands. I shake it out and the patterns are still vivid and beautiful. Even though the material is so delicate now, this fragile remnant still holds its promise of power and strength, a tangible reminder of Eliane's vow to stay true to herself. And I know I'm only imagining it, but a little of that strength seems to seep into my hands from the worn silk scarf and to flow upwards through my scarred arms, making me feel brave too.

Eliane: 1944

The last months of the war were brutal and chaotic across France, with news of battles flaring sporadically as the endgame played out. And in the vacuum left by the Germans' departure, people took the law into their own hands, struggling to restore some sort of order to the traumatised, divided county as it reeled from the legacy of the years of occupation.

It took a while for life to return to normal after the Germans left Coulliac, but Eliane knew that the best way forward would be to try to carry on with the routines and rhythms of life as best they could. So she loaded the last remaining jars of honey and beeswax into the truck and drove them to the square to set up her market stall.

The *place* was busier than it had been for months as people ventured out for the market. They were a little tentative at first, like deer stepping into the open from the shelter of the woods, tense and wary, but then they began to relax as, at long last, they were able to mingle and greet friends and neighbours without feeling the watchful eyes of the German guards upon them. There was very little business to be done – there were only a few stallholders and those who were there had even fewer wares to display – but it felt good to be able to wander freely around the square, to sit at the café and discuss the momentous events of the past week, to talk and to be able to laugh again, hoping, *believing*, that they were free at last. Eliane waved to Mathieu and Yves, who had pulled up chairs on the pavement outside the café from where they greeted a steady stream of friends.

All at once, there was a disturbance at the far side of the *place*, a scuffling and a jostling as a group of men came around the corner, pushing a stranger in front of them. Eliane was rearranging the small pyramid of jars on her stall, trying to make it look as though she actually had something to sell; she looked up, distracted by the sound of their jeers and catcalls. The clustered groups of people parted, stepping aside to let the men through, and the stranger stumbled into the space that was created in the centre of the square.

And then Eliane looked more closely and gasped with horror. Because she'd suddenly realised that this was no stranger after all.

It was Stéphanie the men were goading. But she was almost unrecognisable. Her head had been shaved and her blouse was ripped, hanging loose where it had been torn, exposing the skin beneath. And daubed crudely at the base of her throat was a black swastika. As Stéphanie tried to stand up straight, reaching a hand to the fountain to steady herself against it, Eliane saw that the skin surrounding the stark black emblem was red and painful-looking and she realised that it had been painted on with hot tar.

It was hard to make out what the men were shouting, at first, but then Eliane heard the words 'collaborator' and 'informer'. Stéphanie drew back against the stonework at the base of the fountain as the men drew closer, threatening and spitting, but she still tried to stand up straight and look defiant.

Eliane rushed forward into the space between the men and the girl. 'Stop!' she shouted, spreading her arms wide as if to physically hold them apart. Her heart was pounding with terror, but a bold strength surged through her veins. 'Enough! Don't you think we've all had enough now?'

'Ha! Another collaborator maybe?' jeered one of the men. 'Trying to protect your fellow whore are you? Thought you could get away with it, did you, your *collaboration horizontale*? Sleeping with the Milice – probably the Gestapo too. Denouncing your neighbours in return for a few fripperies.' He stepped closer and flicked the end of the red silk scarf, which was knotted about Eliane's neck. 'And then flaunting them in our faces.'

'Let's get her, too!' another shouted.

One of the men reached out and took hold of Eliane's arm and she screamed at him, like a cornered animal, giving vent to all the fear and rage and pain that the war had inflicted on her, which she'd carried, silently, for so long. As if her voice were a physical force, the man fell backwards away from her and was thrown to the ground.

And then she realised that Mathieu was there.

'Get off her! She's done nothing but try to protect you and your families.' Mathieu's voice echoed around the square as he stepped between Eliane and the mob.

And then Yves was beside him, too, the pair forming an un-crossable barrier, protecting the two girls.

The mob of men fell silent at the sight. It was well known that both Yves Martin and Mathieu Dubosq were seasoned *maquisards* who had fought in the struggle against the Germans. No one in his right mind would have dared challenge either of them, let alone the pair standing there together.

With a shifting of their feet and a few muttered remarks, the men stood their ground uneasily for a few moments more and then began to drift away, leaving the four figures standing in the space at the centre of the square.

'Are you alright?' Mathieu asked Eliane.

'Yes, I'm fine.' She stood with her fists tightly clenched and her whole body was shaking uncontrollably, but otherwise she was unharmed. 'But Stéphanie . . . ?' she turned towards the shaven-headed figure who was now slumped against the fountain.

Eliane knelt beside her and gently touched her arm. Stéphanie flinched and shrank back.

'It's okay. You're alright now. They won't harm you anymore,' Eliane murmured soothingly. Gingerly, she tried to rearrange the flap of torn blouse to cover the blistered, tar-daubed skin. And then she untied the scarf from about her and held it out. 'Would you like this? To cover your head?'

Stéphanie sat up then and ran a hand over the razor-nicked skin of her scalp. Fleetingly, her eyes filled with a mixture of shock and shame. But then she pushed away Eliane's outstretched hand, spurning the scarf, and scrambled to her feet. 'I've never needed your charity, Eliane Martin, and I'm not about to start accepting it now.' She spat the words out, desperate in her pain and her fury. Crossing her arms over her chest and gathering the fabric of her blouse in one fist at the base of her throat, she lifted her chin and walked – just a little unsteadily – out of the marketplace.

She never glanced back, even though she knew that she was leaving it for good.

As the crowd dispersed, Mathieu and Yves helped Eliane back to the market stall and in silence they began to pack away the few remaining jars, the final, pitiful reminders of all that was left of Eliane's bees.

Abi: 2017

It's the middle of October now, and we're preparing for the final wedding of the season at Château Bellevue. Sara explains that this one is for friends of hers, Christiane and Philippe, and it's going to be an especially joyful one. The bride has just come through treatment for cancer. Thankfully, now, she's officially in remission so her wedding is going to be a celebration of her recovery on top of everything else.

I reckon that in the history of all the weddings hosted at Château Bellevue, never has the weather forecast been consulted so often. It's the time of year when it could either be a gorgeous Indian summer, with warm, golden days that bathe the vineyards in a soft light, putting a smile on the face of the wine farmers as they know these last, lingering days of good weather will instil precious roundedness and fullness to the wines they'll soon be making; or the clouds could push their way down from the north, covering everything with their grey dampness, which will mean a difficult, risky harvest – not to mention putting a bit of a downer on Christiane and Philippe's wedding too. The forecast is uncertain, but everyone in Coulliac is willing the weather to remain good. If sheer, human willpower could ensure a perfect day for the couple then we'd be home and dry. But, as Karen often sagely remarks whenever we're getting things ready for the next wedding, you can organise most things – but whether or not it rains on the day isn't one of them.

Thankfully, though, as I hurry up the hill from the mill house early on Christiane's wedding morning, the sky is a perfect, clear blue and the soft veil of mist is already lifting from the surface of the river. If I had the time, I'd linger for a few moments by the willow tree, watching the water gather itself in the dark pool above the weir where the last swallows of summer flit and skim before the river launches itself joyously over the lip of the weir and abandons itself to the onward journey. But I definitely don't have time this morning. I need to get up to the château to help Sara and Karen with the final preparations. We're far more involved in this wedding day than we have been with the others in the season. Usually on the day itself an army of caterers, florists, hairdressers, beauticians and musicians arrive to conduct the proceedings, but this time it's a local, family affair and we're all going to be hard at work.

The kitchen is quiet when I arrive and Sara hands me a cup of coffee. 'Better drink this now – we may not get a chance to have another one later on,' she says with a smile.

And she's right. The château is soon buzzing with activity and Sara, Karen and I are directing a small army of helpers.

In the kitchen, Karen leads a battalion of local ladies who are making roses out of radishes and coronets out of cucumbers to garnish the platters of charcuterie that the butcher's wife and daughters have prepared, which will be handed round with flutes of champagne while photos are being taken after the service.

The pâtisserie delivers a dozen pear and frangipane tarts, gleaming with a rich, golden glaze, which are put on a trestle table in the library for safekeeping.

On a corner of the lawn beyond the marquee, on the down-wind side of the ridge, a shallow pit has been dug by Thomas and Jean-Marc and a huge fire is being lit for the *méchoui*. The tall heap of applewood branches blazes brightly at first but it will continue to burn all day, subsiding into a glowing bed of embers that will cook a whole lamb suspended on a spit above it to succulent perfection. Thomas comes in search of a tarpaulin so that they can rig up an awning over it once the fire's burned down enough, just in case the weather does turn.

I've been assigned to direct table-setting operations in the marquee, at the head of a troop of my own. We spread crisp, lavender-scented cloths over the tables to match the white chair covers, which are tied with jaunty bows – so that the tent takes on the appearance of being filled with a bevy of butterflies. We fold laundered linen napkins into elegant fleur-de-lis shapes and tuck them into the wine glasses at each place; the glasses sparkle and wink like diamonds where the sunlight catches the glass, vying for attention with the glinting of each item of thoroughly polished cutlery.

One of Christiane's aunts consults a carefully considered table plan and she and her daughter set out all the name-cards, which one of the bridesmaids has handwritten in flowing calligraphy. Little net pouches of silver and gold sugared almonds, tied with gold ribbons, are set beside each name as gifts for the guests.

And on a side table we set the wedding cake in pride of place. It is delivered by another aunt, who was up until two o'clock this morning icing it so that it would set in time. Once the cake is safely in place, she carefully ices the final, finishing touches on to the stacked triple tiers, and Sara brings her a length of sweet-scented honeysuckle to arrange around it.

Swags of foliage and flowers, bound with more trailing ribbons of the honeysuckle, have been pinned up behind the top table and now Sara and her band of helpers are arranging posies of roses, lavender, and delicate white gaura flowers, which float like still more tiny butterflies in the centre of each table. And I know – because I couldn't resist taking a peek when I was hurrying past with a pile of tablecloths – that the chapel is bedecked with yet more swags of greenery, and that vast glass vases, loaned by the florist, have been set at the entrance and on the altar, crammed with spectacular, sweet-scented starbursts of every white lily that it's been possible to lay hands on between here and Bordeaux.

By lunchtime everything has been set up and the army of helpers disappears to go and get themselves ready for the ceremony and the party. Sara, Karen and I grab a makeshift lunch of bread and cheese around the kitchen table and Sara runs through her lists, ticking off the jobs that we've completed. 'We're nearly there, I think.' She pauses to consult the weather forecast on her phone yet again and grimaces. 'Still uncertain for later.' She leans back in her chair to see beyond the kitchen door. Some high wisps of cloud are starting to gather, dappling the sky like the markings of the silvered fish that swim in the pool below the weir. 'Hopefully we'll be okay for everyone arriving and then, if it does rain, it will only be once they're all in the marquee. It's going to be touch and go, though. Abi, can you ask Jean-Marc to put the umbrellas out in the barn in case they're needed at the end of the night?' Experience has taught Sara and Thomas to be prepared, whatever the weather, and they have a collection of large, clear plastic brollies at guests' disposal, which are big enough to protect even the most sophisticated hair-dos and the largest of hats.

Thomas comes in, whistling cheerfully and smelling faintly of wood smoke from the fire. He pauses, in passing, to plant a kiss on top of Sara's head and she turns to smile at him. 'There's a bit of lunch if you and Jean-Marc want?' she offers.

He takes two bottles of beer from the fridge and gathers the remains of the baguette into the crook of his arm, then scoops up a chunk of dried *saucisson*. 'Thanks, this will do us fine. We're just about to get the meat on – the fire's perfect.'

'Well you'd better make sure you leave enough time for a shower before you get changed – we can't have the DJ smelling like a roast dinner!'

The wedding party assemble at two o'clock so that they can dress here. Sara and Thomas have made Château Bellevue available to them for the night, so the bedrooms have been prepared and Sara has set out welcoming posies of wildflowers and a bottle of champagne on ice in the master suite to fortify the bride and her attendants.

Christiane looks radiant on her wedding day – although there is a fragility just beneath the surface, which shows in the shadows beneath her eyes and in the sharp definition of her collarbones. Her family and her bevy of bridesmaids flutter around her anxiously, but she bats them away, laughing. 'I'm fine, Maman, don't worry. I slept so well last night. Oh, Sara, everything looks so perfect. Thank you for helping us to do this. I know how much extra work it must have been for everyone.'

Sara tells me that Christiane's wedding dress was bought at a bridal shop in Bordeaux a few weeks ago. It's needed some adjusting as she's put on a little weight following her treatment – a good sign – and Mireille herself, our local Parisian *couturier extraordinaire*, has insisted on overseeing the alterations that have been needed to make it fit perfectly. While her knotted hands and her fading eyesight don't allow her to do fine needlework anymore these days, Mireille has closely supervised the pinning and the sewing done by one of her daughters-in-law. They delivered the dress yesterday and Sara has hung it in the tall wardrobe in the master suite, draped in a clean cotton sheet for safekeeping.

In the event it's perfect: the elegant high neckline and long sleeves are in an ivory lace that flows in soft folds over a slim-fitting bodice and underskirt, emphasising Christiane's figure. Her dark hair is short, as it's only now growing back, but the *gamine* style suits her dress well.

From the chapel, music drifts across the courtyard as the guests arrive. Four of Philippe and Christiane's friends have got together in the past week to form an impromptu string quartet; they are performing in the chapel and will play while the drinks are being served after the ceremony. Once everyone has taken their seats, apart from the soft strains of the music, there is an air of hushed anticipation. There always is at this stage in the proceedings of any wedding, but today it seems to be laden with so much more significance: this is not just a marriage; it's an affirmation of life and hope, of courage and quiet strength, of the defiant joy that exists alongside the sadness and the fear.

I've volunteered to keep an eye on things while the service is under way, so that we can have everything ready for the party immediately afterwards, so I watch from the kitchen door as Sara and Thomas – looking as elegant as any of the other guests now that they've had a chance to shower and change – pause outside the chapel and he gathers her in his arms and kisses her. She smiles at him, and then glances back and gives me a little wave. I give her the thumbs-up sign before making a shooing motion that she should get into the chapel and not worry about anything; I've got this. And suddenly I realise that I feel confident and strong, more certain of myself than I have ever done. I know that I've earned my place as a respected member of Sara and Thomas' team and I see myself, now, through their eyes and realise how capable and resilient I really can be.

I stand and watch, smiling, as the bridesmaids come down the front steps and cross the courtyard to the chapel doorway. And then the bride appears.

Her beauty, in that moment, is simply breathtaking.

And the afternoon sun elbows aside the thickening clouds to illuminate the path, as her father takes Christiane's arm and leads his daughter to her wedding.

Dinner in the marquee has all gone smoothly. The sun stayed out after the ceremony in the chapel so we were able to circulate with platters of charcuterie and warm hors-d'oeuvres among the guests as they sipped flutes of champagne on the lawn. The photos should look great against the backdrop of the warm stones of the château and Sara's soft landscaping.

There must be some good pictures of them cutting the cake, too, which they did early on, Christiane insisting that her aunt be included as a thank you for making such a magnificent creation.

Then everyone found their seats at the tables in the marquee and we brought out the lamb, roasted to succulent perfection, and bowls of salads. The red wine from Château de la Chapelle – made by Thomas' brother – is the perfect accompaniment and the noise level in the tent rises to a happy crescendo that bounces off the canvas roof. It's a warm evening, and still thankfully a dry one, so we are able to tie back the sides of the marquee and let the night air drift in to cool the flushed cheeks of the guests.

As we clear the tables and begin to serve slices of the frangipane tarts, more bottles of champagne are produced and glasses refilled, ready for the speeches. And silence falls as the best man taps a fork against the rim of his glass and stands to introduce the first speaker. To everyone's surprise, it is the bride whom he calls upon.

Christiane reaches down to hold Philippe's hand as she begins to speak. 'I can't even begin to find the words to tell you how glad I am to be standing here,' she says, 'and how much it means to me to see you all here today. This event has been organised so perfectly, thanks to the superhuman efforts of my mother, and the rest of the family, and Sara and Thomas Cortini, and, oh, so many others of you. I know how much trouble you've all gone to in order to make the day perfect for me and my Philippe. I want every single one of you to know how much it means to us. So, this first toast is from me to all of you.'

She pauses to smile at her husband and to give his hand a squeeze, and then she continues. 'When I was at the hospital going through my treatment, Philippe gave me a card, which I always kept with me. It said: "Life is not about waiting for the storm to pass, it's about learning to dance in the rain." That's a lesson we've had to learn. And it's one that we will always remember in our future together. So here's my toast to you all: to dancing in the rain.'

She raises her glass and then adds, with a grin, 'But you're allowed to take a drink too, because heaven only knows how long the other speeches are going to go on for. Cheers everyone!'

Amid a mixture of laughter and tears, everyone stands and raises their glasses back to her.

I smile to myself too. Because I think it's a lesson I've learned as well this summer. Through Sara's telling of Eliane's story, I've learned the importance of staying true to what really matters: to love, to loyalty and to living your life as it's meant to be lived. And then I realise that Jean-Marc is watching me from across the marquee; and that I'm not smiling to myself anymore – I'm smiling at him.

As the guests finish up their dessert and drain the very last drops of champagne, I begin to clear the tables. Sara comes and takes the pile of plates from me. 'Oh no you don't, Abi,' she says. 'We're leaving all this for the morning. You're coming with everyone else to the barn for the party.' She grabs my hand and, bunking off like a pair of giggling schoolgirls, we follow the throng making its way into the barn, where Thomas already has the music playing ready for Christiane and Philippe to lead off in the first dance.

The barn is crammed full. For a moment, hemmed in by the throng, I expect to feel those old, familiar flutterings of panic beginning to rise up in my chest and I wonder if I can do this. But, to my surprise, I find that I don't at all mind being in this packed-out space. All I feel is the excitement of the chattering crowd, the abandon of those who've taken to the dance floor, and the sheer happiness that fills the barn to the rafters high above us all. I notice that Jean-Marc is on bar duty so I go to lend him a hand.

It's so hot in the barn that we've left the doors flung wide open. In a brief lull between two songs, a gust of wind eddies among the partygoers and a woman standing near the door shouts, 'It's raining!' Sure enough, the clouds begin to let fall a soft pattering of drops.

'Outside!' shouts someone else. 'After all, "Life is not about waiting for the storm to pass – it's about dancing in the rain!"'

The barrel-load of umbrellas positioned beside the doorway is completely ignored as the guests flood outside. Hair, make-up, best dresses and formal suits are all forgotten as Christiane and Philippe lead the dancing. High-heeled shoes are kicked off and jackets discarded. Thomas cranks the volume up high and the courtyard is filled with music and laughter and shrieks of joy.

I hang back, watching from the doorway. And then suddenly someone grabs my hand and pulls me out into the melee, twirling me round as the current of the dance draws us in. I look into the eyes of Jean-Marc and the rain falls softly on us as we dance together.

And I feel my heart beginning to unfurl and to reach outwards into the world again, like the delicate tendrils of a plant at the end of a long, long spell of drought.

Abi: 2017

And now the wedding season really is well and truly over at Château Bellevue. We've been busy deep-cleaning everything, packing linens and bedding away for the winter with a scattering of dried lavender flowers between the folds so that next spring they will smell fresh and sweet when they're brought out ready for the new season. Thomas and the builders are still working on the mill house, but the rooms are taking shape and it will be ready in good time for next year, accommodating extra guests. The chapel door is locked and the marquee, which has been the venue for so many happy times this summer, has been dismantled and stored away in the party barn, where the lights have been unplugged and the glitter ball stilled.

I've made a decision. I go to find Sara in the walled garden, where she is tending the raised beds she's created, pulling out the last of the season's salad leaves, which have shot up in the final, hot days of the Indian summer that we've been enjoying. They'll go on the compost heap and be dug back into the soil next spring. Earth to earth.

She straightens up when she sees me and pushes a strand of hair out of her eyes with the back of her wrist.

'I love this time of year,' she says. 'You can sense the garden starting to prepare for its winter rest again after all the hard work of the summer.'

I smile. 'Rather like you and Thomas, too. You must be looking forward to getting your home back to yourselves for the winter.'

She laughs. 'We love our work, but you're right; it will be good to have time to catch up with the rest of our lives.'

I look out at the woods and the hills beyond the garden walls, where the land falls away to the river in the valley far below.

'I'm going to go back to London,' I tell her. 'I've decided it's time to tie up the ends there – sell the apartment, finish my degree. And then I'll see where life takes me.' I can picture myself going back to the city again now and I know I will have the confidence to look up old friends and maybe to make new ones too.

'That's good.' Sara watches me closely for a moment, her eyes the colour of the dark pool in the river above the weir. 'Well, both Thomas and I hope that life may bring you back this way again sometime. You've been a godsend, Abi. You're part of the team now. There's a job here for you next year if you fancy another summer of unremitting graft and no social life!'

'Thank you, Sara. I'll be back.'

And I know that I will. I know that the pilgrim paths and the ley lines and the rivers that all make their way through this corner of the country will draw me back this way sometime soon. And I know that Jean-Marc will be here, waiting for me, and that we will dance together again before too long.

Sara glances at her watch. 'Time we were off. Eliane and Blanche will be expecting us.'

We drive over to the cottage, as we have done several times since that first meeting. With Blanche's help, we've filled in the details of Eliane's story.

It's a story of ordinary, everyday courage. A story about the determination to stay true to your Self through the darkest times so that when, at last, you cross back to safety you can find your voice again and live your life free from fear.

She has taught me about the resilience of the human spirit.

She has taught me about myself.

When we arrive at the cottage, Eliane is sitting in the garden, asleep in the sunshine, a book lying open in her lap.

Inside, Blanche is humming as she prepares lunch. All around us, Eliane's bees hum too, busily collecting sweet nectar from the flowers that she's grown for them. In the valley below, the river, which she's lived beside all her life, for almost a hundred summers, glints with its quiet, golden light.

Up the hill, beyond the acacia trees and the beehives, past the rows of vines whose leaves drink in the last of the sunshine, sweetening the grapes for this year's wine harvest, which will begin any day now, Mathieu waits for Eliane, watching over her from the little white-walled graveyard.

Sara goes inside to find Blanche.

Silently, so as not to wake her, I take a seat beside Eliane. Very gently, I remove the book from her lap so that I can mark her place for her. As I tuck the bookmark between the pages she's been reading, a line catches my eye. I consider the words carefully, letting their meaning sink in.

And then, after a moment, I raise my head and look around at where I am.

I think back to the day that brought me here.

And I realise that I was never really lost at all.

Au milieu de l'hiver, j'apprenais enfin qu'il y avait en moi un été invincible.

In the midst of winter, I found that there was within me an invincible summer.

Retour à Tipasa, Albert Camus (1952)

AUTHOR'S NOTE

The Beekeeper's Promise came about as a result of another of my books, *The French for Always*, which tells the story of Sara's early days at Château Bellevue. Snippets of Eliane's story during the war years are referred to obliquely in that book, prompting many readers to ask to know more.

Other than a few towns that you can find on the map and certain key historical events that took place during World War Two, the people and places referred to in both novels are entirely fictitious. The terrible events at Tulle really did take place, however. As far as possible, I have tried to be true to reports of what happened there, although some of the details vary a bit between accounts. Inevitably, I have taken certain literary liberties for the sake of the story, but where I have done so it is with the utmost respect to the memory of those who died. They are not forgotten: these days, every summer, hanging baskets full of flowers are placed on the lamp-posts in the town to commemorate every single one of the men and boys whose lives were taken on that day in June 1944.

As well as the inspirational stories and memories so generously shared with me by friends in France whose families lived through the years of occupation, the following sources were helpful to me in writing this novel:

Voices from the Dark Years: The Truth About Occupied France 1940–1945, by Douglas Boyd (2007)

SAS Operation Bulbasket: Behind the Lines in Occupied France 1944, by Paul McCue (2009)

Das Reich: The March of the 2nd SS Panzer Division Through France, June 1944, by Max Hastings (2010)

In a Ruined State, Chapter 6: 'Background to the 10th of June', www.oradour.info/ruined/chapter6.htm, by Michael Williams

※

If you have enjoyed this book, I should be very grateful if you would consider writing a review. I love getting feedback, and I know reviews have played a big part in other readers discovering my books.

Merci, et à bientôt,

Fiona

ACKNOWLEDGMENTS

A big thank you to my agent, Madeleine Milburn, for her friendship, enthusiasm and unfailing belief in my writing, and to the rest of the team at the Madeleine Milburn Literary Agency for all their hard work and support in promoting my books.

Thank you to the brilliant Lake Union team at Amazon Publishing and especially to Sammia Hamer, Victoria Pepe and Bekah Graham, as well as to Mike Jones for his editorial patience and percipience.

Thank you to the many friends who have cheered me on and checked up on my word count at regular intervals: the volunteer gardeners at Pitlochry Festival Theatre; my book-club buddies; the bridge group; all my friends in yoga; and to John, Amelia, Wyomia and Nairne for providing such a wonderful refuge at Taymount in which to write.

Special thanks to Annie Fraser, Karen Macgregor, Sally Swann, Marie-Claire Norman-Butler, Mala Saye, Michèle Jobling, Frank Doelger and Bruce Harmon: Friends Indeed.

Love, gratitude and huge hugs to my sons, James and Alastair, as always.

And to Rob too, naturally.

ABOUT THE AUTHOR

Fiona Valpy spent seven years living in France, having moved there from the UK in 2007. She and her family renovated an old, rambling farmhouse in the Bordeaux winelands, during the course of which she developed new-found skills in cement mixing, interior decorating and wine tasting.

All of these inspirations, along with a love for the place, the people and their history, have found their way into the books she's written, which have been translated into German, Norwegian, Czech, Turkish and Slovenian.

Fiona now lives in Scotland, but enjoys regular visits to France in search of the sun.